PRAISE FOR S.

LOST CREATURES

"It's very rare for a story to be uncanny, profound and also enjoy lightness of touch. S.G. Browne somehow manages to do it time after time."

—Michael Marshall Smith

"Beautiful, heart-wrenching, and very funny, S. G. Browne's *Lost Creatures* is the sardonic city-dwelling sibling of Grimm's Fairy Tales. Browne creates deep empathy for his characters, then breaks your heart with the surprising and entirely understandable choices they make. This book is so original, it's breathtaking. I absolutely loved it."

—Loren Rhoads, author of *Unsafe Words*

"Sometimes mythic, sometimes strange, S.G. Browne's *Lost Creatures* is a heartfelt collection of magic and monsters emerging in our world. Each tale can veer between beautiful, funny, honest, startling, surreal, and above all else, fantastic. *Lost Creatures* is ridiculously brilliant."

—John Hornor Jacobs, author of *A Lush and Seething Hell*

"*LOST CREATURES* is a treasure trove of terror, twisted humor and rampant weirdness. Superbly crafted short stories by one of today's most talented writers. Bravo!"

—Jonathan Maberry, NY Times bestselling author of *INK* and *V-WARS*

"*Lost Creatures* is a delight to read. The stories mix humor with the fantastical, along with Browne's unique observations on the foibles of society and pop culture...every one of the stories is a winner."

—Dana Fredsti, author of the Ashley Parker series and Spawn of Lilith series

LUCKY BASTARD

"Wickedly sharp and wildly entertaining. S. G. Browne is one of today's very best writers."

> —*New York Times* bestselling author Jonathan Maberry

"This fast-paced adventure succeeds as both a hard-boiled homage and a paranormal romp. Browne delivers an insightful, intriguing tale."

> —*Publishers Weekly* (starred review)

"Browne hits the funny bone hard with another supernaturally themed comedy."

> —*Kirkus Reviews* (starred review)

"The titular bastard may be in for a very bad day, but Browne's readers are the lucky ones."

> —*New York Times* bestselling author Christopher Golden

BIG EGOS

"A smart and darkly funny thriller that looks at America's obsession with celebrity through a truly skewed lens...Razor sharp."

> —*Kirkus Reviews*

"Fantasy and reality blur in this satirical takedown of celebrity culture."

> —*New York Post*

"Impossible to put down."

> —*Philadelphia Weekly Press*

"A sobering parable of people who don't want to be themselves."

> —*Publishers Weekly*

"Insightful, caustic and irreverent, *Big Egos* is a sharp, smart and immensely entertaining read."

> —*Alibi.com*

LESS THAN HERO

"Hugely entertaining...you've never read a superhero story quite like this one."

—Booklist

"A social-satire-meets-amateur-superhero saga that deftly skewers the money-grubbing slickness of the pharmaceutical industry."

—Kirkus Reviews

"Takes readers on a dark, comic ride through the world of pharmaceutical drug trials."

—San Jose Mercury News

"Browne proves to be a topnotch superhero storyteller...It's great fun."

—Manhattan Book Review

I SAW ZOMBIES EATING SANTA CLAUS

"Hilarious, horrifying...a must for anyone who can't get enough of the undead."

—San Jose Mercury News

"It's *Miracle on 34th Street* meets *Night of the Living Dead.*"

—The Washington Post

"Readers with a certain seasonal sensibility—one that renders zombies appropriate fare no matter the date on the calendar—will be shouting Ho! Ho! Ho!"

—USA Today

"The perfect Christmas read for those who like VERY black comedy in their holiday reading."

—Feathered Quill

LOST CREATURES

Also By S.G. Browne

NOVELS

Less Than Hero

Big Egos

Lucky Bastard

Fated

Breathers

NOVELLAS

I Saw Zombies Eating Santa Claus

The Maiden Poodle: A Fairy Tail

SHORT STORY COLLECTIONS

Shooting Monkeys in a Barrel

To Russell Zisky,

LOST CREATURES

Stories

S.G. Browne

Here's to the past 15 years
living in SF & spending that
time hanging out with you
& deepening our friendship.
I love you, man.

Brownie

Several of the stories in this collection previously appeared in the following:
"Riding the Softland Express": Originally published as "Softland" in *Shooting Monkeys in a Barrel* (Pocket Star, 2012)
"Letters to Santa (from the Arctic Academy for Gifted Creatures)": Originally published in *Naughty or Nice: A Holiday Anthology* (Evil Girlfriend Media, 2015)
"Inside the Monsters Studio": Originally published in *Amazing Stories of the Flying Spaghetti Monster* (Eraserhead Press, 2011)
"The Curse of the Amazing Colossal Thing from Outer Space": Originally published in *Drive-In Creature Feature* (Evil Jester Press, 2016)
"Scattered Showers with a Chance of Daikaiju," "Dr. Sinister's Home for Retired Villains," and "Remedial English for Reanimated Corpses": Originally published as Kindle singles (2016)

ISBN 978-1-7371590-0-1

Cover art copyright © 2021 by Lynne Hansen
LynneHansenArt.com

For David (aka A.J.).
I'm glad I drew the short straw.

Contents

LOST CREATURES

Scattered Showers with a Chance of Daikaiju

My mother stands at the kitchen sink and gazes out the window, the morning sunlight pouring over her as if she's showering beneath it—the sunlight cascading down her black hair and along her cheeks, past her nose and her lips, washing over the scar that runs from her temple to her jaw and just misses her left eye.

I asked her once why she never had plastic surgery to remove the scar. She said she liked to keep it as a reminder.

"A reminder of what?"

"Of what happens when curiosity gets the better of you."

I didn't have to ask her what that meant.

"What's the weather supposed to be like this weekend?" I ask.

My mother lingers at the window a moment longer, the sunlight spilling over her shoulders and pooling at her feet, then she turns to me with her cup of hot tea and smiles.

"Why don't you ask your father, Etsuko?" she says.

I sigh and roll my eyes.

My father is the meteorologist for the local Channel 8 news in Kochi. Whenever I ask him about the weather, instead of just telling me if there's going to be rain or sunshine or a thunderstorm, he performs a forecast like he does on the news.

I used to think it was funny. Now I smile out of daughterly duty, pretending to be delighted. That's what Etsuko means. Child of delight. It's a lot to live up to when you would rather be grumpy or petulant or bored.

"I don't want to ask him," I say.

"Ask me what?" my father says as he enters the kitchen.

My father never walks into a room so much as he makes an entrance, like an actor hitting his mark or a new contestant walking out onto a game show.

My mother tilts her head at me and raises a single eyebrow. I respond by opening my eyes wide and staring at her. This is how my mother and I communicate. Most of the time she doesn't get the message.

"Etsuko was wondering what the weather was going to be like this weekend," she says.

"Mom!"

"Was she now?" My father looks at me over the rim of his cup as he takes a drink of tea.

My parents often address me in the third person when they're in the room together. It's another one of the challenges I face being a child of delight.

"Why are you so interested in the weather?" my father asks.

"Aiko is having her eleventh birthday party this weekend," I say.

Aiko is the most popular girl in my class, maybe in the whole school, and this is the first time I've been invited to one of her birthday parties, so I want everything to be perfect. Especially the weather. If it rains, she and the other girls will probably blame me because I'm the daughter of the weatherman and then I'll never get invited to another one of Aiko's parties.

I don't explain this to my mother and my father because they wouldn't understand.

"She's invited me and some of the other girls in class to go to Katsumirahama Beach and then to the Obiyamachi shopping arcade," I say. "So I'm hoping for good weather."

"Well then." My father puts down his tea and slips into his suit jacket seemingly all in a single move, then he tugs once on each of his shirt cuffs and spreads his hands out like a magician getting ready to perform his next amazing trick. "Let's see what the weather gods have in store for us this weekend, shall we?"

My mother smiles her little smile that she reserves for my father when he's not looking, the one that says she loves him for all of his silly antics and theatrics, while I roll my eyes and wait for the show to be over and hope there aren't any thundershowers or freak typhoons in the forecast.

"The current high pressure system that has been keeping temperatures above average for this time of year is going to back off a bit," my father says, motioning to an invisible map of Shikoku on a non-existent blue screen behind him, with Kochi, Susaki, and Muroto among the highlighted cities along Tosa Bay. "This should lead to a bit of a cooling trend as we head into the weekend, with some clouds and even some scattered showers moving in from the Pacific."

In spite of the fact that my father's weatherman bit has lost most of its charm on me, I let out a little groan.

"However," my father says, with a theatrical wave of his left hand that culminates in a single index finger held up for emphasis. "There will be enough of a northerly wind moving across the mountains to push the precipitation south along the coast, where it will fall over the southern tip of Shikoku, missing Kochi and leaving blue skies with some scattered high clouds for the weekend."

I don't realize I'm holding my breath until I let it out.

"So no rain or thunderstorms or typhoons?" I ask.

"No rain or thunderstorms," he says.

I stare at my father, not blinking or moving, waiting for him to finish his answer, but he just drinks his tea.

I'm trying to be a child of delight but with a father like mine, it's not always easy.

"Dad!"

"And no typhoons," he says.

My mother gives my father another smile, this one meant for him to see, and he returns it with a smile and a wink.

3

"Promise?" I ask.

"When it comes to the weather, there are no promises, Etsuko," he says. "Only predictions and forecasts based on patterns and satellite data."

"Yes, father," I say.

"But don't worry about your party," he says. "You and your friends should have perfect weather for Aiko's birthday."

This should put my mind at ease but it doesn't. I look at my mother who gives me a smile, my glance lingering on her scar before I ask my next question.

"What about daikaiju?" I say.

My mother's smile falters, then recomposes before she hides it in her cup of tea.

"We don't tend to get daikaiju this far south," my father says, his smile and good humor gone like a magic trick. Now you see it, now you don't.

"But sometimes we do," I say, remembering my history.

"Yes," he says. "Though not for many years."

The last daikaiju attack in southern Japan occurred on January 17, 1995, in Hyōgo on Awaji Island, though that was more of a quarrel between Hedorah and Gojira than an attack. Before that was April of 1968, when Gamera came ashore on Okinoshima to lay some eggs. The only other confirmed daikaiju attack in the region took place along the coast of northern Shikoku in late December of 1854, though there are conflicting accounts as to whether it was Kubadon or Kingugidora.

So yes, my father is right. We don't often get daikaiju this far south.

Most of the daikaiju attacks take place along the coastal cities and prefectures of northern Honshu, with Tokyo taking the brunt of the punishment. Unofficially, Tokyo has been attacked by daikaiju more than forty times, though many Japanese historians believe the first daikaiju attack dates back as far as 1293, in what is officially known as the Great Kamakura Earthquake.

I always wondered why my father became a meteorologist rather than opening his own construction company. Construction does a booming business in Japan, especially during daikaiju season, creating working class millionaires. Most of the kids I know whose fathers or grandfathers are in construction have seven figure trust funds.

I don't care about having a trust fund. I just wish my father didn't have a job that the other kids could use to blame me if Aiko's birthday party gets ruined.

"So no chance of daikaiju this weekend?" I say.

I can tell from the expression on my father's face that I'm pressing my point, but it's his job to know these things.

"Forecasting daikaiju is much more difficult than forecasting the weather, Etsuko," he says. "They are much less predictable."

In Japan, meteorologists not only forecast the weather, they also read the daikaiju radar and provide warnings of possible attacks. So during daikaiju season, it's common to hear weather reports that combine the two:

Mostly sunny with a chance of Garuganchua.

Increasing afternoon winds, with a Rodan trend taking us through the weekend.

Scattered thunderstorms late this evening, with the possibility of Megaro or Barugon by morning. So get out your umbrellas and your emergency survival kits!

"What about the daikaiju radar?" I ask.

"While the radar is helpful, it doesn't always give us much advance warning," my father says. "Daikaiju move a lot faster than weather fronts."

Due to trade winds and water currents, the daikaiju generally tend to come in from the east, though every now and then you hear about an attack in Niigata or Kanazawa off the coast in the Sea of Japan.

"But you didn't see anything on the radar for this weekend?" I ask.

"No," he says. "The seven day forecast calls for mostly clear skies and less than a five percent chance of daikaiju."

"Even Gigalar?" I ask.

Of all the daikaiju, Gigalar scares me the most. I've only seen it on YouTube and on archived news footage, but its shriek sends chills down my spine every time.

"Yes," he says. "Even Gigalar."

"Promise?" I say.

My father looks at my mother, who is still hiding behind her cup of tea, then he turns back to me with a smile that looks as if it was hastily painted on with an unskilled hand.

"Promise," he says.

I'm sitting in the classroom late Friday morning with the other students for our English language studies, learning about objects and predicates and dependent clauses, when the first raindrops start to fall.

Aiko, who is sitting behind me, kicks the back of my chair. I glance toward the front of the room where Mr. Kasama writes a sentence in English on the dry erase board, his back to us.

Aiko kicks my chair again.

"What?" I whisper over my shoulder.

Aiko leans forward. "I thought you said your father promised good weather this weekend."

"He did," I whisper.

She glances at the windows, then looks back at me—her eyes wide and her expression demanding. "Then why is it raining?"

My first thought is that it's raining because water evaporated, condensed into ice in the clouds, then fell back to earth as precipitation due to a localized warm air mass and a strong updraft.

My father's nightly instructional discussions on meteorology haunt me, though apparently the northerly wind blowing down from the mountains that my father mentioned wasn't strong enough to push the rain further south.

"It's just some scattered showers," I whisper. "They'll pass."

Aiko purses her lips, then says aloud, "They better."

"Etsuko!"

I turn back around and see Mr. Kasama watching me, his arms folded in front of him.

"Yes sir," I say.

"Did you have something new to add to the lesson?" he asks.

Behind me, several of the girls giggle.

"No sir," I say.

"Good," he says and points to the sentence he's written on the board. "Then perhaps you can tell me the object and predicate in this sentence."

We spend the next thirty minutes going over the elements of English sentence structure. Five minutes before the end of class, I glance outside and see that the showers have stopped and there are pockets of sunlight drifting across the schoolyard. Although there are still some lingering stratocumulus clouds with a threatening gray pallor, the emerging blue behind them appears to be winning the battle for supremacy of the sky.

Maybe my father was right. Maybe the weekend weather will be perfect for Aiko's birthday and I'll finally get to know what it's like to be one of the popular girls.

Then the warning siren goes off outside.

Everyone looks out the classroom windows, all of our heads turning in unison like a choreographed shot in a movie or a music video. Two of the boys, Shinji and Takeru, stand up and leave their desks to get a closer look but are admonished by Mr. Kasama to return to their seats before he picks up the phone to call the administration office.

"What's going on?" Kumiko says, twirling one of her long black braids.

Kumiko means 'girl with braids.' I've known her for almost three years now and I've never seen her without her signature hairstyle.

"It's probably just a test," Ichiro says.

Ichiro means 'first born son,' though if you ask me it should mean 'first to answer' because he always has his hand in the air before any of the other students. "They test the siren every now and then to make sure it works."

We all sit and listen to the siren, waiting for it to stop.

"What if it's not a test?" Miki says, looking worried. Miki is a big hulk of a girl whose name means 'tree trunk.'

"Then we can all hide behind you for safety," Ichiro says.

A bunch of the kids laugh, including Miki, who always laughs when anyone makes fun of her. I don't laugh because I don't think it's funny. Also because after more than a minute, the siren is still blaring.

"Attention students," Mr. Kasama says, once he's off the phone. We all quiet down and turn toward him. "I've been informed that we're all to remain inside the classroom until we receive further word."

Ichiro raises his hand. "Did they say what's happening?"

"Just that we're all to remain inside and stay clear of the windows," Mr. Kasama says.

When the bell rings signaling the end of class, no one moves or seems to know what to do.

"I have been asked to come to administration," Mr. Kasama says. "I won't be long. Takeru, you're in charge until I get back."

Takeru responds with a self-important smile and immediately looks for someone to boss around. His name means 'fierce and unbending.' Takeru is not one of the more popular students.

"What about lunch?" Miki asks.

"We will take lunch once we're given the all clear," Mr. Kasama says as he walks to the classroom door. "Until then, if anyone brought snacks, you're free to take them out."

After Mr. Kasama leaves, most of the students dig into their backpacks and remove nori and senbei, daifuku, Yan Yan, and other snacks. I didn't bring anything so I sit and wait, listening to the siren, wishing it would stop. While I'm wishing, Aiko kicks the back of my chair again. When I turn around, she's scowling at me.

"You better hope this is just a test, Etsuko."

Aiko means 'beloved' in Japanese. Sometimes I wonder if her parents made a mistake when they named her.

"Hey!" Hiroki has taken out his portable radio and is listening to it with his headphones. "I've got some news about what's happening!"

Everyone gathers around Hiroki, like pigeons flocking to an old woman with a bag of birdseed.

"What are they saying?" Katsumi asks.

Katsumi is Aiko's best friend. Her name means 'victorious beauty,' which is fitting since she often excels over everyone else, both in academics and athletics. Most of the girls can't stand her, though they all wish they could be just like her.

Hiroki doesn't answer Katsumi but holds up his left hand to silence everyone while pressing his right hand against his ear. Ichiro starts to say something but Yuko shushes him, placing a single finger against her lips to emphasize her point. Takeru comes over to throw his weight around, saying, "Move aside, I'm in charge," until someone tells him to go stick his head in a toilet.

Hiroki's eyes go wide. "Kubadon was spotted ten miles offshore!"

There are five seconds of shocked silence as everyone looks around at one another, eyes wide in disbelief. Not even Ichiro has anything to say, which is a first. Meanwhile, Aiko stands with her arms crossed, staring at me as if all of this is my fault.

When the school bell rings again, some of the girls scream in terror. A couple of the boys, too, though they'll deny it. Then everyone starts talking and shouting at once.

"I can't believe it!"

"What should we do?"

"Is he heading this way?"

Some of the girls cluster together and cast glances of worry in the hopes of catching one of the boys, most of whom are too busy laughing and running around in a display of pre-adolescent bravado, excited at the idea of seeing a real live daikaiju.

While Kubadon is no Gojira, he still strikes an intimidating image with his indestructible carapace, taloned feet, and upper appendages that are more blades than arms. I neither join the other girls in their worry nor the boys in their excitement but close my eyes and pray—not because I'm afraid for myself or for my friends or for my family and not because I hope to save our city from wide scale destruction. I'm praying because I don't want Kubadon to ruin Aiko's birthday.

Please let the currents and trade winds take him south. Let him attack Tosa or Susaki, instead. Anywhere but here. Anywhere but Kochi.

"Kubadon just came ashore at Katsumirahama Beach," Hiroki says. He pauses several moments before delivering the punch line. "They say the entire area has been decimated!"

When I open my eyes, Aiko is glaring at me as if trying to will me to drop dead. Katsumi stands next to Aiko and attempts to do the same in a show of anti-Etsuko solidarity.

"Attention students," Mr. Kasama says as he returns to the classroom. "Attention! We are all going down to the daikaiju shelter, so please grab your backpacks and line up at the door. Quick quick!"

We all do as we're told, lining up as if we're going to eat lunch instead of going to hide in a shelter while our city gets attacked by a giant monster. Even though none of us has ever experienced an actual daikaiju attack, no one is crying or hysterical. Like people who live in regions with tornados or hurricanes or earthquakes, daikaiju attacks are just part of our upbringing. It's something we're taught to expect. So we listen to our instructor and trust that he knows what he's doing.

"Attention students," Mr. Kasama says. "Attention. Does everyone have a partner?"

We're all lined up in pairs to make sure no one is left behind. My partner is Yuko, whose name means 'gentle child.' While I get along with Yuko more than any of the other girls, we're not what you would call close friends.

Mr. Kasama counts to make sure we're all here, then nods his approval. "Attention students, please follow me."

We file out of the classroom and march in two columns, side-by-side behind Mr. Kasama like tiny little soldiers heading off to battle, armed with backpacks and nori snacks and braids. Other students file out of other classrooms, no one saying a word, the only sound that of the instructors giving directions and the siren continuing to blare. Then Hiroki shouts out:

"Gigalar was just sighted over Mt. Kuishi!"

Everyone turns and looks north in the direction of Mt. Kuishi, even though it's more than twenty-five kilometers away. For several moments I don't move or breathe, frozen in place by the thought of seeing Gigalar, even just catching a glimpse of him in the distance. But instead of a giant winged creature with pincers and fangs who looks like the mutant offspring of a bat and a scorpion, half a dozen JASDF fighter jets roar past overhead, headed toward the coast.

A moment later to the south, a different type of roar fills the air. Having heard that same roar dozens of times on YouTube and as ringtones on cell phones, I expect it to have lost any sense of novelty. But the electronic reproductions of Kubadon's roar fail to capture its strength. It explodes in the air, rattling windows and shaking the earth, causing goose bumps to break out on my arms and along the back of my neck, my hands flying protectively to cover my ears. When I look around, I see all of the other students have covered their ears, as well. Even Mr. Kasama is holding a hand to each side of his head.

More than anything—more than Kubadon's roar, more than

the JASDF fighter jets, more than the prospect of seeing Gigalar—the sight of Mr. Kasama covering his ears makes me wish my mother and father were here.

"Attention students!" Mr. Kasama shouts as if he's trying to be heard over the ghost of Kubadon's roar, his adult veneer stripped away. "Run!"

Any sense of orderly composure we'd maintained vanishes in Mr. Kasama's naked urgency. We all start running, the boys for the most part faster than the girls, but gender doesn't play any favorites when it comes to terror. Boys and girls alike shout and scream or cry; some do both, while some of the students in the lower grades urinate in their school uniforms.

I don't scream, cry, or urinate. I do, however, run faster than everyone in my class except for Katsumi, Ichiro, and Mr. Kasama.

When we reach the shelter, we find the entrance clogged by students and instructors, like a backed-up sink that's slowly draining.

"Kubadon just destroyed the Obiyamachi shopping arcade!" Hiroki shouts.

Gasps of shock and cries of concern rise up from the crowd, orchestral notes of distress that are a prelude to the symphony of impending fear. I barely have a chance to react to the news before a hand grabs my shoulder and turns me around and I'm face-to-face with Aiko, who points a single index finger at me, her face dark with anger.

"You are *so* uninvited from my birthday party!" she says.

It's times like this when I really hate that my father is a meteorologist.

Students and instructors press forward toward the clogged shelter entrance. It takes a few minutes but the drain finally clears, allowing the rest of us to flow inside the shelter and down the stairs to safety. Moments after the last of us are inside, the doors close and we're all gathered one story underground, beneath the gymnasium and the ceiling lined with fluorescent lights.

There aren't any chairs to sit on, but the benches along the walls are occupied by the students from the lower grades, most of them sniffling or crying while being consoled by the instructors. The students from the older grades stand around or sit on the floor in cliques and gangs of friendship, attempting to cultivate a façade of pre-adolescent indifference.

"Do you think we'll be safe down here?" Yuko asks.

I answer with a shrug. I suppose I could do more to comfort Yuko, who wears her concern on her face like a fresh bruise, but I'm too wrapped up in my own distress to offer any comfort.

Kumiko, Hiroko, Katsumi, and a few of the other girls have huddled around Aiko, attempting to console her. I think about going over and apologizing but decide that would just make things worse. I want to explain to her that no one can control the weather, that they can only make predictions based on available data. But my father's scientific rationale doesn't stand a chance against a popular eleven-year-old girl's crushed sense of birthday entitlement.

Principal Okuma walks around the shelter, speaking in a low whisper, telling everyone to stay calm and to refrain from making any loud noises. Some of the other instructors take up the mantra and repeat it to their students, including Mr. Kasama, who seems to be saying it more to calm himself than any of us.

Outside we hear the sound of more fighter jets roaring past, followed a short time later by several distant explosions, though caused by the jets or by Kubadon, we can't tell. Hiroki is still giving us updates but even without his play-by-play, the sound of Gigalar's shrieks growing closer are unmistakable.

"This is your fault," Miki says, pointing an accusing finger at me. "Your father is the weatherman. You should have told us this was going to happen."

I've never done anything mean to Miki or made any rude comments about her size or her name, so I don't know why she would attack me like that and single me out. Then I see Katsumi and Kumiko and Aiko all nodding their heads in vigorous approval and

I realize Miki saw an opportunity to improve her standing in the eyes of the other girls and took it at my expense.

She'll probably get invited to Aiko's birthday party instead of me.

Mr. Kasama admonishes Miki to stay quiet, as do the other instructors to their students, most of whom avoid making eye contact with me. Some of the instructors look away, as well. Even Principal Okuma gives me a disapproving shake of his head. Other than Yuko, no one else stands within a three-foot radius of me, as if being the daughter of the local weatherman is contagious. After a few moments, Yuko decides she doesn't want to catch anything, either, and moves further away.

Gigalar shrieks again, the high-pitched cry so close it sounds as if he's directly over the school. We all sit in silence, looking up at the shelter ceiling, waiting for the roar of the fighter jets to respond. Instead, Kubadon's roar answers, reverberating throughout the shelter. A moment later comes a faint vibration, followed a few seconds later by another—not the sound of bombs exploding but of giant footsteps, growing closer.

Soft cries and whimpers turn to shouts and wails, the chorus of terror building toward full-fledged panic, making it more and more difficult for the instructors to keep the students on key. It's not long before the shrieks and roars from outside combine with the rhythmic and swelling vibrations to shatter the façade of pre-adolescent indifference and adult supervision, causing everyone in the shelter to hold hands and hug one another, students and instructors seeking and offering comfort, while I stand alone in shame.

Part of me longs for my mother, for the soothing comfort of her embrace. But another part of me, the part that hates being ostracized because my father is the local meteorologist, decides I need to show everyone that they're wrong. I need to prove that I'm better than what they think of me.

"Aiko!" I shout, but she doesn't notice me, so I shout her name again. "Aiko!"

She looks my way, her face pinched in disappointment and fear. When she sees me, her expression turns to a dark scowl accompanied by a sullen stare. I smile and stick my tongue out at her before I turn and walk to the stairs.

"Hey!" Miki shouts. "Look at Etsuko!"

No one runs up from behind to stop me or shouts for me to come back as I ascend the stairs, not even Mr. Kasama or Principal Okuma. It's as though they're all too shocked to know what to do. For a moment, I think about turning around and taking a bow or giving a small curtsy, but decide that would be too pretentious.

When I reach the top of the stairs, the shelter has grown silent behind me. From the other side of the door I hear the shrieks of Gigalar and the roar of Kubadon, not right outside but close enough to cause my arms to break out in goose bumps. Beneath the soles of my feet, the top stair vibrates with every one of Kubadon's earthshaking steps.

My heart is pounding and my mouth has gone dry. Somewhere below my waist, my knees are shaking, although they seem so far away that they might as well belong to someone else. A song of doubt whistles through my thoughts. I glance back down the stairs, half-expecting to see faces looking up at me in awe but no one is watching.

Had someone come after me or called out for me to stop, I might have listened. Not at first, but maybe I would have turned back after I'd made it halfway up the stairs. It probably wouldn't have been enough of a gesture for everyone but it might have been enough to impress most of them. But now that I'm here, I can't turn around and return to the shelter, not even if Aiko appeared at the foot of the stairs and begged me herself. Now that I'm this close, I don't have any choice but to see what's on the other side of the door.

For a moment I see my mother standing at the kitchen sink, bathing in the light pouring through the window, the scar on her face lit up like a warning. I think about how my mother touches the scar whenever she's reading or watching television or lost in thought—her index finger tracing the length of the scar from her hairline to her jaw and past the soft, vulnerable pocket of her left eye.

I guess I'm more like my mother than I realized.

A shriek from Gigalar fills the air, answered by another of Kubadon's roars. I take a deep breath and let it out, then I turn the handle, open the shelter door, and step outside.

Riding the Softland Express

Grandpa only had one finger left and it was pointing at the door.

He was leaning forward in his chair, his gaze turned away from the marathon of *Gilligan's Island* reruns, that single, remaining digit on his left hand pointing across the room.

"Someone's comin'," he said.

Before I could reach my Smith and Wesson sitting on top of the television, the front door crashed open.

Wait a minute. Let me back up.

Ten hours earlier, my little brother Ben and I had just returned from the Centr-O-Mart with some bread, eggs, and beer. Not that we had anything to celebrate. But both of us had been craving fried egg sandwiches and it was Saturday morning, so Ben and I decided to live it up while Grandpa settled in to watch the *Gilligan's Island* marathon on Nickelodeon.

"Nice!" he shouted from his chair as Tina Louise bent towards the camera in a low cut, gold sequin dress.

Ben cracked open three beers and gave one to each of us, then joined Grandpa while I prepared breakfast. Before I could get the pan on the burner, the cell phone rang.

The phone hadn't rung in nearly three months, so Ben and I exchanged glances before Ben got off the couch, downed half his beer, plucked the phone off the counter, flipped it open, and pressed the ANSWER button.

"Softland."

I watched Ben's expression to see if I could read the order. We hadn't had any customers, not since Grandpa's accident, so when Ben said, "What grade?" it looked like our fortunes had turned.

Good luck comes in grades.

People with high-grade good luck win the lottery, get discovered by a talent agent, and always manage to escape serious injury. Medium-grade good luck helps people win progressive jackpots, marry the right person, and be in the right place at the right time. Those who possess low-grade good luck win money and prizes on game shows, become friends with a celebrity, and get an occasional hole-in-one.

While low-grade good luck seldom sells for more than five grand, high-grade good luck can command up to six figures on the open market.

Bad luck comes in grades, too, but it's not a good idea to poach bad luck. It's like inviting an unwanted guest into your home and asking him to spend the rest of his life with you. Of course, just because it's a bad idea doesn't mean someone hasn't tried it. Look at the Edsel. Or *Battlefield Earth*. History is full of bad decisions.

Ben wrapped up his conversation and flipped the phone shut.

"What's the order?" I asked.

"Soft," he said, downing the rest of his beer in three gulps. "Top-grade soft."

Good luck is soft and warm. The higher the grade, the softer the luck. Bad luck, conversely, is curdled and heavy—used motor oil with the consistency of hot asphalt. Except bad luck isn't warm. It's cold, like death. And whereas good luck is the color of alabaster, bad luck is as black as the shadows in the barrel of a gun.

Ben rubbed the stubble on his chin and looked my way. "That woman in Gilroy who won the lottery last week?"

I nodded. "Dolores Santos."

Even though we hadn't had a paying customer for more than three months, we still kept on top of current events. But other than people coming into large amounts of money or flirting with death, it wasn't easy to find hosts for high-grade good luck, especially within driving distance.

Ben got the gear together while I finished making the fried egg sandwiches, which we washed down with a couple more beers. Normally Grandpa would have come with us, but after what happened last time, we decided to leave him home. Besides, there was no way we could drag him away from the television.

"Nice!" Grandpa shouted at the sight of Dawn Wells bending over in a pair of tight denim shorts.

Gilroy was an hour and a half away, so by the time Ben and I pulled up across the street from Dolores Santos's, the August afternoon sun was beating down on the roof of our '73 Charger. Driving through the valley during the summer in a suit and tie was about as much fun as wiping up the toilet after one of Grandpa's accidents, but sometimes you did what you had to do.

Dolores Santos lived at 151 Magnolia Lane, a few blocks from a strip mall where Ben and I had picked up some powdered doughnuts and Budweiser. Sugar and beer help with the transference of luck into a marketable form. We don't know why, since neither Ben nor I ever got better than a C in chemistry, but powdered sugar doughnuts and Budweiser was always our best combo.

While Ben got the transference equipment ready, I polished off another doughnut and drained the last of my beer, then climbed out of the car and walked across the street, stopping beneath the shade of an elm tree to blot the perspiration from my face. Anxiety had nothing to do with my sweat glands working overtime to cool my body. Wearing a suit in ninety-five degree heat was to blame for that. But poaching luck is a lot like a job interview—if you don't make a good first impression, you're probably not going to get what you came for.

Not just anyone can poach luck. It's not a skill you can pick up with practice or learn in a weekend seminar. Great Grandma passed it on to Grandpa, who passed it on to Mom, who passed it on to us— though Mom refused to use it. Said it wasn't right, stealing someone's luck.

Had Mom used her gift once in a while, she probably wouldn't have pulled out of the parking lot an instant before that bus ran a red light.

I can still see her sometimes, broken and bleeding in the driver's seat, safety glass in her hair, her head twisted to one side. Nothing happened to me. Not a scratch or a bruise. Even at the age of nine, I'd already learned the art of poaching.

That's one of the reasons Ben and I poach for hire instead of poaching luck for ourselves. Out of respect for Mom. Though if we truly wanted to respect her ideals, we wouldn't use our gift at all.

But if we're being honest, the main reason we sell the luck we poach is because using poached luck can create its own problems. The addictive properties aside, you win the lottery or hit a bunch of progressive jackpots and suddenly you're drawing attention to yourself and having to report your income on a tax return. The last thing we want is to have the IRS or the government poking around in our lives. But just because you take precautions doesn't mean you can avoid the consequences.

The problem with poaching luck is that sooner or later, karma is bound to catch up with you. After all, you can't take something from someone without eventually paying a price.

After a quick adjustment of my tie, I walked up to the front door and rang the bell. I hoped Dolores didn't have any children at home. Parents are more wary and distrustful of strangers when their children are present. But when Dolores answered the door alone, I knew this would be a simple hit and run.

"May I help you?" she said.

"Good afternoon." I extended my right hand. "My name is William Kennedy and I'm running for the Gilroy city council."

When you're poaching luck, you can't just pick a random name or crusade and expect someone to trust you when she's just won seven million dollars and a stranger knocks on her door. It's an art form, like being an actor. All you have to do is convince your audience that you are who they want you to be.

"Nice to meet you," Dolores said. She still didn't trust me enough to offer her own name, but I didn't require that level of acceptance. All I needed was her hand, which she gave to me.

A simple hit and run.

Physically, my skin looks and feels like anyone else's. I sweat, get sunburned, and have had my share of cuts, abrasions, and rug burns. But my skin heals faster than most people. Same with Ben and Grandpa. Maybe we have more keratin. Or collagen. Or a greater abundance of cells that are involved in immune defenses. But whatever helps our skin heal also allows it to absorb another person's luck simply by grasping his or her hand.

Most people don't notice when their luck runs out, so to speak. It leaves without fanfare, like sweat through your pores or air from your lungs. Dolores might have noticed a slight temperature change or a momentary acceleration of her heart rate, but it's nothing the human body doesn't go through multiple times each day.

I, on the other hand, felt a surge of adrenaline through my veins and tendons. It had been more than six months since I'd poached top-grade good luck and I staggered back a step from the front door with Dolores's hand still clasped in mine.

"Hey, let go of me!" she said and yanked her hand away. Before I could offer up an apology, the front door slammed and the deadbolt clicked into place.

The initial moments after a successful poaching are intense. Colors turn rich and vibrant. Half a block away, you can hear a crow take flight, hear its wings flap, then a car engine comes to life. You can smell the oil on the street and the beer on your breath and the honeysuckle in the yard next door. Your pores release perspiration to cool your skin as the sun heats the air around you. You feel this. You experience every moment, every fraction of time. It's as if existence has slowed down and you're moving at twice your normal speed.

In spite of the rush of invincibility that accompanies poaching,

I knew I'd be pushing my luck by sticking around. So after one last inhale of honeysuckle, oil, and beer, I turned around and headed toward the street, feeling the pavement through the soles of my shoes and the blood rushing through my veins. I didn't pay attention to the humming of tires on asphalt until it was too late.

A white SAAB braked to a sliding stop in front of me. The driver and passenger doors opened and two men wearing Ronald Reagan masks emerged from the SAAB. Just before they grabbed me, I heard tires squealing and saw the Charger take off. An instant later, I was on the ground. A couple of zip ties around my wrists and ankles and a knit beanie over my head later, and I was sitting in the back of the SAAB between two bodies who smelled like garlic and Wild Turkey.

I could hear muffled breathing but no one spoke. I should have been scared. After all, it's not like I get tied up, blindfolded, and kidnapped on a regular basis. Try never. But I was riding The Softland Express, the high of having one hundred percent top grade luck pumping through my system.

Although good luck won't solve all of your problems, it gives you the confidence things will work out.

Bad luck, naturally, swings the pendulum the other way. Everything that will go wrong does—sickness, bankruptcy, divorce, hair loss, impotency, sterility, car accidents, shark attacks, cancelled flights, termites, flood damage, and herpes.

When it's top-grade heavy, the pendulum not only swings the other way, it gets stuck. Imagine the worst thing that can happen to you short of death, then dip it in oil and set it on fire. Even a trace amount of the stuff will stick around like a bad infection—making you and your brother sick for two weeks, causing your business to go into the tank, and elevating fried egg sandwiches to a gourmet meal. Sometimes it'll take away four fingers on your Grandpa's left hand.

But when someone hands you a bag full of money that comes to more than you made poaching the past two years, you figure you're young enough to handle it. Of course, it doesn't enter your mind that all that money might get lost or stolen or fall into a black hole. We still don't know what happened to it. The next day, the money was gone.

As devastating as top-grade bad luck can be, Grandpa used to tell us stories about something worse, a bad luck in vapor form—a black cloud bearing a malevolent storm that makes plague and pestilence seem like a light, refreshing summer rain.

Who needs the bogeyman when you have stories like that to keep you in line?

After what felt like an hour, the SAAB finally came to a stop. A car door opened and the body pressed against my right side stepped out and closed the door. A few moments later, the car started forward and the warmth of the sun through the windows vanished. The engine shut off. Two car doors opened. Hands grabbed me and hauled me out of the backseat and across what felt like a bare concrete floor before turning me around and shoving me into an unpadded metal chair.

A few minutes of silence passed before the knit beanie was removed from my head. Once my eyes adjusted to the overhead fluorescents, I realized we'd driven into a warehouse. Two of my abductors stood near the SAAB a few feet away, still wearing their Reagan masks. One was shorter and the other held a tire iron. The third Reagan stood behind me, breathing like Darth Vader. Except for the SAAB and us, the warehouse was empty.

I laughed. I couldn't help myself. It was so cliché. The roadside abduction, the masks, the abandoned warehouse. The only thing missing was a briefcase full of money.

"What's so funny?" asked the shorter Reagan.

"Nothing," I said. "Just nervous."

"Yeah, you should be nervous, you freak," said the Reagan with the tire iron. "After what you did to our sister."

"Shut up," said the shorter Reagan.

The short one's voice sounded older, worn out by either age or tobacco. Or both. He also appeared older—beer gut, hairy knuckles, the works. At least twenty years older than Tire Iron. Probably his father. Darth Reagan, still breathing behind me like an obscene phone call, was odds on Tire Iron's brother. And I'd done something to their sister and Dad's daughter to piss them all off.

"So, you like stealing other people's luck?" Father Reagan said, his voice muffled behind the mask.

I shrugged. "It pays the bills."

"It pays the bills," he said, nodding. "That's good, because we've got a debt that needs to be settled."

"Your daughter," I said.

Tire Iron stepped forward and raised his weapon. "You're going to pay for what you did to Melissa."

"Will you shut up!" said Father Reagan.

An image floated through my head. A woman in her mid-twenties, two years ahead of me in high school. Melissa Benedetto. Italian. Dark hair. Fair skin. Blue eyes. Her picture had been in the newspaper a few months back, not long after Grandpa lost the four fingers on his left hand. Something worse had happened to her. Some kind of freak accident. Whatever beauty she'd had was taken away. And it was our fault.

Another benefit of poaching top-grade soft: it gives you omniscient clarity, an almost godlike perception. Moments that seemed disconnected suddenly become related, a series of events leading up to right now.

We never should have poached bad luck.

While the majority of our clients are interested in improving their own luck, every once in a while we get a call from someone with a vindictive side. Someone who wants to take away someone else's good fortune. Maybe it's a competing business that's cutting into your profits. Or a star athlete on a rival sports team. Or a popular high school beauty queen.

I don't know what kind of personal vendetta someone had against Melissa Benedetto, but apparently it was serious enough to warrant something worse than toilet papering her house.

We had no idea what our client wanted to use the bad luck for. We never know the motives of our clients, good or bad. The money is just too good to pass up to worry about consequences.

Sometimes, bad decisions catch up with you.

"That luck you stole from the Mexican woman," Father Reagan said. "We want it."

Another insight: this entire job had been a setup to get some good luck in hopes of reversing what had happened to Melissa. Or at least make things better. So these three had waited for someone to win the lottery and then made their move. Since no one knows where we live, the only way to find us is to call our cell phone and send us out on a job where you could lay in wait in a SAAB Turbo and Ronald Reagan masks.

"How did you get our phone number?" I asked.

"Let's just say the person responsible for what happened to Melissa didn't have a high threshold for pain," Tire Iron said.

Behind me, Darth Reagan's breathing hitched up a notch, like a squeal of delight.

"Give us the luck," Father Reagan said.

"I can't just give it to you," I said. "It has to be processed from my system."

"Bullshit," said Tire Iron.

Father Reagan gave his son a look, holding up a single warning finger, then turned back to me. "What do you mean *processed*?"

The last thing I wanted to do was explain the physiology of luck transference into a consumable form to three grown men in Ronald Reagan masks. Maybe if they'd been wearing JFK or Jimmy Carter masks. But Reagan? Come on. Like I'd ever vote Republican.

Before I could offer up an answer, my cell phone rang. Father Reagan plucked it from my inside coat pocket and answered.

"Yeah?"

Silence again, broken only by the heavy breathing of Darth Reagan.

"Yeah, he's here," said Father Reagan. Another pause. "All right. But the conversation's one way."

He held the phone toward me. "Say something so he knows you're okay, but keep it short or you'll need stitches in the back of your head."

"I gotta pee, bro," I said.

Father Reagan put the phone back to his ear. "You hear that? Good. Now here's what we want..."

I listened to Father Reagan demand the delivery of top-grade soft if anyone wanted to see me alive again, wondering what Ben was saying in response. Not that I didn't trust him, but I really did have to pee and it was only a matter of time before I decided to give in to my bladder and let go, which wouldn't be a good idea considering that most of Dolores Santos's luck would run down my leg.

He pissed it all away isn't just an expression. Though technically, you can't piss it *all* away. And those who are born with luck never lose it through urination or perspiration or masturbation. Luck stays in their system until a poacher comes along. Those who aren't born with it have to settle for the residue of other people's good fortunes.

In order for ordinary people to use poached luck, it has to be extracted using a catheter and a series of double tubes that run through a portable centrifuge, where the luck is separated from the urine and deposited into a plastic container.

Kind of like apheresis, only without the movie or the free cookies or the American Red Cross T-shirt.

Up until the 1960s, poachers collected urine in a glass flask with a rubber stopper and condensation tube, then let the urine and water boil off, leaving the luck behind. Trouble was, some of the luck always got lost in the evaporation process. Plus burned luck doesn't hold its market value. And it tastes horrible. Might as well just drink the urine straight.

After including a few more details about a meeting time and

location, along with a demand that my brother come alone, Father Reagan said, "How do I know you won't try to screw us?" Whatever my brother said seemed to satisfy him because he answered, "We'll be there in twenty."

Father Reagan walked up to me, reached into my other coat pocket, and retrieved my wallet. He flipped it open, pulled out my driver's license, then tossed the wallet and cell phone on my lap.

"Put him in the back seat," Father Reagan said.

The next moment the knit beanie went back over my head and everything went black. Two minutes later I was riding in the back of the car, listening to Father Reagan explain what was going down, hoping my brother knew what he was doing.

When the SAAB finally came to a stop, Darth Reagan hauled me out of the backseat and across what felt like asphalt until Father Reagan said, "That's good."

Before I could ask if my brother was there, I heard his calm, mellow voice.

"Do you think you could take that off him?"

The beanie was pulled off and I squinted into the glare of the sun reflecting off the windshield of the Charger, in front of which stood Ben holding a brown paper bag in one hand and a crowbar in the other. I glanced over at Tire Iron, who held his own weapon in front of him like an adolescent who's just realized his penis isn't as big as he thought.

"Do you have it?" Father Reagan asked.

Ben held up the crumpled brown paper bag. Father Reagan stepped forward and took the bag from my brother, opened it and glanced inside, then pulled out a plastic water bottle filled with a white liquid.

Father Regan held up the bottle. "This is it?"

Ben nodded. He was never one for making small talk.

"Looks like a jar full of sperm to me," said Tire Iron.

His father didn't respond, just returned the bottle to the bag and motioned to Darth, who flipped out his fold-up hunting knife.

For a moment I thought he was going to plunge it into my back. Five seconds later, the zip ties around my ankles and wrists fell away and I walked over to Ben and the Charger.

We didn't say a word or embrace or high five or anything, just nodded to each other and climbed into the Charger—Ben behind the wheel and me riding shotgun. Father Reagan stepped forward and leaned into my open window.

"This better be what you say it is. If not," he pulled out my driver's license and held it up for effect, "we'll be stopping by for a visit before you can change your shorts."

He stepped away and Ben turned on the ignition, put the car in drive, and took off. I watched the three Reagans and their SAAB grow smaller in the side view mirror.

"What was in the bottle?" I asked.

"Sugar water," he said. "And milk."

"Won't they figure that out as soon as they try to use it?"

"Probably," he said.

"Won't that make them angry?"

Ben shrugged.

"Shouldn't we be worried?" I asked.

Ben shrugged again. "Grandpa's not."

"Grandpa's not worried?"

Ben shook his head. "He said he's done this before."

"Done what before?"

"This," he said, as if that explained everything.

"When?"

"I don't know," Ben said. "But he's the one who told me to fill the bottle with sugar water and milk. And to tell them to take your driver's license."

"Why would he do that?"

"He said not to ask any questions. Oh, and he said not to let you go to the bathroom."

That was one part of the plan I didn't have to question.

When we got home, Grandpa was still parked in his chair six

feet from the television, watching the *Gilligan's Island* marathon. A four-foot tall floor fan hummed on HIGH behind him. A bowl of prunes and a stainless steel thermos sat on the table beside him.

"Hey Grandpa," I said.

He waved his right hand at me, the one with all five fingers—not in a welcoming greeting but in an effort to get me to shut up. His eyes never left the television.

"Nice!" he shouted as Tina Louise jumped up and down in a white, tasseled, hip hugging dress.

I still couldn't pee, not until the situation with the Reagans was resolved, so I retrieved my Smith & Wesson .38 Special from the kitchen and walked back into the family room.

"Grandpa..."

He gave me a quick, irritated glance and pointed his single, left index finger at me like a witch casting a spell, then returned his attention to the television. I looked at Ben, who'd grabbed a beer from the refrigerator and was standing a few feet behind Grandpa's chair. He shrugged and took a swig.

I walked over to the television, set my gun on top of it, and turned the television off.

"What the hell are you doin'?" Grandpa said.

"I want to know what's going on."

"You don't need to know what's going on," he said. "You'd just screw things up. The both of you. Now go stand over there with your brother and stay the Christ out of my way."

I remained where I was, trying to stare Grandpa down, but eventually I gave up and retreated into the kitchen to sulk.

Grandpa turned on the television and set the remote control down next to the thermos, then plucked a prune from the bowl. The next instant, the prune dropped into his lap and Grandpa leaned forward in his chair, his attention turned away from the television, that single finger on his left hand pointing at the front door.

"Someone's comin'," he said.

I started to make my way around his chair. Before I could get halfway to my Smith and Wesson sitting on top of the television, the front door crashed open, spraying splinters of wood across the floor.

Tire Iron came in first, screaming and waving his namesake in front of him like a scythe. Just behind him, Darth Reagan shoved the broken door aside with one arm while in his other hand he wielded his hunting knife. Coming through the threshold after them was their father carrying a Louisville Slugger.

Ben raised his half-finished bottle of beer and prepared to throw it, while Grandpa grabbed the thermos. Before I could reach my gun, Grandpa twisted the lid off and held the thermos up in front of the fan. A black cloud rose out of the thermos like a swarm of flies and was propelled forward by the force of the fan. The cloud flew in front of me, brushing across my face, clinging for the shortest of moments before sliding past.

Although it touched me for barely a second, and even with Dolores Santos's luck to protect me, it felt as if my life force had been sucked from my bones. I dropped to the floor an instant before the cloud enveloped the three Reagans.

I don't have a complete recollection of what happened after that. It's kind of hard to be a reliable eyewitness when you're lying on the floor in a fetal position. All I could hear were the voices of the Skipper and Gilligan on the television. Otherwise, the room had fallen silent. In front of the broken door, the black cloud seemed to pulse. The next thing I knew, the cloud was gone and the Reagans right along with it. After that, I blacked out.

When I came to, Ben was in the kitchen packing what food we had into boxes and an ice chest, while Grandpa was sitting in his chair watching *Gilligan's Island*.

"Don't lay there like a useless cat," he said. "Get your stuff packed."

Against the wall by the broken front door that had been shoved back into the frame, Grandpa and Ben's suitcases sat packed and ready to go. No surprise there. After all, we couldn't exactly stick around after what had gone down. Still, it would have been nice to sit down and have a beer. Which reminded me, I had to pee.

When I walked past him, Grandpa smiled as Dawn Wells bounced across the television screen wearing a pair of tight white shorts and a red and white polka dot shirt.

"Nice!"

I didn't have time to use the catheter and centrifuge, so I peed into an empty Vitamin Water bottle for safekeeping until I could process the good luck from the urine.

The initial rush of poaching top-grade soft is offset by a feeling of complete abandonment when you release it from your body. It's as if all of your confidence and strength just drains away. But the feeling is only temporary. Gradually, you return to normal, which isn't so bad if the luck you just released has been converted into a sugar water mixture that you can drink for a quick fix.

Twenty minutes later, the Charger was packed with three suitcases, two boxes of food, one ice chest, one garbage bag of dirty clothes, and a half case of beer. Everything else, all the furniture, appliances, and other stuff we'd bought over the last three years, got left behind.

I wasn't sad or wistful about leaving. None of us was. It was just the nature of poaching. We rented a house, filled it with stuff, and when circumstances dictated, we moved. We moved around a lot. Sometimes, we moved farther away than others.

As we pulled out of town, I asked Grandpa what happened to the Reagans. He said the bad luck had devoured them, bones and all, and then "flown out the front door like a legion of bugs from hell."

Bad luck feeds on anger. It's a living organism. And when it gets hungry, it likes to eat.

The reason it left me alone was because I still had the protection of Dolores Santos's top grade good luck. Grandpa and Ben had avoided infection by consuming some top grade soft before Ben had come to get me.

Unknown to Ben and me, Grandpa kept a couple of pints of

high-grade good luck and one thermos of thermonuclear bad luck around for emergencies. He hadn't told us about them because he said we wouldn't know an emergency from a hangnail.

We drove north to Interstate 80, then headed east until we reached a motel on the outskirts of Reno. We booked two rooms, one for Ben and me and one for Grandpa, then grabbed some fast food and headed to the casinos to do a little poaching and win some money. Ben and I each came back with over five grand.

The next day we found a house to rent in a neighborhood south of downtown. With what was left from our winnings, we bought two beds, linens, and a sofa bed. A few more days at the casinos and we managed to completely furnish the house, including a flat screen HDTV for Grandpa and a killer stereo system with surround sound.

With more than a dozen casinos and saloons in downtown Reno, plus another two-dozen casinos in the outskirts and in Sparks, we can earn a comfortable living without having to poach for hire. But we probably won't be able to stick around much longer than a couple of months. Even if you spread your winnings out among the casinos, you can only leave with the house's money so often before someone notices.

Of course, with an ability like ours, it's hard not to draw attention. And even when you keep a low profile, people have a way of finding you.

The cell phone has started ringing again. We haven't answered it yet, but it's just a matter of time. The lure of the score and its incomparable rush is too great a temptation to deny. Not to mention the money. People are willing to pay good money for good luck. And with a nearly limitless supply of customers, the decision is pretty much a no-brainer.

When you have the ability to make six figures off of someone else's good luck without having to declare your income, patience becomes a nagging virtue that suppresses your potential. And Mom always told us to live up to our potential. I know this isn't what she had in mind, but we can't help it. It's just the way we're built.

We're poachers.
Thieves for hire.
And our customers are waiting.

Periodic Table of the Elements
Weekly Singles Mixer

"Atomic" by Blondie is playing on the sound system when I walk through the front door.

I'm decked out in a low-voltage vacuum discharge tube dress that really brings out my deep reddish-orange complexion, causing a number of heads to swivel my way. Drawing attention has never been an issue for me, especially since I'm very rare on Earth. My problem is that I can't seem to sustain a lasting relationship. Silicon says I have commitment issues, but I think it has more to do with a lack of chemistry.

"Hey hot stuff," Nickel says, invading my personal space, his speech slurred and his breath thick with the smell of beer. "Where have you been all of my half-life?"

It's bad enough he's using a stale pickup line. But mixed in with his beer breath I detect more than a hint of Francium—a useless, radioactive, highly unstable metal. I don't care if Nickel does have a lustrous sheen. Beer goggles or not, I don't respect any element who would hook up with that contaminated, crazy bitch. But that doesn't mean I can't have some fun.

I run a playful finger along Nickel's hard exterior. "Did you know that if you combine our atomic symbols, you get NiNe?"

Nickel nods, mesmerized by my finger, which I put under his chin to bring his gaze up to meet mine. Transition metals have a habit of staring at my isotopes.

"Do you speak German?" I ask.

Nickel shakes his head.

I lean forward as if to kiss him but instead whisper in his ear. "Nein means no," I say and then walk away, leaving him to contemplate his incompatibility.

On my way to the bar, I catch Hydrogen checking me out over the top of his margarita, his eyes glassy and full of mischief. While Hydrogen has a good sense of humor and a spontaneous personality, there's never been any mutual attraction between us. Plus he has commitment issues. You put enough pressure on him and he turns into a liquid metal, so if you're looking for a serious relationship, he's not exactly husband material. He's also prone to violent reactions and is highly flammable. I know more than a few elements who have been burned by him.

Even though I know nothing will come of it, I give Hydrogen a playful smile just to be flirty. But when he returns my smile and beckons me to join him, I wonder if he's had one too many margaritas. Then I glance over my shoulder and see Fluorine making ions at Hydrogen, seductively sucking on the straw sticking out of her half-finished piña colada.

Fluorine is the lightest of the halogens, with a pale yellow complexion the color of diluted urine. Like all halogens, Fluorine only has nine electrons. In Periodic Table parlance, she's one electron shy of a full shell. Not to mention she's highly toxic. So caveat emptor.

Not that I'm judging or anything, but Fluorine is a reactive, electronegative, poisonous skank who looks like she's suffering from jaundice. But when it comes to bonding, Hydrogen has never had much in the way of standards. Sulfur. Iodine. Selenium. Nitrogen. Bromine. Phosphorous. Doesn't matter if you're male or female, noble or poor, stable or monoatomic. If you're ionizing, Hydrogen is synthesizing.

Not to be outdone, Fluorine has formed compound bonds with nearly all of the other elements. She's kind of the resident Periodic Table slut.

She saunters past, not noticing me on purpose if you know what I mean, and cozies up to Hydrogen, who looks her up and down and says, "Damn girl, you're looking good enough to combust."

"I bet you say that to all of the halogens," she says and flashes her pearly whites.

I have to admit, she does have great teeth.

These two definitely have a history together and I don't want to be around if that history repeats itself. Hydrogen fluoride is a poisonous gas that can cause a variety of adverse long-term health effects. And if the two of them end up getting aqueous, their resulting bodily fluids can be downright corrosive.

I look around for the nearest exit, just in case, but other than the front door and a couple of windows, the options are limited. Considering this place is filled with a bunch of volatile chemical elements, the owner should invest in more windows or better ventilation, maybe a couple of emergency safety showers and eyewash stations. And they don't have nearly enough fire extinguishers.

Before things can progress to the point where I have to worry about getting any hydrofluoric acid splattered on my new dress, I make it the rest of the way to the bar and order a whiskey sour— mostly because it's my favorite drink but also because *sour* fits my mood.

I know I shouldn't be such a Negative Neutron. After all, I'm not the only element who can't make a commitment to anything that lasts much longer than a spontaneous exothermic reaction. The other noble gases don't form permanent bonds, either—although Radon, Xenon, and Krypton have all hooked up with Fluorine. Big surprise.

Xenon tells me I should lower my standards and just get down and nasty with someone, morning-after regrets and walk-of-shames be damned. She stops short of suggesting I get together with Technetium or Promethium, which is good since neither one of them have any stable isotopes. The last thing I need is a stalker.

Argon, my therapist, tells me I shouldn't compare my love life to that of other elements but should focus on my own prospects for romance. Argon is nonflammable and nontoxic, both big selling points when picking a therapist. He's also stable and resistant to bonding, which cuts down on the likelihood he'll become involved with one of his patients, unlike Oxygen, who lost her license because she readily formed oxides with more than half of her clients.

So in spite of my inability to form any lasting connections or meaningful bonds, I take Argon's advice and keep coming back to these weekly mixers hoping to find my ionic soul element. Although at this point, I've all but given up on the idea of romance and would settle for some clumsy covalent foreplay.

On cue, Aluminum approaches me wearing an awkward smile and a suit he bought off the rack. While intelligent and versatile, Aluminum doesn't have what you would call a magnetic personality.

"Hey," he says.

"Hey," I say, trying to be aloof so he doesn't think I'm interested. Which I'm not.

On the sound system, Blondie has been replaced by The Sweet singing, "Love is Like Oxygen."

"You here by yourself?" Aluminum asks, not wasting any time.

While I appreciate his forthright approach, sometimes a girl likes some subtlety and nuance in her romance. Just not from him.

"I'm meeting someone," I lie.

"That's cool." Aluminum nods and looks around as if this was all part of his plan, then he points at me and winks. "I'll catch you on the flipside, babe."

I hate being called *babe*.

As Aluminum walks away, I catch a glimpse of my reflection in him and stare at myself, wondering why it is that I can't develop a real, emotional connection.

I've tried online dating—H_2OKCupid, Plenty of Electrons, Solid Meets Gas—but none of those resulted in anything that went beyond a first date. Silicon suggested I try my luck with

AtomicTinder, but everyone there is too busy rock climbing, snowboarding, wine tasting, or oxidizing. Not to mention that half of the elements I swiped right on sent me lame text messages such as:

Baby you give my electrons a positive charge.

Girl you are one charged atom, because I've got my ion you.

I'd give you one of my electrons but you're already a perfect 10.

Are you made of Fluorine, Iodine, AND Neon? Because you are FINe!

Either that or they just send me dick pics.

Cue the theatrical sigh.

I went out with Thulium a little over a year ago, but it didn't last. He's nice enough. Non-toxic, bright, a good conversationalist, with a pleasant silvery-gray complexion that gives him a distinguished look. And, like me, he's a rare find on Earth. But he's soft and malleable, whereas I prefer someone who's more of a take-charge kind of element. A little more dominating between the electrons, if you get my drift. Plus he never wanted to try any position other than missionary, which was disappointing considering his atomic number is sixty-nine.

After Thulium I went on a couple of dates with Titanium, who is corrosion resistant and has a great strength-to-density ratio, but he's narcissistic and a poor conductor of heat. I followed up Titanium with Tungsten (robust but very dense), Tantalum (too pliable and soft when in his crystalline alpha state), and Tellurium (brittle and mildly toxic), before Manganese pointed out I was serial dating elements with the same first letter. So I broke the cycle by going out on dates with Platinum (stable but highly unreactive), Gold (great eye candy but only one stable isotope), and Silver (versatile and bright but lacking any covalent character). But they're all transition metals, so I knew the dates wouldn't lead to anything serious.

Eventually I ended up in a short-lived, highly toxic relationship with Beryllium, which was when I started going to therapy.

"Here you go," Copper says, setting my whiskey sour in front of me.

While he tends to tarnish easily, Copper is resistant to corrosion, making him better suited to bartending than most other metals. But I've been to singles mixers where Mercury, Arsenic, or Lead have been pouring drinks, which is a lawsuit waiting to happen.

I give Copper my American Express Iridium card. "Keep it open."

"Sure thing," he says with a smile.

It's a nice smile: warm, sincere, unpretentious. The kind of smile that can charge an element's protons. But his teeth have a constant green patina that makes it impossible to think about kissing him, let alone forming a compound bond together.

I take my whiskey sour, then turn around to check out the room and peruse my options for romance or hookups.

Nickel and Cobalt stand in the middle of the room, laughing conspicuously as if to prove they're a couple of regular ferromagnetic elements who know how to have a good time. While Nickel and Cobalt are two of only four elements who are magnetic at room temperature, I'm not feeling the pull. Based on the empty space around them, neither are any of the other female elements in attendance.

Not far from them, Zinc and Cadmium stand next to each other in matching bluish-white suits drinking Coronas. Rather than laughing like a couple of attention whores, they don't say a word but survey the crowd with casual indifference, as if they're the prize.

On the surface, Zinc and Cadmium both seem like good prospects for either a casual hook-up or an ongoing friends-with-benefits situation. But while Cadmium is resistant to corrosion and can form complex compounds, he has a toxic personality. Zinc, meanwhile, has five stable isotopes and is hard at room temperature. But according to Sulfur, he becomes soft when things start to heat up.

Maybe Xenon is right. Maybe I need to lower my standards and give someone like Zinc or Cadmium a chance. I mean, we're talking a one-night stand, not a full-time relationship. In spite of his performance anxiety issues, I'd probably go with Zinc. At least he's an essential mineral. But like Cadmium, he's a poor metal, so chances are we'd end up eating at Chipotle.

At the other end of the bar, Hydrogen, who apparently bailed on Fluorine, is doing tequila shots with one of his brothers. I've lost track of how many brothers he has, which isn't surprising since Hydrogen is the most abundant element in the universe.

Oxygen has joined them, laughing and fawning all over the two Hydrogen brothers as she tries to match them shot for shot, rubbing up against first one of them and then the other. It doesn't take a doctorate in chemistry to know where this little party is headed.

Trapped between them and the far wall sits Iron, neurotically drinking his Scotch and soda through a straw, looking anxious and annoyed.

"Hey, watch what you're doing!" he shouts as Oxygen and one of the Hydrogen brothers stumble into him, causing him to spill his drink. "Stop touching me!"

While Iron is stable and hard in all of the right places, he definitely has some OCD issues when it comes to other elements causing him to oxidize. I don't know why he bothers to come to these mixers.

The sound of shouting draws my attention to the other side of the room, where Thorium has apparently said or done something inappropriate because Sulfur, Fluorine, and Iodine are all attacking him.

"You do *not* get to speak to me that way," Iodine says, one hand on her hip and an index finger jabbing at Thorium's chest. "You got that, asshole?"

"Yeah, you radioactive prick," Fluorine says, getting all up in Thorium's face. "You got that?"

Sulfur doesn't say anything but just dances around Thorium, lighting matches and flicking them at him as she sings along to "Uranium Rock" by The Cramps.

Before the situation can escalate, Carbon intercedes, playing the role of peacemaker. While Hydrogen or Chlorine might end up making the situation worse—in part because they're both egotistical assholes but also because they have a tendency to cause explosions—Carbon manages to avoid creating additional conflict because he's strong and stable enough to avoid chemical attacks.

"Let's all just try to calm down and not get negatively charged," Carbon says.

Telling three agitated and highly volatile female elements to calm down isn't the most prudent approach. But since he's a common element of all known life, Carbon gets along with just about everyone, so it doesn't take long before Fluorine, Iodine, and Sulfur are all going back to their drinks while Carbon escorts Thorium outside.

Along with his easygoing nature and his two stable naturally occurring isotopes, Carbon has a soft side and a hard side, a nice combination of the feminine and the masculine. Plus he's capable of forming multiple stable covalent bonds, which makes him an ideal candidate for a long-term relationship. And, at atmospheric pressure, he has no melting point, so you know he's cool and rational even when faced with someone as volatile as Nitrogen or as unstable as Francium.

While Carbon seems like relationship material, he does have his flaws. For one thing, he can be opaque one moment and completely transparent the next, so you're never exactly sure what you're going to get. Not to mention that he's formed more compounds than any other element, almost ten million if you believe the rumors, so I'd always wonder if he practiced safe bonding. Plus he's into all of that organic crap and wears nothing but turtlenecks and flannel, which is too granola for my tastes.

With a sigh, I go back to scoping out the bar, my options for a potential bond running low. But I'm not the only one here having trouble finding Mr. Right.

Palladium stands on the other side of the room, looking rare and luminous as always in her silvery-white sequined dress with a plunging neckline, casually sipping a martini and making furtive glances while Tin, Lead, and Aluminum lurk nearby, pounding beers, trying to drink up the courage to talk to her.

Cesium sits by herself at a table for two, sipping a cosmo, looking like the loneliest element in the universe. I've never seen her interact with anyone at these mixers, probably because she's one of the least electronegative elements. Plus she's one of only five elemental metals who are liquid at room temperature, which isn't something you want to put on your dating profile. The fact that she only has one stable isotope might be a deal-breaker, too. But in spite of her atomic shortcomings, she's here hoping to make a connection, to find that special someone. Or at least a one-night stand.

I raise my glass to Cesium in a show of solidarity. She sees me and returns my gesture with a wan smile, the two of us sharing a nice little moment. I'm about to walk over to commiserate with her on our lack of successful bonding when someone taps me on the shoulder.

I turn around expecting to find Calcium or Lithium ogling my ass. It wouldn't be the first time. Instead, Thulium stands there next to Bromine, holding her hand, which is a neat trick considering that in her current state she's a fuming red-brown liquid.

Thulium and I haven't spoken since we broke up over a year ago, mostly because it was always too awkward but also because I'm skilled at avoiding intimacy. But I've heard through the Period Table grapevine that he and Bromine have been dating for a couple of months, so this isn't totally unexpected.

"Hey," he says with a sheepish smile.

"Hey," I respond, trying to breathe through my mouth.

Bromine has a stench that is sharp and disagreeable and

irritates the eyes, lungs, and throat. I have no idea how Thulium can stand to be around her for more than a couple of minutes at a time, let alone have sex with her.

After a few moments, Bromine clears her throat and says she needs to freshen up, which is the understatement of the year. She kisses Thulium on the cheek and shoots me a glare before sloshing off toward the non-metals room, leaving Thulium and me to enjoy an awkward silence.

"So how have you been?" he finally asks.

"Great," I lie. "How about you?"

"I'm good," he says. "I'm with Bromine now."

"So I see." I take a drink of my whiskey sour, trying to come up with more small talk, which is always fun. "How's that going?"

"Great," he says. "We're great. She's great."

Like all halogens, Bromine is one electron short of a full octet, so she reacts with numerous other elements in order to complete her outer shell. While not as big of a slut as Fluorine, she still gets around. Again, not that I'm judging.

"Neon Tiger" by The Killers plays over the sound system as another awkward silence ensues. Thulium glances toward the direction of the restrooms—probably hoping for Bromine to return to save him from having to say anything else—before he turns back to me and says, "I'm sorry things didn't work out between us."

Great. One of *those* conversations. Just what I needed to make my night.

"Yeah, well, you know," I say, trying to think of something to say that won't hurt his feelings or make me sound like a bitch. "It wasn't you. It's me."

"I know," he says, which annoys me because it was most definitely *him*. "But sometimes I still think about you, you know?"

I don't nod or smile but hide my non-reaction in my whiskey sour, which I drain before I place the empty glass on the bar and signal to Copper for a refill, stat.

"Let me get that for you," Thulium says, reaching for his wallet.

"That's okay," I say. "I've got it."

"Oh, okay. But if you want to get together for coffee sometime..." His gaze wanders to my isotopes and lingers there. "Or maybe a drink..."

"What the hell is going on here?" Bromine says as she comes sloshing up to us, fuming like always.

"Nothing's going on," Thulium says. "We were just talking."

"Just talking?" Bromine says. "Then why do you look like *that*?"

While Thulium's default state is a pleasant silvery-gray, whenever he gets excited his ions emit a strong blue luminescence. And right now, he's the color of Cobalt.

"Just look at yourself!" Bromine sloshes over and grabs Aluminum—who appears to enjoy the attention because he's probably hoping to casually synthesize some aluminum bromide—then drags him over and shoves him in front of Thulium, his blue luminescent reflection staring back in shocked embarrassment.

"I don't..." Thulium stammers. "It doesn't...I mean..."

"Shut up!" Bromine shouts at him, boiling with anger, which is problematic since she evaporates readily. "Just. Shut. Up!"

By this point, most of the other elements in the bar are watching us and waiting to see what happens next. It's rare that there's not at least one explosive chemical reaction at these mixers, which always makes for a memorable evening. But when the others see that a noble gas is involved, they lose interest and go back to what they were doing.

While I may be pretty to look at, I'm definitely not the life of the party.

Bromine continues to boil and seethe with anger, which only causes Thulium to grow a brighter shade of blue. Displays of dominance and bondage always did turn him on, although he didn't have much of a tolerance for pain and he could never remember our safe word.

I look around for Carbon to see if he's interested in playing peacemaker again, but he's nowhere to be found. Typical. There's never a stable element around when you need one.

"Listen," I say, trying to calm Bromine down. "Nothing happened. We were just..."

"I know what you were *just*." Bromine gives me a look of contempt. "I may not be as bright or as flashy as you, but I'm not an idiot."

"I didn't say you were an idiot," I say. "I just meant..."

"I don't care what you meant!" she screams, continuing to boil, drops of her splattering everywhere. A couple of the drops get on my dress, which is just great. There's no way I'm getting the smell out. "Just stay away from him, you colorless, tasteless bitch!"

Then she evaporates into a reddish-brown gas and floats toward the exit.

Thulium looks at me helplessly, his bright blue luminescence dimming a couple of shades until he's the color of a faded violet, before he turns and goes after her. "Bromine, honey, wait!"

I watch him go, knowing that I dodged a bullet when I got out of that relationship, then I turn back to the bar to find my second whiskey sour waiting for me.

"For the record," Copper says, "I don't find you colorless or tasteless."

"Thanks," I say. But he's just being nice.

All noble gases *are* colorless and tasteless, as well as odorless, which is a big selling point when you're competing for attention with the likes of Sulfur. But even though noble gases have our shortcomings, most elements, especially the halogens, secretly want to be us.

Take me, for example. I have ten electrons symmetrically arranged around my nucleus like the petals of a flower. Bromine, meanwhile, has thirty-five electrons, giving her a skewed orbital arrangement. She's completely out of balance and desperately wants that one little extra electron to make her symmetrical and happy, which is one of the reasons why she's so jealous of me. The same goes for Fluorine, who only has nine electrons, which is probably why she's such an indiscriminate whore.

Sodium on the other hand, has eleven electrons. While she's not as burdened with electrons as Bromine or Rubidium, she's not as svelte or as perfectly balanced as I am. No matter how much she exercises or how many proton diets she goes on, Sodium can never manage to shed that one extra electron. Unless, of course, she hooks up with a halogen like Chlorine.

I look up at the mirror behind the bar and start in on my second whiskey sour as I watch the other single elements continue their drunken pursuit of covalent and ionic bonding. In the back corner at a table for two, Sodium and Chlorine canoodle, as happy as two full atomic shells, which isn't surprising considering alkali metals and halogens are the most reactive of all elements.

Halogens have a tendency to rip an electron from other atoms because, well, they're selfish assholes. But alkali metals like Sodium, most of who are Leos, have an equally strong tendency to give an electron away. It's just their selfless nature. Still, I have no idea what Sodium sees in Chlorine. He's toxic, gassy, irritating, and chemically promiscuous. I wonder if Sodium knows that Chlorine has, at one time or another, combined readily and eagerly with nearly all of the other elements at the bar.

The jealous bitch in me wants to send Phosphorous, Nitrogen, or Magnesium over to their table just to open Sodium's goo-goo eyes to the fact that Chlorine is a man whore, but then I remember Argon's advice to focus on my own happiness as separate from the happiness of others. So instead, I raise my glass to their reflection and wish them a happy and healthy bonding before I drain half of my drink.

From the corner of the bar, Iron lets out a drunken war cry when Black Sabbath's "Iron Man" comes on. He tries to high-five Hydrogen but misses and stumbles into him and his brother, his hand inadvertently landing on one of Oxygen's breasts.

"Easy there, pal," Hydrogen says. "You might end up oxidizing."

"You know, you guys aren't so bad," Iron slurs, putting an arm around each of the Hydrogen brothers while Oxygen does another shot of tequila. "Hey, do the three of you want to come back to my place and play Trivial Pursuit?"

Before I can drain the other half of my whiskey sour, a high-pitched voice cuts through the music and babble of conversation. "Oh. My. *God!*"

I turn around to see Helium walking toward me—all smiles and wide-eyed enthusiasm. That's all I need: Helium's perky, sunny disposition to try to cheer me up when I just want to wallow in my unreactive solitude.

"Hey girl!" She embraces me in a gassy hug. "What's up with my favorite noble gas?"

"I'm great," I say, not bothering to hide my sarcasm.

"Well, you look *fabulous!*" Helium says, her voice rising to an almost ear-splitting pitch. "It's so great to see you!"

I just give her a thin smile.

"Can I get you something to drink?" Copper asks Helium, flashing his green patina smile. He really needs to invest in a good toothbrush. Maybe a Sonicare.

Helium looks over the menu of Happy Hour cocktails, then she points at my glass. "What are you drinking?"

"Whiskey sour," I say.

She wrinkles her nose ever so slightly, which is the closest she gets to anything resembling a negative reaction, before she turns to Copper with a radiant smile. "I'll have a pomegranate mimosa, please."

"One pom-mimosa," Copper says. "Coming up."

Helium laughs, then turns to look around the bar. "I love this place! It's so much fun!"

I don't know why she's always in such a good mood considering that she's just as unreactive as I am. It's probably because she leads a fulfilling existence working in MRI and satellite technology, fiber optics, semiconductors, and airbag safety systems—not to mention the Large Hadron Collider and the Apollo space vehicles—while I've primarily made my living via ubiquitous, flashy advertising. Although I have dabbled in lasers and cryogenics, so at least my existence isn't completely meaningless.

"Here you go," Copper says, delivering Helium's pomegranate mimosa. "Enjoy."

"I will!" she says and takes a sip of her concoction of sweetness, the yang to my whiskey sour. "It's yummy! You want a sip?"

"No thanks," I say and down the rest of my drink.

At the other end of the bar, Iron has passed out in the corner while the Hydrogen brothers draw on him with a permanent red oxide marker. Oxygen stands nearby, giggling uncontrollably.

I don't know if it's the spectacle of watching the Hydrogen brothers humiliate Iron or the numerous awkward encounters I've had with unsuitable suitors, but I decide that I am *so* over this whole singles bonding scene. I'd rather be home by myself, curled up on the couch with a glass of red wine, binge-watching *GLOW* on Netflix.

"Will you watch my drink?" Helium asks. "I need to use the little noble gases room."

"Knock yourself out," I say.

Helium's high-pitched laughter cuts through Black Sabbath's grinding guitar finale. "You're so silly! When I get back you have to catch me up on everything you've been up to!"

"Can't wait," I say.

As soon as Helium leaves, I close out my tab, pay for her drink and give Copper a generous tip, then I call for an Uber on my phone and head toward the front door before Helium can return and harangue me with her annoying, nonstop optimism. On my way out, Potassium comes stumbling into the bar wearing sunglasses and nearly runs into me, obviously drunk or stoned or on some kind of intoxicant, his usually silvery-white sheen tarnished with a dull oxide coating.

"Hey Red." He lowers his shades to look me up and down, his

eyes glassy and at half-mast. "You look absolutely incandescent. Want to play a game of hide the proton?"

I give him the finger and continue past him to the front door, glancing back when Iron cries out in a drunken fury.

"You guys are fucking assholes!"

He's looking at himself in the mirror behind the bar, atomic symbols and the phrase RUST ME drawn all over him in red oxide, while Oxygen and the Hydrogen brothers stumble away from the scene of the crime, laughing hysterically.

Potassium continues to check me out, distracted by my reddish-orange glow. He gives me a parting wink, then he turns around, not watching where he's going, and walks right into Oxygen and the Hydrogen brothers. The next instant, the bar is filled with a bright flash and a loud *bang* followed by a thick cloud of hydrogen gas. When the smoke finally clears, all that's left is a puddle of water and bunch of potassium hydroxide scattered across the floor.

While I'd like to find an element I could bond with, someone I could wake up next to in the morning without having to worry about feeling a sense of regret or wondering where I left my bra, moments like this make me appreciate that I'm so unreactive.

As Copper grabs a mop and a broom to clean up the mess and Nirvana's "Lithium" blares from the speakers, I make like an atom and split.

While waiting outside for my Uber, I scroll through the various dating apps on my Samsung Galaxy, contemplating all of my unappealing matches and failed relationships, thinking about my lack of reactivity and inability to bond with other elements, and I wonder if I should just delete my dating profiles altogether and get a dog instead.

Letters to Santa (from the Arctic Academy for Gifted Creatures)

January 15
From: Elizabeth Wolfe, Headmaster
To: Santa Claus, CEO, Kris Kringle Enterprises, LLC

Dear Mr. Claus,

It's always a delight to hear from a former graduate of AAGC, especially one with such a storied and celebrated history as yourself. I believe I speak for the entire staff when I say it's an honor to count you among our prestigious alumni. Once a Narwhal, always a Narwhal. Thank you for the candy canes, by the way. Everyone in the office appreciated them.

We were delighted to receive the admission application for Rudolph, who we understand is a bit of a prodigy. If he's even half as gifted as any one of your other reindeer who have graced the hallowed halls of AAGC, he'll be a welcome asset to the student body.

As you know, AAGC has a rich tradition of providing the finest education north of the Arctic Circle, offering unparalleled instruction and unmatched educational opportunities while graduating such luminaries as Frosty the Snowman, the Winter Warlock, and, of course, yourself. So obviously, we have high standards to which our students aspire.

Of course, we do need to follow proper admission protocols for every applicant in order to avoid any implication of impropriety or favoritism. But considering the academic and leadership records of Dasher and Dancer and Prancer and Vixen, the application process for Rudolph should be nothing more than a simple formality.

As a representative of the faculty and administration of the Arctic Academy for Gifted Creatures, I would like to thank you once again for your continued support of our educational institution, both financially and through the generous outreach you have done with so many of our students. We will be in touch regarding Rudolph's application for admission soon.

Sincerely,
Elizabeth Wolfe

"Change is inevitable; progress is optional."

March 2
From: Elizabeth Wolfe, Headmaster
To: Santa Claus, CEO, Kris Kringle Enterprises, LLC
Cc: Terry Puffin, Assistant to the Headmaster

Dear Mr. Claus,
It is with great pleasure that I share with you Rudolph's official acceptance into the Arctic Academy for Gifted Creatures. We are all looking forward to welcoming him to campus for the new school year beginning this fall. From what I've heard, the members of The Reindeer Guild are literally champing at the bit in anticipation of his arrival.

My previous assistant, Hermey, who over the years facilitated the paperwork and registration for all of your other reindeer, has moved on to pursue a career in dentistry. My new assistant, Terry Puffin, will be following up with you shortly regarding all of the requisite paperwork and forms, as well as information on registering for classes and summer orientation. As you are well aware, orientation provides an invaluable networking opportunity for all of the new students, while at the same time allowing them to get acclimated to the campus so that their first day of school isn't quite so overwhelming.

If you have any questions or if you need any assistance, please don't hesitate to reach out. In the meantime, you are in good hands with Terry.

Thank you. And congratulations to you and to Rudolph on his acceptance.

Sincerely,
Elizabeth Wolfe

"Change is inevitable; progress is optional."

March 7
From: Terry Puffin, Assistant to the Headmaster
To: Santa Claus, CEO, Kris Kringle Enterprises, LLC
Cc: Elizabeth Wolfe, Headmaster

Dear Mr. Claus,

Attached please find all of Rudolph's registration materials for his introductory year at the Arctic Academy for Gifted Creatures, as well as the Orientation Packet for New Students. Summer orientation takes place on one of two weekends (one in July and the other in August) and it's recommended that you sign up early, as spots tend to go fast. You also have the option of registering Rudolph to participate in several special orientation activities—including Snow Castle Building, Ice Floe Skating, and Klondike

Karaoke. These activities are designed to help our students develop new friendships and learn team-building skills. Did I mention they're also loads of fun?!

In addition, I've attached the syllabus so Rudolph can get a head start on selecting his classes. There are half a dozen core classes all reindeer are required to take in order to graduate (e.g. Introduction to Flying and Ergonomics of Sleigh Pulling), so he'll want to make sure he signs up for at least one of these classes during his first semester.

I think that's about it. If you have any questions or concerns, please don't hesitate to ask. I'm here to help facilitate Rudolph's enrollment at AAGC in any way I can.

Go Fighting Narwhals!

Cheers,
Terry Puffin

"You can't control the wind, but you can adjust your sails."

March 30
From: Terry Puffin, Assistant to the Headmaster
To: Santa Claus, CEO, Kris Kringle Enterprises, LLC
Cc: Elizabeth Wolfe, Headmaster

Dear Mr. Claus,

We are in receipt of Rudolph's registration materials as well as his preferred class schedule for the upcoming semester. This is a friendly reminder that all classes are on a first-come, first-served basis and are not guaranteed until we've received all of the student applications, so Rudolph will want to make sure to check in with registration upon his arrival at orientation to verify his class schedule.

Preferred housing requests are also based on availability and are not guaranteed, but we try to accommodate as many students as possible with their choices. We'll be sure to notify you if for any reason Rudolph's preferred dormitory is not available.

If you have any questions, please don't hesitate to reach out to me. In the meantime, we're looking forward to having Rudolph here for our August orientation.

Go Fighting Narwhals!

Cheers,
Terry Puffin

"You can't control the wind, but you can adjust your sails."

April 1
From: Elizabeth Wolfe, Headmaster
To: Santa Claus, CEO, Kris Kringle Enterprises, LLC
Cc: Ramona Fox, Assistant to the Headmaster

Dear Mr. Claus,

My sincerest apologies for the confusion regarding Rudolph's classes and preferred accommodations. Rest assured that there is nothing to worry about. Rudolph has been confirmed and registered for all of the classes he selected and he has a dormitory room reserved for him in Caribou Hall, as requested. There is no need for him to check in with either registration or housing when he arrives for orientation.

If I can be of any further assistance, please don't hesitate to ask. In the meantime, my new assistant, Ramona Fox, will be happy to answer any questions you may have.

Thank you again for your understanding and patience in this matter.

Sincerely,
Elizabeth Wolfe

"Change is inevitable; progress is optional."

May 14
From: Ramona Fox, Assistant to the Headmaster
To: Santa Claus, CEO, Kris Kringle Enterprises, LLC
Cc: Yukon Cornelius, Office of Financial Aid

Dear Mr. Claus,
We have received your inquiry regarding Rudolph's financial aid. As this office does not process applications for scholarships or grants, I have forwarded your inquiry to Yukon Cornelius in the Office of Financial Aid for further assistance.

Thank you,
Ramona Fox

Please consider the environment before printing this email

May 17
From: Yukon Cornelius, Office of Financial Aid
To: Santa Claus, CEO, Kris Kringle Enterprises, LLC

Hey Mr. C,

Good to hear from you, big guy. How's life in the North Pole these days? Cold as a witch's you-know-what, I bet. The missus and I bought a timeshare in Maui and we get out there a couple of times a year just so we can thaw out. You and Mrs. C should join us sometime.

As for your questions about scholarships, all incoming freshman are automatically eligible for a handful of academic awards and scholarships, like the Narwhal Scholarship and the Rankin/Bass Award. Bad news is, Rudy's grades and test scores aren't quite up to snuff for any of the academic scholarships. Plus the deadline for financial aid applications was January 15, so even if Rudy qualified for any of the other awards or grants, that proverbial ship has pulled out of port and sailed off into the sunset.

There are still some options available for student loans and work-study programs if you're interested in going that route. Sorry I can't give you better news, big guy, but that's how the Bumble bounces! If you need anything else, just give me a shout. And let me know about the timeshare. Wahooooo!

Best,
Yukon

"You eat what you like and I'll eat what I like."

June 24
From: Walter Rangifer, President, The Reindeer Guild
To: Santa Claus, CEO, Kris Kringle Enterprises, LLC

Dear Mr. Claus,
Greetings! As acting President of the AAGC chapter of The

Reindeer Guild, I would like to extend my formal invitation for Rudolph to attend our Fall Rush Social Mixer coming up in September.

As you know, The Reindeer Guild has been a mainstay at the AAGC since the school's inception and as such has been the standard-bearer for the academy's social organizations. So it's no surprise that every notable reindeer who has graduated from this institution is a member of The Reindeer Guild. The one exception, of course, being Prancer, who had the misfortune of attending the Arctic Academy during a time when The Guild, shall we say, had a far more conservative and less inclusive mindset when it came to its membership. I can assure you that we have adopted much more liberal policies to reflect the changing times. Adapt or perish, as the saying goes.

Needless to say, we are all looking forward to having the opportunity to meet Rudolph and introduce him to the possibilities of what The Reindeer Guild has to offer.

Respectfully,
Walter Rangifer

"More rapid than eagles his coursers they came..."

July 31
From: Deirdre Jingle, Office of Admissions
To: Santa Claus, CEO, Kris Kringle Enterprises, LLC

Dear Mr. Claus,
This is a courtesy reminder confirming Rudolph's registration for the New Student Orientation scheduled for the weekend of August 14 and 15. We at the Arctic Academy for Gifted Creatures are

looking forward to welcoming Rudolph to campus and providing him with a memorable and enriching experience.

If you have any questions, we are at your service.

Sincerely,
Deirdre Jingle

"After all is said and done, more is often said than done."

August 17
From: Ramona Fox, Assistant to the Headmaster
To: Santa Claus, CEO, Kris Kringle Enterprises, LLC
Cc: Elizabeth Wolfe, Headmaster

Dear Mr. Claus,

We have received your inquiry about the unfortunate incident that took place during orientation weekend and we are looking into the matter. We can assure you that the AAGC does not tolerate discrimination nor does it take your concerns lightly. Every effort will be made to insure that those responsible for what happened at the bonfire are held accountable.

We appreciate your patience and understanding.

Thank you,
Ramona Fox

Please consider the environment before printing this email

August 22
From: Yukon Cornelius, Office of Financial Aid
To: Santa Claus, CEO, Kris Kringle Enterprises, LLC

Hey Mr. C,

Rudy's been approved for the work-study program, although just being in the program doesn't guarantee him a job. He'll have to go on the Narwhal Jobs online job board once it opens August 31. In the meantime, he might want to go to the web site and give the Student Employment FAQs a read and prepare his résumé.

If he has any questions, have him come find me at the Financial Aid Office when he gets here and I'll be sure to walk him through everything. Wahooooo!

Best,
Yukon

"You eat what you like and I'll eat what I like."

September 3
From: Ramona Fox, Assistant to the Headmaster
To: Santa Claus, CEO, Kris Kringle Enterprises, LLC
Cc: Elizabeth Wolfe, Headmaster

Dear Mr. Claus,

After speaking with campus security and several dozen witnesses, we have determined the identity of the students who took part in the incident at the bonfire during orientation weekend last month. Please know that those responsible have been disciplined according to the AAGC's code of conduct.

If you have any additional concerns, please don't hesitate to let us know. In the meantime, we hope this unfortunate incident does not adversely affect your perception of the AAGC.

Thank you,
Ramona Fox

Please consider the environment before printing this email

September 21

Dear Santa,

All of the other reindeer are dicks!

None of them like me because of my stupid nose. They all laugh at me behind my back and call me names like Pinocchio and Cherry Top and Road Rash. It's worse than what happened at the bonfire! That was a tropical vacation compared to this! Yesterday someone taped a drawing to my dorm room door that showed a proctologist using my nose as a light while he gave you a rectal exam.

My roommate bitches at me all the time to cover up my nose and says that rooming with me is like living on Mars. He complains that my nose gives him migraines and when he gets drunk he threatens to chop it off. And don't even get me started on the girls around here. They all think I'm some kind of genetic freak.

To top things off, The Lamedeer Guild won't even acknowledge that I exist. No one talked to me at the mixer. Not even Comet or Cupid. They all treated me like a pariah. And when I tried to sign up for the annual Reindeer Games, they told me all the spots were filled, which was total bullshit. I could see the sign-up sheet and there were tons of open spots for the Sleigh Pull and the Chimney Slalom.

Oh, and in case you're wondering, work-study is a complete

bust. I can't even get a job making minimum wage as a janitor. Apparently, no one wants to work with Rudolph the Red-Nosed Freak. I'm a fucking pariah around here. The only friend I've made so far is this dude named Heat Miser.

I hate this place. It sucks. I want to come home.

Rudolph
Sent from my iPhone

September 23
From: Ramona Fox, Assistant to the Headmaster
To: Santa Claus, CEO, Kris Kringle Enterprises, LLC
Cc: Elizabeth Wolfe, Headmaster
W. Warlock, Dean of Students

Dear Mr. Claus,

Thank you for your email. We are as troubled as you are by the descriptions of Rudolph's treatment by the other reindeer and apologize for any grief you and he may have experienced. However, as this is a student body matter, I have passed the details of your situation along to Dean Warlock, who I have Cc'd on this email. He will be handling this situation moving forward.

In the meantime, we have transferred Rudolph to a single occupancy room in Kringle Hall, per your request.

If there is any other way I may be of assistance, please know that I am here to help.

Thank you,
Ramona Fox

Please consider the environment before printing this email

❄ ❄ ❄

September 26
From: W. Warlock, Dean of Students
To: Santa Claus, CEO, Kris Kringle Enterprises, LLC
Cc: Elizabeth Wolfe, Headmaster
Ramona Fox, Assistant to the Headmaster

Dear Kris,

I'm disheartened to learn of the trouble Rudolph has encountered with some of the other students. As you know, here at the AAGC we emphasize teamwork, respect, and friendship—something I learned a long time ago from a certain someone who taught me the value of caring (unlike that Meisterburger fellow, who was a real horse's ass, pardon my French).

But back to the dilemma at hand.

I've personally spoken to several of the students identified in Rudolph's letter, which Liz and Mona forwarded to me. While I'm of a much warmer temperament than I was when you and I first met, I can still get my freeze on, so I don't think they'll be bothering Rudolph again.

However, with regard to the allegations of discrimination against The Reindeer Guild, I'm afraid my hands are somewhat tied, as The Guild is not obligated by the AAGC to offer membership to any students, no matter their pedigree. If you feel there is overt and deliberate bias going on there, you may want to take it up with their national board. I should warn you that proving malice or intent to discriminate when it comes to The Reindeer Guild is more of a challenge than melting a frozen warlock's heart. But if anyone is up to the task, it's you.

If there's anything else I can do, please let me know. You have my cell phone and I can be reached day and night. My door and heart are always open.

By the way, I still have the train.

Warmly,
Winter

"Put one foot in front of the other..."

October 1

Dear Santa,
When I told you about all of the crap I was dealing with here at the Arctic Academy for Giant Cocksuckers, I meant for you to get me the hell out of this shithole. I didn't mean for you to write a bunch of letters to the administration and have them discipline my roommate and a bunch of the other students and then transfer me to my own room in another dorm. Now not only am I the freakish reindeer with the radioactive nose, but I'm a fucking snitch and self-entitled whiner. Everyone on campus knows about the letter I wrote to you. Everyone! Things are worse than ever!

At least I have Heat Miser and Snow Miser to cheer me up. They're the only friends I have, no thanks to you. Asshole.

Rudolph
Sent from my iPhone

October 16
From: Walter Rangifer, President, The Reindeer Guild
To: Santa Claus, CEO, Kris Kringle Enterprises, LLC

Dear Mr. Claus,

My apologies for not responding sooner but apparently your email ended up in my spam folder, which I don't check on a regular basis.

Unfortunately, I'm unable to provide any information regarding Rudolph's denied membership in The Reindeer Guild, as I'm not personally involved in the selection process. However, I can assure you Rudolph was provided with as equal an opportunity as any other reindeer.

If you have any further inquiries regarding this matter, please address them to our national charter.

Respectfully,
Walter Rangifer

"More rapid than eagles his coursers they came..."

November 3
From: Karl Krampus, Chief of Security
To: Santa Claus, CEO, Kris Kringle Enterprises, LLC
Cc: Elizabeth Wolfe, Headmaster

Dear Mr. Claus,

This letter is to inform you of several incidents that took place during the annual Reindeer Games held at the Arctic Academy for Gifted Creatures during the week of October 20-27.

1) During the Opening Ceremonies, more than a dozen students were hospitalized after drinking Reindeer-ade® that had been spiked with LSD. Several of those students are still experiencing hallucinations.

2) Multiple competitors were injured during the Chimney

Slalom and sent to the campus health center for medical attention, one of them in serious condition, due to injuries caused by fishing line that had been strung between multiple rooftop chimneys.

3) Cinderblocks were found in more than a dozen sacks that had been loaded into the sleds for the Sleigh Pull competition. Fortunately, the cinder blocks were discovered before any injuries or damage occurred.

In addition to the above incidents, someone defecated on the Comet and Blitzen lawn, melted the Ice Sculpture Garden, and sawed portions of antlers off two Reindeer Games participants while they were asleep.

While none of the perpetrators have been apprehended or charged as of yet, several witnesses mentioned seeing a bright or shiny red light during the times in which the above criminal activities occurred.

To be clear, this is not a legal indictment of Rudolph, but a formal courtesy to alert you to the incidents and the investigation into his conduct. If you would like to speak with me further about this, I can be reached at this email address or via the main number for Campus Security.

Regards,
Karl Krampus

"The devil is not as black as he is painted."

November 5
From: Elizabeth Wolfe, Headmaster
To: Santa Claus, CEO, Kris Kringle Enterprises, LLC
Cc: Ramona Fox, Assistant to the Headmaster
Jack Skellington, Interim Chief of Security

Dear Mr. Claus,

Please accept my apologies for the recent letter you received from Karl Krampus, our former Chief of Security. He was by no means authorized to contact you regarding Rudolph's alleged activities or behavior, so I hope his actions do not reflect poorly on your opinion of our institution. We do not condone the accusations made by Mr. Krampus, nor do we encourage members of the administration and campus staff to contact alumni on sensitive issues without vetting the letters through this office first.

Regarding the circumstantial evidence mentioned in the letter sent by Mr. Krampus, rest assured that Rudolph is not under suspicion and we are investigating these allegations thoroughly. I would also like to mention that Mr. Krampus has been suspended from his duties as Chief of Security pending a school board hearing. If you have any questions relating to the contents of his letter, please contact my office. If you would like to speak with Campus Security directly, you may ask for Jack Skellington, the interim Chief of Security, who I have Cc'd here.

Once again, I apologize for this breach of etiquette and any grief it may have caused you and Rudolph.

Sincerely,
Elizabeth Wolfe

"Change is inevitable; progress is optional."

November 17

Dear Santa,

You'll be glad to know I've made some new friends here and we've been hanging out a lot, having some laughs, and making our own kind of fun. Our own kind of music. Singing our own special song. Even if nobody else wants to sing along.

Fa la la la la, la la la la.

Where was I? Oh yeah. My new friends!

They're great! Jack Frost and I hit it off almost right away and now we hang out all of the time with Heat Miser and Snow Miser, who are brothers in case you couldn't tell. They're always setting each other on fire or freezing each other whenever one of them gets mad at the other one. They totally crack me up!

Oh, and then there's The Grinch. Man that is one cool cat. He's almost as good at getting into places as you without anyone seeing him. And he has this amazing collection of handguns and semiautomatic rifles. He took me out to the shooting range and taught me how to use them and everything. We're like total buds now! He even offered to take me Abominable Snow Monster hunting. How awesome is that?

Someone's knocking at my door. Gotta run!

Rudolph
Sent from my iPhone

November 29
From: W. Warlock, Dean of Students
To: Santa Claus, CEO, Kris Kringle Enterprises, LLC

Dear Kris,

Sorry to be the bearer of bad news, especially at this time of year when you have your busiest month coming up, but it appears as though young Rudolph has fallen in with the wrong crowd. As is the case at any institution where large numbers of strangers come together in a microcosmic melting pot of society, there are bound to be a few bad apples. And Rudolph has apparently taken a bite out of all of them.

Over the past couple of months, Rudolph has been seen keeping company with Heat Miser and his brother Snow Miser, both of whom are, in my professional and personal opinion, misanthropes with sociopathic tendencies. While I'm not a psychologist, I am a warlock, so I know a thing or two about what makes someone tick. And these two have "Future Prison Inmates" written all over them.

This is, of course, between you and me.

Rudolph has also been seen on numerous occasions smoking cigarettes out behind the quads with Jack Frost, who has been in this office for disciplinary reasons more often than any other student in the time I've held this position. To top things off, Rudolph has apparently struck up a friendship with The Grinch. You and I both know that whole story about his heart growing three sizes in one day is hogwash. He's a schemer that one, and no good can come of Rudolph spending time with him.

As for the investigation into the events that transpired during The Reindeer Games, the information I've received points to several of Rudolph's new BFFs. While there is so far no physical evidence tying Rudolph to any of the juvenile and malicious pranks that were pulled, there is mounting testimony from dozens of witnesses that places Rudolph in, at best, a tenuous and compromising situation—both academically and legally.

While others here at the AAGC may be more concerned about protecting the school's image than following due process, I won't lie to you, Kris. There is a serious chance that criminal charges will be pressed against Rudolph, so you might want to think about hiring a good lawyer.

I tell you this not as the Dean of Students but as your friend. I realize these are troubling developments, but please know I'm here to help in any way I can.

Warmly,
Winter

"Put one foot in front of the other..."

December 4

    Dear Santa,

    Sorry I'm such a disappointment to you. "An embarrassment and stain on the Kringle name" as you put it. But I don't feel like a disappointment. I feel like I've found my calling. Call it fate or destiny or whatever, this is what was meant to happen. What *had* to happen.

    Besides, you had your chance to get me out of here but instead of listening to me, you told me I needed to suck it up and learn how to be a reindeer. Earn my antlers. At first I was pissed. Like, really pissed. Gut-you-with-my-antlers pissed. But now I'm glad you made me stay. The past couple of months have been some of the best of my life. I've become a stronger reindeer. I've learned how to deal with rejection and ridicule and merciless teasing and channel my anger and resentment into something positive. Something I can control. Something I can own. But hey, if you want to point fingers and make accusations, I turned out this way because you left me here. So I guess whatever happens next is on you.

    Catch you later, fat man. Ho ho ho!

Rudolph
Sent from my iPhone

December 12
From: Ramona Fox, Assistant to the Headmaster
To: Santa Claus, CEO, Kris Kringle Enterprises, LLC
Cc: Elizabeth Wolfe, Headmaster

Dear Mr. Claus,

We regret to inform you that effective immediately, Rudolph has been expelled from the Arctic Academy for Gifted Creatures due to actions in violation of the AAGC code of conduct for criminal activity. Please arrange for Rudolph's return to the North Pole as soon as possible, as he no longer has campus housing provided to him.

Should you have any questions, please direct them to this office.

Thank you,
Ramona Fox

Please consider the environment before printing this email

Reminiscences of
My Childhood Centaurs

My father gave me my first centaur when I was nine years old.

The centaur had auburn hair, blue eyes, and a pale human torso, with the lower body of an Arabian horse colored a deep chestnut red that made me think of curling up by the fire on cold winter nights. I'd never seen such a beautiful creature before, not in real life or up close, anyway, and I adored him immediately.

"Thank you Papa!" I said, hugging my father. "Thank you! Thank you!"

"You're welcome," my father said, hugging me back. "Happy birthday, Pumpkin."

That's not an endearing nickname. My name is Pumpkin. It was my father's way of honoring my mother, who died after giving birth to me on All Hallows Eve in 1956.

"You think she's old enough to handle him?" my brother Gourd asked.

My father had a thing about herbaceous vines.

"You're only ten," I said. "And you have a minotaur."

My brother received a pet minotaur for his birthday six months earlier.

"I'm older than you," my brother said, as if I didn't know.

"Only by a year," I countered.

"A year and *a half.*" My brother always lorded that half a year over me as if it were some kind of medal he'd won in a contest.

"Yeah, but I'm mature for my age," I said. "Isn't that so, Papa?"

My father, who rarely took sides even when I was right, smiled and nodded. "You're both older than your years."

"See?" I said to my brother, taking a victory where I could.

"Doesn't matter," my brother said. "I'm still older than you."

While some people considered nine years old to be too young to raise a centaur, my father believed in teaching responsibility early in life. But he wasn't the only open-minded parent in town. Dozens of my friends and classmates were nine or ten years old when they received their first centaur, gryphon, harpy, unicorn, or chimera.

Personally, I'd never want a chimera. Not because I find them repulsive or frightening like a lot of the other girls do, but three-headed, fire-breathing monsters tend to cause a lot of property damage. Although my friend, Fenwick, got a chimera for Christmas last year and hasn't had to file a single insurance claim.

While I've always appreciated that my father entrusted my brother and me with responsibility at a young age, some parents are a little too trusting, giving their sons and daughters mermen, sirens, or cyclopes as birthday or Christmas presents. Even the most mature eleven or twelve-year-old shouldn't be trusted to make good decisions when it comes to raising a mythological creature that can lure you to your death or crush you with its fist.

This one middle-school girl I heard about, Samara, received a gorgon for her bat mitzvah. Samara was apparently on the chunky side and was often teased about her weight. When two of the popular girls in school who regularly teased Samara and called her names were found in the girls' locker room turned into stone, Samara was expelled and her gorgon was sold to a masonry and concrete supply company.

"What are you going to name him?" my father asked as I ran a brush along my centaur's hindquarters.

My father believed that choosing a name for a mythological creature shouldn't be taken lightly, especially since it was common knowledge that the name would have an influence on the development of the creature's personality.

I pretended to ponder my options, but I knew right away that I wanted to name my centaur Ajax after the great Greek warrior in Homer's *Iliad*. One, I was a big fan of the Trojan War. And two, Ajax was my favorite mythological hero. At the time, a lot of the other girls in my school were infatuated with Achilles or Odysseus, who were fine and all as far as Greek heroes go, but they were easy and obvious choices. It was kind of like picking Paul or John as your favorite Beatle.

I didn't think I could go wrong choosing the name Ajax, who was always described by the poets as being of great stature, the strongest of the ancient Greeks, a fearless warrior with great intelligence. Plus he received less assistance from the gods than most of the other Greek heroes, which made him more self-reliant. All good qualities to have in a centaur.

"I'm going to name him Ajax," I said, certain that I had chosen the best name possible for my centaur.

My brother laughed. "Why don't you name him Clorox instead? Or Lysol? Or Mr. Clean?"

"Not *that* kind of Ajax," I said as I continued to brush my centaur. "It's the name of a Greek warrior."

I didn't elaborate any further because trying to explain *The Iliad* to my brother was a pointless endeavor.

"What do you say, Ajax?" I said to my centaur. "Do you like your name?"

My centaur whinnied and nodded, then stamped one of his front hooves in approval.

"See?" I said. "He agrees with me."

While centaurs understand human language, unlike their mythological counterparts they don't have the gift of speech. Instead, they neigh, whinny, and bray much the same as horses. They also grunt, snort, laugh, cry, and have been known to scream when in pain.

"Whatever," my brother said. "I still think it's a stupid name."

"It's better than Prince Charming," I said.

While I was a student of Greek mythology, my brother preferred Grimm's Fairy Tales, so he named his minotaur after the ubiquitous romantic hero. I would have chosen something like Hansel or Rumpelstiltskin, but my brother had a thing for damsels in distress.

"I think they're both fine names," my father said, attempting to defuse the situation while maintaining his neutrality. "Now, who wants some birthday cake?"

For the first few months, Ajax lived up to his mythological counterpart. He was strong and resourceful, helping around the farm wherever needed, especially during a couple of early winter storms that knocked down some trees. He was a quick learner and could even solve simple arithmetic by counting out the answers using his hooves. Plus he was fearless as he was intelligent, chasing off coyotes and crows, along with one surprised drifter who picked the wrong barn to bed down in for the night.

It didn't take long for me to grow attached to Ajax. I've always been quick to develop emotional bonds, especially with animals. The various cats and dogs and other creatures who lived on the farm over the years weren't just pets to me, but members of the family. My brother, on the other hand, treated them as if they were interchangeable pieces of property, which was probably one of the reasons why Prince Charming had anger management issues. Of course, minotaurs by their nature tend to be hotheaded, so maybe it wasn't all my brother's fault.

Ajax, on the other hand, was kind and even-tempered and he made me feel protected and safe whenever I was with him. And when I sat on his back and he galloped through the pasture, I felt as if I was flying. He was the best birthday or Christmas gift I'd ever received.

Unfortunately, I neglected to take into account that the mythological Ajax went a bit mad at the end and slaughtered a flock of sheep before taking his own life. Not that *my* Ajax committed suicide or killed a bunch of sheep. But by the time 1966 rolled around, he'd begun to develop an unhealthy fascination with some of the neighboring livestock. We tried to redirect his focus with a regular regimen of exercise, archery, and music lessons, but eventually we had to sell him to the circus after he impregnated several of Mr. Willoughby's prized unicorns.

In the real world, centaurs are nothing like the ones portrayed in fiction. Most of them are not wise or noble creatures, nor are they skilled in healing and astrology. The truth is centaurs are wild, untamed creatures who are prone to indulgent drinking and who can become rather belligerent when intoxicated. So it's a good idea to keep them away from the wine cellar. And, in some cases, untended livestock.

I blamed myself for Ajax's actions. After all, I was the one who had chosen his name. My father tried to convince me I wasn't responsible, but I wasn't easily swayed.

"It's all my fault, Papa," I said, fighting back my tears, but it was a losing battle and the tears knew it. "I should never have chosen that name. Gourd was right. I'm too young to raise a centaur."

"You're not too young, Pumpkin," my father said, sitting down next to me. "You're just short on experience."

"But this is so...so...*hard*," I said, the tears finally breaking through my defenses.

My father put an arm around me. "Life comes with its share of triumphs and disappointments. This just happens to be one of the disappointments. But you'll feel better before you know it and when you do, we can go pick out a new centaur."

Even though I'd only had Ajax for six months, the idea of getting another centaur seemed like an insult to his memory. I didn't blame my father for thinking of Ajax as replaceable. He was just trying to make me happy.

"I don't think I'm ready for another centaur yet," I said, snuffling and wiping my nose. "I think I'd like to wait until I'm a little bit older if that's okay."

"Of course it's okay," my father said. "Whatever you want, Pumpkin."

And so it wasn't until a year and a half later, on my eleventh birthday, when my father gave me my second centaur.

"What are you going to name this one?" my father asked as he, my brother, and I stood in the barn around a blue-eyed, platinum-blond human combined with a Camarillo White horse, which had a coat that reminded me of the first winter snowfall.

"I don't know." I scratched my centaur behind his ear, causing his right rear hoof to stamp repeatedly. "I'm still thinking about it."

The truth was that I was afraid to choose a name. I didn't want another Ajax fiasco, which turned out to be a boon for Mr. Willoughby since centaur and unicorn mixes are rare and fetch a pretty penny at livestock auctions.

"What about Theseus or Perseus?" my father asked. "Those are good names, right?"

My father didn't share my love of Greek mythology, but he encouraged my interest and did his best to have a basic understanding of the various gods and heroes so he could feel as if he was holding up his end of the conversation. To my father's credit, Theseus and Perseus were both Greek heroes of high character, but I knew of two other centaurs named Perseus, while Theseus was one of the most popular choices for mythological creatures five years running.

"Yeah, those are good names," I said. "But they're kind of ordinary."

"Sometimes ordinary is good," my father said.

I nodded and didn't offer up a rebuttal.

"Why don't you name him Snoopy?" my brother said, not being helpful at all. "Or how about Rex? Or Mr. Peanutbutter?"

76

"He's not a dog," I said. "He's a dignified, majestic creature."

My centaur chose that moment to relieve himself, creating a dignified, majestic pile of manure.

"Maybe you should call him Mr. Stinky," my brother said, snorting out laughter. I could see my father fighting to suppress his own smile, but I didn't feel like humoring my brother.

"Why don't you go tend to Prince Charming?" I said to my brother. "I'm sure his diaper needs changing."

After two and a half years, Prince Charming still wasn't housebroken.

My brother's mood turned sour and he sulked off, grumbling under his breath.

Part of me considered naming my new centaur Theseus just to spite my brother, since in Greek mythology, Theseus slayed the Minotaur by chopping off its head. But I didn't have anything personal against Prince Charming, just my brother. Plus I was kind of squeamish when it came to violent bloodshed.

"Maybe you could name him Pegasus," my father said. "That's a nice, safe name."

I rolled my eyes. If I'd had a dollar for every one of my classmates who named their centaur or unicorn Pegasus, I would have been able to buy my own Phoenix.

"Thanks," I said. "But I think I'll choose another name."

"Okay, I'll leave you to it, then," he said, ruffling my hair the way he liked to do even though I hated it. "And Pumpkin?"

"Yes Papa?"

He pointed at the majestic pile of centaur dung on the ground. "Don't forget to put his droppings into the compost for the crops."

To make a living, we grew magic beans that we harvested and sold at farmer's markets and to amateur giant hunters from neighboring villages. At the time, we were the only magic bean farm for fifty miles in any direction. Unlike some of the new factory farms that had begun to pop up around the country, we only used natural fertilizers. And centaur dung is especially rich in nitrogen, as well as in potassium and phosphorus—nearly three times as much as regular horse manure.

"I won't forget," I said.

"Good girl," my father said. "And Pumpkin?"

"Yes Papa?" I said with another eye roll. Even at the age of eleven, I'd already mastered the art of teenage exasperation.

"Happy birthday." My father gave me a wink, then he turned and walked out of the barn, leaving me alone with my attitude and my new centaur. With his strong limbs, compact build, and alabaster coat, he was a striking creature. I understood why my father suggested I name him Pegasus.

"So what should I name you, boy?" I said, picking up a body brush and running it across his back and flank. "What do you think about Pegasus?"

He shook his head with a snort, his curly blond locks swirling about his face.

"How about Snoopy then?" I said. "Or Rex? Or Mr. Peanutbutter?"

My centaur looked at me and rolled his big blue eyes, causing me to break out in laughter. At least he had a sense of humor.

When it came to choosing a name for my new centaur, Chronos and Hyperion sat at the top of my list. I wasn't sold on naming him after the god of time or the Titan of light, mostly because both seemed like a lot to live up to. I'd also considered Oedipus and Icarus because I loved the way they sounded, but after Ajax, I needed to choose a name with a less tragic association.

Eventually I decided to name him after the Greek centaur Pholus, who, like the mythological Chiron, was more civilized and intelligent than your standard centaur, which I hoped would bode well for his demeanor and personality.

"How about Pholus?" I asked him.

He nodded and clapped his hands.

"I'll take that as a yes." I walked around until I stood in front of him. "It's nice to meet you, Pholus," I said and held out my hand.

"I'm Pumpkin."

He snorted once and took my hand in his, shaking it twice.

"So are you hungry?" I asked.

He whinnied and stamped his front hooves.

While the average horse eats close to twenty pounds of hay a day, centaurs are about half the size of a horse, on average. But rather than having a standard equine digestive system, centaurs are omnivorous and can eat just about anything, including fruit, vegetables, rice, pasta, oats, soybeans, and eggs. In general, centaurs aren't fussy eaters, although they're not big fans of beets or radishes. And they hate broccoli.

I fed my centaurs a lot of cabbage and potatoes, which helped to keep the cost of feeding them manageable, although I'd occasionally throw in some waffles or peanut butter sandwiches. Centaurs love peanut butter. And honey. Especially when it's fresh, so it's not a good idea to get a centaur if you live near a bee apiary. Same thing goes if you're downwind of a dairy farm, as most centaurs tend to be lactose intolerant, although that doesn't stop them from getting into refrigerators or freezers and gorging on milk and ice cream.

Centaur milk farts are the worst.

It didn't take long for us to realize that Pholus was going to be a lot less trouble than Ajax. For starters, he wasn't much of a drinker, which made him considerably less belligerent and more agreeable, not to mention less likely to break out of his stable and molest the local livestock. And other than a mild curiosity that he cultivated from a distance, he didn't show the least bit of interest in Mr. Willoughby's unicorns. Overall, he was a fast learner and a hard worker, which not only made him easier to train but also made him rather useful around the farm, especially during harvest time.

As with Ajax, it didn't take long for me to grow attached to Pholus. There wasn't any one specific thing he did. It was more a collection of acts and actions, a combination of behaviors and mannerisms that endeared him to me.

It was the way he greeted me with a bow of his head and a scrape of his hoof when I fed him each morning and how he would nudge me with his head when he wanted something. It was the way he would rear up on his hind legs to celebrate the completion of some task and how he would stamp his hooves and flare his nostrils whenever my brother raised his voice in anger. It was the way he ran around in small circles whenever I came home from school and how he would prance about in the pasture during a spring rain.

I looked forward to seeing him first thing in the morning when I woke up and to grooming him each night before I went to bed. I couldn't remember what my life was like before he'd come into it or what it might look like without him.

"I love you, Pholus," I told him almost every day.

By *love*, I don't mean in a romantic way. Even though Pholus was half-human, I didn't think of him as anything other than an animal, but that didn't make my feelings for him any less real. And although he couldn't voice his feelings for me, he would grunt and hug me with his human arms in reciprocation.

Pholus brought me joy, laughter, and a sense of belonging that I'd never experienced before. He was my constant companion and my best friend, never judging me for my faults or condemning me for my mistakes, always supportive, loving, and appreciative of my company. In turn, he taught me to treat him with the same unconditional love and respect, which had a positive impact on all of my other relationships. Even with my brother.

He was the best thing that ever happened to me.

And then, one spring Sunday in 1972, he didn't come home.

He'd gone out for an early morning run after breakfast, something he'd done countless times over the past four and a half years, racing to the far reaches of our property and staying out to bask in the sun or to nap beneath the shade of a tree before returning in the early afternoon just in time for lunch.

When lunch had come and gone and Pholus hadn't returned, we went out to look for him, figuring he must have fallen into a deep sleep or lost track of the time. Instead, we found him lying motionless in the shade of an oak tree next to the remains of a beehive, his body cool to the touch.

"No!" I cried, running my hands over him, searching for a pulse or any sign that he might still be alive. "No, no, no, no, no!"

It was the only word I could manage to speak.

As I sobbed over my lifeless centaur, my father took my brother aside. "Run back to the house," I heard him say in a low voice. "Call Animal Control. Tell them to bring the flatbed."

"No!" I shouted, turning away from Pholus, my face hot and wet with tears and snot. Had I been the eleven-year-old version of myself, I probably would have gone along with my father's decision. But I was fifteen and full of hormones and I wasn't in any mood to agree. I pointed an accusing finger at my brother like a witch casting a spell. "You are not calling Animal Control!"

"Pumpkin," my father said as he squatted down next to me. "We can't just leave him out here. And we don't have the equipment to move him ourselves."

"But we have magic beans," I said, wiping the snot from my upper lip. "We can make an elixir, like the one Mrs. Potter used on one of her flying monkeys."

"But it was just really sick," my brother said. "It wasn't..."

I shot a look at my brother that stopped him from finishing his sentence.

"I'm sorry, Pumpkin," my father said, putting a gentle hand on my head. "It's too late for magic elixirs."

I knew my father was right, but I was in no mood to listen to reason.

"I have to try," I said, tears running down my cheeks. "I can't let him be dead. Let me try, Papa. Please, just let me try."

So instead of calling Animal Control, my brother fetched a tent, a sleeping bag, and some blankets while my father mixed up an elixir of magic beans. My brother pitched the tent around us and brought out a lantern along with a grilled cheese and tomato sandwich and a thermos of peppermint tea. He never said a word but just tried to make things as easy for me as possible, for which I was grateful.

I stayed with Pholus all night, applying dropper after dropper of the magic elixir into his mouth. Once the bottle was empty, I curled up next to him and cried until, at some point, I drifted off to sleep. In my dreams, Pholus woke up and I climbed upon his back and the two of us went running off through the fields, the wind blowing back our hair, both of us smiling and laughing. But when I woke up the following morning, my dreams were just dreams.

And so it came to pass that four and a half years after he had come into my life, my beloved Pholus left me.

Rather than calling Animal Control to remove the body, my father and brother helped me to bury Pholus beneath the oak tree, which I would visit every day, even when it was raining or so cold that the tears froze on my cheeks.

I cried nonstop for two weeks.

While honey isn't normally poisonous to centaurs, it turned out that the beehive Pholus found had been built by bees that fed on the nectar from a nearby field of rhododendron flowers. And rhododendron flowers, even in small quantities, are toxic to horses and centaurs alike, causing their respiratory systems to fail within hours after ingestion. Even had we found him earlier, chances are it would have been too late.

So like his mythological counterpart, my Pholus had met his tragic end by accidentally poisoning himself, although he had been done in by honeybees rather than by the prick of an arrow dipped in the venomous blood of Hydra.

By the end of the summer, the shock of losing Pholus had begun to subside, along with the frequent outburst of tears. But the dull heartache remained as a constant reminder, especially first thing in the morning after I woke up and each night before I went to bed.

I was still grieving Pholus when I turned sixteen.

"Are you ready for your big birthday surprise?" my father asked as he and my brother led me out to the barn, which I'd avoided as much as possible for the previous five months. The idea of seeing the empty stall was too much for me to bear.

We'd already had cake and ice cream and opened up all of the presents my friends had brought. Once the festivities had concluded and my friends had all gone home, I'd planned to go upstairs to my bedroom and wallow in my memories of Pholus until it was time to go to bed, but my father told me I had one more gift to open.

"I bet you can't guess what it is," my brother said as we approached the barn.

Ever since the death of Pholus, my relationship with my brother had improved, but that didn't mean I still didn't find him occasionally annoying.

"I bet I can't," I said.

For all I knew, my father had bought me a satyr or a unicorn, or a hairy humanoid like a sasquatch or an abominable snowman. Those were all the rage. I hadn't spoken to my father about wanting another mythological creature, but it *was* my sixteenth birthday, which was kind of a big deal, so I guess I should have expected that he would get me something special.

From atop the barn came the roar of a lion followed by the cry of an eagle. I didn't have to look up to know that the creature making those sounds was not my birthday present.

A couple of years ago, my father surrendered Prince Charming to The Minotaur Rescue Society in the hopes that they would be able to place him in a more suitable home, as my brother had grown increasingly frustrated with Prince Charming's inability to understand basic commands or learn how to use the toilet.

Minotaurs aren't the brightest of creatures, mythological or otherwise.

So for my brother's fifteenth birthday, my father bought him a gryphon—a menacing creature with the head, wings, and talons of an eagle, and the body and hind legs of a lion. My brother named him Grimm, which wasn't very original but it fit, as Grimm was hideous, ill tempered, and had no sense of humor. Mostly he sat on top of the barn or on the roof above my brother's window, watching and leering at everything and everyone with his soulless black eyes. He also left enormous gryphon droppings everywhere, which my brother constantly neglected to clean up.

My brother's lack of remorse at having to give up Prince Charming was something I never understood. Even though Prince Charming required a lot of patience and energy and would often get his head stuck between the fence slats, he was part of our family and I was sad to see him go. Ajax was only around for six months but I bawled like a baby when they took him away. And when it came to Pholus, no mythological creature could ever take his place. Especially not another centaur.

"Surprise!" my father said with a smile and a flourish as he opened up one of the stables to reveal an olive-skinned, dark-haired human mixed with a Friesian, whose black coat reminded me of a starless midnight sky.

"Isn't he a beaut?" my brother said.

While the centaur was, indeed, a beautiful creature, my initial reaction was less than enthusiastic, which I could tell wasn't lost on my father. So in an effort to appear appreciative, I walked up to the centaur and started half-heartedly petting him.

"Do you like him?" my father asked.

"Yes," I said, running my hand along his flank. "He's a fine specimen."

"Fine?" my brother said, offended. "He's more than fine. He's magnificent!"

My brother had helped to select my centaur and convinced my father to go with the dark-haired Friesian. Had they gone with my father's choice of another Camarillo White mix like Pholus, I probably would have spent the rest of my sixteenth birthday crying in my bedroom, so I had to give my brother credit for that. But even though this centaur didn't have the same coloring or demeanor as Pholus, it was all I could do to hold in my tears.

"Come on," my father said to my brother, apparently sensing my conflicted emotions. "Let's leave the two of them alone so they can get acquainted."

Once my father and brother had gone, I continued to pet my new centaur, though it was almost perfunctory, as if I was just going through the motions of being happy. It wasn't the centaur's fault, but I just couldn't bring myself to muster the joy I wish I could have felt. Instead, all I could think about was how much I missed my beloved Pholus.

A small sob escaped me, almost like a hiccup, which was quickly followed by another sob. Before I could stop myself, the tears I'd been holding in started flowing and the next thing I knew, I was sitting on the dirt floor of the barn, my legs pulled in against my chest and my knees poking through the holes in my jeans, sobbing into my hands.

At that moment, in my most melodramatic teenage angst, I decided I was suffering through the worst sixteenth birthday ever.

As I sat there, sobbing and miserable and wishing Pholus was still alive, an arm wrapped around me and held me tenderly. I figured my father had returned to check on how I was getting along, saw me in distress, and was doing his best to try to console me. But when I took my hands away from my face and opened my eyes, my father was nowhere to be found. Instead, my centaur was kneeling beside me, looking at me with his big, dark, soulful eyes. After a few moments, I put my head on his shoulder.

We sat that way for a while: him with one arm around me and me with my head on his shoulder, neither one of us making a sound except for the occasional sob that escaped me. Eventually my sobs tapered off and I began to accept the idea that maybe this wasn't the worst sixteenth birthday in history and that maybe I could appreciate my birthday present rather than wishing for Pholus to return from the dead.

When my father returned to check on me, I was brushing my new centaur and scratching him behind the ears, letting out a little laugh whenever he would stamp one of his rear hoofs.

Later that evening, as my new centaur was finishing his dinner of potatoes and cabbage, I sat on the floor of the barn watching him and trying to come up with a name that would be a good fit and hopefully not result in a fate of poisoned honey or pregnant unicorns. My brother had gone into town to meet a couple of friends and my father was puttering around the barn, trying to stay out of my way while sticking around for support, just in case.

"Have you come up with a name yet?" he asked.

I shook my head. "I'm still thinking about it."

"What about Odysseus?" my father said. "Or Theseus?"

My father had either forgotten that he'd suggested Theseus five years earlier or else he really liked the name.

After Ajax and Pholus, I was reluctant to go to the proverbial well a third time for obvious reasons. Plus I'd outgrown my Greek mythology phase about a year earlier and I was more into English rock bands like the Kinks, the Rolling Stones, and, of course, the Beatles. Like most teenage girls, I was devastated when they broke up.

"I'm kind of done with Greek mythology," I said.

"Oh," my father said, though I couldn't tell if he was more confused or relieved. "Okay." Then he went back to puttering.

I had my transistor radio tuned to the local radio station, which was playing a mixture of popular music including The Beach Boys, Chicago, and Elton John. I was hoping to hear some David Bowie but wasn't having any luck. His new album had been released just a couple of months earlier and Ziggy Stardust had crossed my mind as a possible name. But I decided that naming my centaur after a fictional wild, hedonistic, alien rock star with a massive ego probably wasn't a good idea.

While I was considering other Bowie-inspired names such as Major Tom and Starman, "Octopus's Garden" came on the radio, which got me to thinking about names from Beatles' songs, like Sergeant Pepper, Rocky Raccoon, Maxwell, and Jude. I was leaning toward Sergeant Pepper when I noticed my centaur moving back and forth to the song, tapping one of his front hooves, a contented expression on his face, and the name finally came to me.

"Ringo," I said.

My centaur looked over at me and smiled, as if he'd been waiting for me to speak his name all along.

"What did you say?" my father asked.

"Ringo." I stood up and walked over to my centaur, who let out a whinny and clapped his hands. "I've decided to name him Ringo."

Ringo was always my favorite Beatle. And my centaur apparently liked the name. Plus it seemed like a safe choice since as far as I knew the real Ringo hadn't slaughtered a bunch of sheep or poisoned himself on a venomous arrow.

"It's a pleasure to meet you, Ringo," I said with a curtsy.

He returned my curtsy with one of his own.

It's difficult to compare one centaur to another, especially when one of them held such a special place in your heart and the memories of what he meant to you were still so fresh. For months after his death, I would find myself reminiscing about Pholus and the way he would run around in circles whenever I came from school. Or how he would prance about the pasture during a spring rain. And it was years before I could see a jar of honey without bursting into tears.

But while Pholus was prone to overt displays of affection and playfulness, Ringo had a more nuanced and understated temperament. He didn't greet me with enthusiastic antics or playfully nudge me or stamp his feet and flare his nostrils to get my attention. Instead, he gave me my space and let me come to him. At the same time, he always seemed to sense when I was feeling blue and would sit with me and hold my hand or put an arm around me to offer comfort. Sometimes he brought me wildflowers to brighten my room or to put in my hair. Other times he would leave me little hearts that he'd woven out of magic bean vines.

He was a sweet and gentle creature with the soul of a poet.

It didn't take long for Ringo to steal his way into my heart. I resisted at first because it felt like a betrayal of my feelings for Pholus. But the more time I spent with Ringo, the better I felt about myself and the more I realized how much I appreciated him. He helped me to find my way through my grief. Eventually, he became the favorite part of my day.

After graduating from high school, I worked full-time on the farm with my father and brother—tending to the crops, ordering supplies, maintaining the equipment, and helping to manage the finances. Other than when I was eating, sleeping, bathing, or selling magic beans at the farmer's market on Saturday mornings, I spent every possible moment with Ringo. He helped me when I was working in the fields, and I bathed and groomed him and cleaned his hooves. He brought me flowers and other tokens of appreciation, and I took him for walks into town. We did almost everything together. My father called the two of us a matched set. All for one and one for all. I was his human and he was my centaur. And nothing could ever come between us.

Nothing, that is, but time.

The lifespan of centaurs in classic mythology is around eighty-to-one-hundred years. But in real life, the mortality rate of centaurs is much higher due to a variety of viruses, diseases, and infections that affect both humans and horses alike, reducing their lifespans to an average of around twenty-five years. Some centaurs have been known to live as long as fifty years. Most, however, live much shorter lives.

At the age of ten, and nine years after coming into my life, Ringo contracted a combination of pneumonia and horse colic. It started out as a dry cough and restless pawing at the ground but quickly progressed to fever with sweating, shortness of breath, and irritated kicking. We took him to the vet, Dr. Sullivan, who prescribed some medication for the colic to help relieve the discomfort but otherwise he couldn't do much for the pneumonia, as he didn't have the medical training to treat the human half of Ringo. And human doctors were notoriously discriminatory when it came to treating centaurs.

So we had no choice but to treat Ringo ourselves.

Although we didn't have a lot of extra money in the bank due to the factory farms that had been eating into our profits for more than a decade, my father spent as much time and money as he could to create magic bean elixirs for Ringo. Even Gourd helped out, selling his baseball card collection to help cover expenses and building me a makeshift bed in the barn so that I could sleep in the stable.

I spent every possible moment I could with Ringo, brushing him and bathing him, spoon-feeding him magic elixirs along with oatmeal and honey, and doing whatever I could to make him more comfortable. I even brought in a portable turntable and played *Rubber Soul* and *Abbey Road*, which were his favorite Beatles' albums.

Sometimes I sang to him, which brought a smile to his face even though I couldn't carry a tune. Other times I just sat and talked to him.

"I love you, Ringo," I told him, wrapping my arms around him, his body shaking with chills as I struggled to hold back my tears. "You need to get better because I can't stand the thought of losing you."

But as the days progressed, his breathing grew more rapid and shallow and his fever and discomfort waxed as his appetite and energy waned.

In the end, nothing we did could prevent the inevitable.

Ringo died in my arms on a warm September evening, a little more than a month before my twenty-fifth birthday, his head in my lap as I tried to comfort him, leaving me in much the same way that he'd come into my life, only with the roles reversed.

We buried him beneath the oak tree next to Pholus. While the idea was mine, I had no idea how the gesture would exacerbate my grief, causing me to mourn both of my lost centaurs. It was as if an emotional scab had been ripped open, the wound as fresh as it had been nearly ten years ago. No matter what my father and brother did to try to comfort me, I was inconsolable.

I cried almost daily for a year, more often in the spring when the wildflowers bloomed. Or whenever I came across a deformed magic bean vine that I thought resembled the shape of a heart. But even when I was at my happiest, my tears were never far from the surface.

It took more than three years after Ringo's death before I considered the idea of getting another centaur. But once I was emotionally ready and could afford the cost of raising one, I adopted a four-year-old, brown-haired Clydesdale mix from the Chiron Centaur Rescue. I named him Mercury, not after the Roman equivalent of Hermes, the fleet-footed messenger of the gods, but after the lead singer of Queen, who I was a big fan of at the time.

By then I had married a goose farmer named Gavin, who rented his geese out to other organic farmers to weed and fertilize their crops. He'd initially bought the geese in the hopes that one or more of them might start laying golden eggs, but the more practical side of his investment paid the bills.

We lived about two miles down the road from my father's farm, which allowed me to continue to help with the farm's finances and the harvesting of the magic beans. Although we had plenty of land upon which we could have built a barn and a stable, I kept Mercury at my father's farm because Gavin was allergic to centaurs.

Over the years I adopted and raised several other centaurs, one of which I named Theseus in remembrance of my father after he succumbed to prostate cancer. Theseus was brave and strong like his Greek mythological namesake and mostly stayed out of trouble, but I would occasionally wake up in the morning to find a minotaur head waiting for me on the back porch.

While I loved Theseus, Mercury, and all of my other centaurs, each in his own way, I never felt as deep of a connection to any of them the way I did with Ringo and Pholus. There was something special about the two of them, something that set them apart from the others and made me long for their company whenever I felt sad or lonely. Or when the wildflowers bloomed.

Maybe it was because of the formative ages at which I had Ringo and Pholus. Or because of how each of them helped me to become a better person. Or because they not only made me feel special and appreciated, but tapped into a form of love that I hadn't experienced before.

While I loved my father and my brother (in spite of how he would tease me, even as an adult), Ringo and Pholus taught me how to open up my heart and love another creature unconditionally. They taught me how to deal with life's pain and disappointment and come out stronger on the other side. Although I didn't give birth to them, they were my four-legged children. My adopted offspring. In a way, I suppose you could say they helped to prepare me for motherhood.

My husband wasn't thrilled with the idea of naming our twin sons Pholus and Ringo, especially since he was a bigger fan of the Rolling Stones and preferred the name Mick, but he relented because he loves me. And because I agreed that if we ever had a little girl, we would name her Ruby Tuesday.

We never ended up having a daughter due to some health complications I experienced that made it impossible for me to have any more children. And although I would have loved a little girl, raising my sons has been the most rewarding experience I have ever known. I love them more than I imagined possible. More than I love my husband or my brother. More than I loved my father. More than I loved any of my centaurs.

But even though my centaurs Pholus and Ringo have been gone for years, I still think about them often. Some mornings, I sit with a cup of coffee and my old books on Greek mythology and read about the adventures of Pholus. Other days, I listen to my Beatles library while working in the fields and get sentimental whenever I hear "Octopus's Garden" or "With a Little Help from My Friends." One day, I nearly called the poison control center when I found my son Pholus asleep next to a half-empty jar of honey. Another day, I burst into tears when Ringo gave me a heart made out of magic bean vines.

More and more, I find myself thinking about how my father told me choosing a name shouldn't be taken lightly and about how, when it comes to mythological creatures, names can have a significant influence on the development of their personalities. Even though my sons are one-hundred-percent human, sometimes I wonder if my father's advice applied only to my centaurs.

I wonder this when Pholus comes home from school and gets so excited to see me that he runs around in circles. Or when Ringo brings me wildflowers to cheer me up on days I'm feeling blue. Or when the two of them run outside trailing bubbles of laughter and prance around in an early spring rain.

Maybe it's my imagination. Maybe I just miss my centaurs more than I realize. But lately, whenever I watch my sons chase each other around the yard or go running through the fields, I swear I hear the sound of hooves galloping through the grass.

Dr. Sinister's Home
for Retired Villains

Moriarty sits on my right, picking at his Salisbury steak, inspecting it with the tines of his fork and peering underneath it as if his lunch is booby-trapped and might explode at any moment.

Moriarty has trust issues.

"This is disgusting," he says. "A culinary abomination. They might as well just poison us and get it over with."

He also tends toward the melodramatic.

"If you don't like what they've prepared, don't eat it," I say around a mouthful of Salisbury steak and mashed potatoes.

Moriarty raises a single eyebrow and gives a patriarchal look down his nose to let me know he doesn't approve of me talking with my mouth full.

My table manners have admittedly taken a turn for the worse—a consequence of my long-term accommodations and lack of English propriety that would otherwise provide a sense of adequate social structure. Moriarty finds my excuses wanting and suggests my barbaric alternate personality is to blame, pointing to his own high standards for proper etiquette that he has managed to maintain. He might have a valid point. But although I've learned to temper my expectations about the food service and to accept the sub-standard quality of the cuisine, Moriarty still complains.

"It's as if someone scraped this off the pavement, heated it up in the microwave, and covered it in gravy," he says, holding his Salisbury steak up with a thumb and index finger as if it were contaminated.

I go back to eating my lunch, attempting to do so without breaching proper dining etiquette as Moriarty drops his Salisbury steak back on to his plate and then impales several green beans with his fork.

"Overcooked," he says, plucking one of the green beans from his fork and holding the offending vegetable up for emphasis. "This is unacceptable."

Moriarty flings the overcooked green bean across the dining hall, hitting Captain Hook in the back of the head. Hook turns around, a scowl on his face, his gaze darting back and forth before he raises his namesake in the air and shouts, "Curse you, Peter Pan!"

He's always cursing Peter Pan.

Hook continues to glare around the dining hall, which teems with the lunchtime crowd. Dozens of the infamous and the nefarious stand in the food line, fill up their plates, and sit down to eat beneath the racks of fluorescent lights that flicker and buzz throughout the room, which has all the charm of a prison cafeteria. Six-foot long, industrial-grade tables with attached hard plastic blue chairs are arranged in uniform rows and bolted to the linoleum floor, as if to prevent any of the occupants of Dr. Sinister's from stealing them, while the off-white walls remain sterile and barren save for the signs about death rays posted on all sides.

DEATH RAYS ARE NOT ALLOWED
IN THE DINING HALL!
—The Management

"Death rays." Moriarty gives a derisive snort as he plays with his bread pudding. "Since when did weapons make for a convincing villain? Tell me Doc: What happened to good, old-fashioned treachery?"

"Times have changed," I say. "Villains today have more

technology at their disposal. They would be remiss not to consider making use of it."

Moriarty lets loose with a raspberry before he takes a bite of his bread pudding.

When it comes to our trade, Moriarty leans toward the snobbish. He believes the only true villains are those who use their intellect and other natural-born talents rather than relying on technological tools to get the desired results.

While I understand his point, I believe there has always been a place in our line of work for ingenuity and innovation. Not every villain has the ability to outthink his or her adversary. Sometimes you have to use the tools at your disposal, be that brains, brawn, death rays, or supernatural powers.

"Good evening," the Count says as he sits down across from Moriarty.

The Count always says 'Good evening' no matter the time of day. I used to think it was an affectation bred from the Count's love for early twentieth century cinema, but lately I've begun to wonder if it might be something more serious.

Dementia and senility are unfortunate side effects of growing older, even if you happen to be an immortal creature of the night. When you've celebrated more than half a millennia of birthdays, the mind can begin to reshape reality. And I know a thing or two about reshaping reality.

"It's afternoon, genius." Moriarty pulls out his pocket watch and shows it to the Count to emphasize his point.

"Of course." The Count gives a strained smile, either out of embarrassment or because he's sizing up Moriarty's blood type. It wouldn't be the first time. Moriarty has a way of bringing out the worst in people.

Moriarty points across the dining hall. "Hey, isn't that Van Helsing?"

The Count turns to look with a start, his face blanching. You wouldn't think he could get any paler but he somehow manages the trick.

While the Count remains preoccupied with his paranoia, Moriarty grabs the Count's bread pudding off his tray and sets it on his own.

"My mistake," Moriarty says. "It was just the Sheriff of Nottingham."

The Count turns back with an expression that's a mixture of relief and annoyance. "The two look nothing alike."

Moriarty shrugs and digs into the Count's bread pudding with a self-satisfied smirk.

The Count regards Moriarty a moment as if considering an afternoon snack, then he picks up his fork and looks down at his tray, an expression of confusion clouding his face.

In spite of the Count's frailties, Moriarty should know better than to tease him. Even though he's not as agile or as strong as he used to be, the Count can still hypnotize the trousers off Svengali. And when it comes to transmogrification, my abilities pale in comparison.

The three of us continue to eat our meals in relative silence, with the occasional derogatory complaint from Moriarty about the quality of the food and the odd apology from the Count for his audible flatulence.

"My god." Moriarty waves a hand in front of his face. "It's as if something died."

The Count glares at Moriarty, who glares back.

"I wouldn't recommend that," I say to Moriarty. "Remember what happened last time."

Two months ago, Moriarty challenged the Count to a staring contest, only to end up stripping naked and strutting around the shuffleboard court like a rooster. When he came to, he was perched on the roof and crowing at the sunrise.

Moriarty relents and breaks eye contact, looking past the Count and rolling his eyes. "Oh joy. Here comes Mr. Wonderful."

I follow Moriarty's gaze to find Mr. Blank walking past the

other tables, headed our way—his thick helmet of black hair covering his oversized head. While more than a few villains possess above-average craniums, Mr. Blank is an unusual specimen in that regard. However, I have my doubts that it's a reflection of a superior intellect.

Mr. Blank is one of the newest arrivals at Dr. Sinister's, what the old-timers refer to as *cubbies*. And like many cubbies, Mr. Blank operates under the assumption that he's still a bear. Every time he walks into the room, he wears the smirk of someone expecting to do battle. His eyes narrow, assessing potential threats and identifying easy conquests. It's a hard habit to break. A survival skill that's fostered and nurtured until it becomes second nature. Like breathing. Or swallowing. Or planning world domination.

Mr. Blank hasn't yet figured out that his plans for planetary supremacy have been reduced to outdated blueprints and filed away in the archives.

Not everyone who ends up at Dr. Sinister's is a candidate for hip replacement surgery or on a steady diet of high-blood pressure medication and Ensure. Sometimes even the best of us meet our match before we're ready to hang up our black capes or monocles. When that happens, denial and anger perform a hostile takeover, leaving reason and acceptance as collateral damage.

No one wants to admit that his or her time has passed, especially villains. When it comes to holding on to our glory days, we're a singularly obstinate species. Worse than child actors and high school jocks.

At Mr. Blank's approach, the Count turns and gives a courteous nod. "Good evening."

"It's afternoon, Grandpa." Mr. Blank nods toward the sunshine pouring in through the windows. "Shouldn't you be in your coffin or crypt or something?"

Mr. Blank suffers from an ignorance born of pop-culture misinformation.

"Contrary to any propaganda you may have seen or read,

sunlight does not affect me in an adverse manner," the Count says.

"But cut off his head and drive a stake through his heart and you're in business," Moriarty says.

The Count fixes Moriarty with another stare.

"Thanks for the tip." Mr. Blank gives a menacing smile and eyes each of us in turn, but we avoid direct eye contact, just to play it safe.

Mr. Blank has the ability to steal people's memories, which isn't particularly threatening in a place where more than half of the residents teeter on the precipice of Alzheimer's and senility. That's the main reason for the signs posted everywhere, shouting orders at us about death rays and other off-limit activities. Not as a warning for residents who break the rules with malice or contempt, but more as a reminder, in case we forget.

PORTALS BETWEEN DIMENSIONS ARE
TO REMAIN CLOSED AT ALL TIMES!
—The Management

Plus in these litigious times, even retirement homes for scoundrels and evildoers have to worry about lawsuits. More so considering the clientele. So there's a liability concern that has to be taken into consideration.

Mr. Blank nods at the open seat next to the Count. "Mind if I join you?"

"Yes," Moriarty says without hesitation, never one to add any sweetener to his bitter rejoinders. "We do mind. Go find another table to pollute."

"We're somewhat particular as to our preference for dining companions," I say, attempting to clarify Moriarty's antisocial behavior.

"Perhaps if you had a title...," the Count adds, leaving the implication hanging like an unfinished confession.

While the three of us have been something of a literary

triumvirate for more than a century, we have had numerous other infamous characters share our table over the years.

Dr. No. Dr. Evil. Dr. Manhattan.

Judge Doom. Lord Voldemort. General Zod.

So yes, we do tend to be somewhat exclusive when it comes to the company we keep.

Mr. Blank studies us a moment. "I get it. It's like that old joke: A doctor, a professor, and a count walk into a bar..."

"I don't believe I've heard that one," the Count says with a good-natured smile.

For a creature of darkness, the Count tends to be a bit of a dupe.

"You'd like it, Grandpa," Mr. Blank says. "You're the punch line."

The Count's bright smile transforms into a dark scowl.

"The only joke around here is you," Moriarty says.

Mr. Blank lets out a laugh to rival that of Skeletor. But at Dr. Sinister's, evil laughs are akin to vanity license plates: more show than substance.

"Nice laugh," Moriarty says. "Does it come with a money-back guarantee?"

Mr. Blank points a menacing finger. "I'd watch your step, Professor. Or the next time we have this discussion, you won't remember your own name."

"Ooooh!" The Count waves his fingers in the air theatrically. "Such a threat!"

Mr. Blank turns his finger on the Count. "That goes double for you, Grandpa."

The cubbie points his finger at each of us in turn as if playing *eeny meeny miny moe* before he walks away in a huff looking for an open table, finally sitting down with Bluebeard and the Wicked Witch of the West. What the three of them could possibly have in common I have no idea, but they seem to hit it off and within minutes they're laughing like old college chums. When they glance our way, Mr. Blank whispers something and the other two howl like hyenas.

I don't take it personally. This is, after all, a retirement home for villains, so it's not as if we're all sharing our feelings in support groups or participating in team-building exercises.

While the general nature of being a villain precludes any of us from developing honest and loving relationships with each other, out in the wild we do share a general sense of camaraderie as we're all united in the single-minded purpose of spreading evil throughout the world. Not exactly a noble undertaking, but common ground, nonetheless. However, gather us together to live under a single roof and force us to share limited personal space and resources along with questionable meals served by an underpaid and indifferent staff, and the camaraderie unravels like a failed diabolical plot.

"Cretins." Moriarty gestures toward the other tables. "They're all nothing more than cretins."

"I believe they can hear you," the Count says, looking over his shoulder.

Indeed, those sitting nearest to us glance our way with sneers, leers, and general expressions of iniquity. While it's true that Moriarty, the Count, and I are among the longest-tenured residents at Dr. Sinister's and have occupied a position of respect and power for more than a century, the influx of modern pop-culture villains and antiheroes has altered the current social landscape, causing us to lose some of our long-standing stature.

Reputation can only get you so far in this business. Eventually, more sophisticated and powerful villains emerge, spreading a new and improved brand of evil, and before you know it you've become obsolete. Relics of the villainous past. Quaint in your outdated version of treachery. Where people once quaked in their proverbial shoes at the thought of us, appalled by our immoral exploits and terrified by our very existence, we now live in a world where villains eat their victims, shoot lightning out of their fingertips, and have developed the ability to control magnetism.

Criminal masterminds and alter ego sociopaths can't compete with today's crop of villains. And although his supernatural powers would seem to give the Count some added cachet in the modern world, his legacy has been diluted by parodies, adaptations, and updates that have rendered him little more than a caricature of his former monstrous self.

Eventually, we all find ourselves staring into the abyss of irrelevance. Some of us sooner than others.

Once we've finished our lunch, Moriarty goes outside to take his afternoon stroll around the grounds to smoke his pipe while the Count and I retire to the grand lounge, which is more plebian than palatial. Stuffed with second-hand furniture and decorated with cheap lamps and threadbare area rugs, the grand lounge suffers from an identity crisis. In spite of its less-than-opulent décor, it's where many of the residents of Dr. Sinister's gather to plot, scheme, and play the occasional not-so-friendly game of backgammon or Parcheesi. Blood has been spilled more than once over claims of cheating and telepathic mind reading.

As a rule, villains tend to be sore losers.

Other than playing board games and cards, the residents of Dr. Sinister's often pass their time in the grand lounge with one of the numerous books that have been donated or left behind by previous residents. There's a lot of Stephen King and Clive Barker among the paperbacks, along with classics like *Frankenstein*, *Dracula*, and *The Haunting of Hill House*. You won't find any Danielle Steel or Stephanie Myers on the shelves. If you did, chances are there would be a riot.

Every Friday we have Movie Night on the antiquated forty-two-inch CRT that's hooked up to a DVD player in the corner of the lounge, where some of us gather to watch films like *Rosemary's Baby*, *The Silence of the Lambs*, and *The Usual Suspects* because who doesn't like a happy ending? Occasionally, someone will pop in a Batman or a Superman film and we all boo and hiss at the spandex-clad heroes. It's all good fun, though every now and then someone gets carried away. Two weeks ago, Lex Luthor drank a little too much absinthe and threw a lamp at the television, cracking the screen.

"Fucking Superman!" he screamed.

We're still waiting for a new television.

At least Luthor took out his frustrations on an inanimate object, unlike Magneto, who has anger management issues, especially when he loses at chess.

PLEASE REFRAIN FROM TURNING THE OTHER RESIDENTS INTO MUTANTS!
—The Management

The Count and I sit down in a couple of wingback chairs that smell of disinfectant and stale urine (incontinence strikes even the most villainous among us) and proceed to pursue our own post-lunch activities—the Count picking up where he left off in *Interview with the Vampire*, while I open my journal and continue writing my autobiography. Perhaps it's just wishful thinking, but I have aspirations that someone will want to publish my memoirs.

Moriarty mocks my endeavors and doesn't think anyone is interested in reading the self-indulgent ramblings of a discarded and obsolete villain. On numerous occasions, he has told me my ideas are trite and my writing is overly florid and filled with clichés. I think he's just jealous that I've found a hobby, something that makes me happy and fulfilled, and he's attempting to drag me down into his morass of negativity. But I'm not going to let him deter me. I have a story to tell and I plan to tell it. There's a great deal of personal experience I feel I can impart to others, not to mention a unique insight into the lives of some of the most notorious villains of literature, television, and film.

Norman Bates, Emma Frost, Agent Smith, Walter White, Dr. Belloq, Annie Wilkes, The Joker, Patrick Bateman, Morgan le Fay, Emperor Palpatine, Gordon Gekko, Randall Flagg, Bellatrix

Lestrange, Ernst Blofeld, Hans Gruber, Two-Face, Lady MacBeth, Bill Sikes, Milo Mindbender, the Green Goblin, and Nurse Ratched are among the villains who have passed through the doors of Dr. Sinister's at one time or another. Not to mention the various wolves, witches, and other classic villains of the brothers Grimm variety who ended up here.

While they know how to enjoy a party, fairy tale villains aren't much on conversation—most of which revolves around cooking children, devouring elderly women, and terrorizing pigs.

Not a lot of common ground to be had there.

I suppose that's the main reason the Count, Moriarty, and I have maintained our friendship: familiarity. We've known each other for so long that we've grown comfortable with one another. Our habits. Our traits. Our threats. You can only promise to strangle someone or beat them to death or drink their blood so many times before it becomes predictable. Once you reach that point, the threats lose their teeth and become a source of dark amusement. Especially when you've been smoking medical marijuana.

Although most of the villains who end up here eventually fade into obscurity, some of Dr. Sinister's infamous residents have gone on to make new lives for themselves. Cruella de Vil was a mainstay here for years until she decided to open up an exclusive bed and breakfast for dog owners, while The White Witch teamed up with Hannibal Lecter to open a chain of fast-food restaurants called Hannibal and Gretel's.

On the other side of the grand lounge, the Big Bad Wolf and the Queen of Hearts sit across from one another at a scuffed oval tea table, playing a game of cards and alternating promises of disembowelment or beheadings. They do this every day after lunch, their threats escalating until one of them wins and the other lets out a scream or a roar of frustration and storms off.

"I'll fucking eat you," the Big Bad Wolf growls, baring his teeth like a promise, saliva dripping from his lips.

"Poppycock," the Queen of Hearts says with a dismissive wave of her hand. "I'll chop off your furry head before you can get so much as a nibble you mangy, flea-infested jackal. Do you have any Queens?"

"Go fish!" the Big Bad Wolf shouts, spit and foam spraying from his muzzle.

I write down the scene in my journal, taking notes, thankful that I don't need to get their permission to use their names and likeness since they're both in the public domain.

The Big Bad Wolf and the Queen of Hearts aren't the only regulars who like to hang out in the grand lounge. Dorian Gray comes moping around on an almost daily basis, complaining about his portrait. Every now and then, the Wicked Witch of the West flies through on her broom, a handful of monkeys trailing behind her, chattering and flinging their feces at everyone. And it's not unusual for Captain Hook and Long John Silver to spend the afternoon lounging on a couch, reminiscing about their glory days, sharing a bottle of cheap rum and singing "Fifteen Men on a Dead Man's Chest" before getting into an argument that eventually escalates into a drunken swordfight.

As you can imagine, we don't receive many visitors.

Next to me, the Count lets out a contented sigh as he continues to read *Interview with the Vampire*, one hand holding the paperback while he absentmindedly bites at the back of his other hand and makes soft sucking sounds. He started doing this a couple of years ago. He says he does it for comfort but considering that the Count has admitted to deriving sexual pleasure from sucking blood, it's probably something he should do in the privacy of his room.

While the Count continues to suck his own blood, Svengali and Don Juan stroll through the grand lounge in matching Under Armour athletic T-shirts and compression shorts like a couple of fashion models on a catwalk, neither one of them saying a word. *Prima donnas*, Moriarty calls them. None of the other residents care much for either Svengali or Don Juan, who stop and flex for the Evil Queen, but she's too preoccupied with her magic mirror to notice them, so they pretend as if they don't notice her, either, and continue on their way to their afternoon workout.

Along with the prison-themed dining hall and the less-than-grand lounge, Dr. Sinister's boasts a rundown gym filled with obsolete exercise equipment, a weed-infested garden that has been the cause of several outbreaks of poison ivy, and an outdoor booby trap otherwise known as the Recreation Center.

The Recreation Center consists of two ping-pong tables held together with duct tape, a dilapidated shuffleboard court with several treacherous cracks, and an unsupervised swimming pool. While the ping-pong tables and shuffleboard court are often put to good use in spite of their condition, most of the residents have avoided the swimming pool ever since the Dr. Kananga incident.

THE POOL IS NOT A SHARK PIT!
ALSO, NO RUNNING OR DIVING ALLOWED!
—The Management

"I win again!" shouts the Queen of Hearts, laying the last of her cards on the table, which the Big Bad Wolf immediately overturns with one of his giant paws, scattering cards across the floor as he lets out a howl of rage and storms off.

"Loser!" the Queen of Hearts yells after him, her finger and thumb held up to her forehead in the shape of an "L," her derisive laughter filling the grand lounge. She emits a couple of triumphant clucks, then rights the table and cleans up the scattered cards to make a show of being a good winner. After tidying up, she pulls out her compact, powders her face, puts on a fresh coat of blood-red lipstick, then stands up and straightens her petticoats and collar, glancing around the lounge with disdain, as if the rest of us are beneath her, before she tilts her chin in the air and strolls toward the exit.

Out of nowhere, the Phantom of the Opera appears at my side.

"The phaaaaaaantom of the opera is heeeeeeeeere," he sings.

"Beside your chair."

I liked him better before he became enamored with the Andrew Lloyd Webber musical.

"What do you want?" I ask, as if I didn't know.

Several months ago, the Phantom convinced me to accompany him into the Big Bad Wolf's bedroom closet to play a prank. I thought we were going to jump out at him when he opened the closet door. Or perhaps wait until he went to sleep before we snuck out to frighten him—the proverbial monsters in the closet. Although frightening an ill-tempered and violent carnivore probably isn't the smartest idea.

Instead of jumping out of the closet, the Phantom cracked open the closet door just enough for us to get a glimpse into the room, where the Big Bad Wolf was lying naked on the bed, pleasuring himself. Before I could object or scrub the image from my mind, the bedroom door opened and the Queen of Hearts snuck in, closing and locking the door behind her.

"Oh my," she said to the Big Bad Wolf. "What a big cock you have."

"The better to fuck you with," he growled.

Faster than you could say *I'll huff and I'll puff*, the Queen of Hearts burst out of her corset and royal undergarments and climbed on top of the Big Bad Wolf, where she rode him like a mechanical bull until he let loose with an orgasmic howl.

Those are three minutes of my life I will never get back.

"Want to watch the freak show again?" the Phantom asks from beside my chair, smiling at me with deranged glee.

"I think I'll pass," I say.

"Suit yourself." The Phantom does a theatrical wave of his black cape and disappears into the shadows.

"I like his cape," the Count says with a hint of envy. "I wish I had one like that."

I return to my memoirs while the Count goes back to his book and resumes his soft, masturbatory sucking sounds. While I know he's not attempting to annoy me on purpose, sometimes I just want to give in to my inner evil nature and bash in his skull with a hammer.

Before I can allow Mr. Hyde to come out and play, there's a commotion outside, voices shouting along with maniacal laughter. At Dr. Sinister's, there's always maniacal laughter, so chances are it's a false alarm. But in addition to my dissociative identity disorder, I also suffer from FOMO: the fear of missing out. And I'm not the only one.

The Count and I abandon our chairs and exit the grand lounge through the French doors to find a small crowd standing at the edge of the pool. Bluebeard, Lady Macbeth, Rumpelstiltskin, Norman Bates, and Hans Gruber are there, along with Pennywise the Clown, who is the source of the maniacal laughter. He's always laughing maniacally about something.

When we reach the others, I stand next to Bluebeard and glance into the swimming pool, where Mr. Blank floats face down in the deep end, his arms outstretched, scattered brown leaves drifting in the water around him, a ribbon of red flowing out from his neck.

In a retirement home full of villains, you're bound to make an enemy or two, and Mr. Blank made more than his share in short work, so I can't say this is a surprise.

"Did anyone see what happened?" I ask.

"Not me," Rumpelstiltskin answers, quick and high-pitched, his right index finger halfway up one of his nostrils.

Rumpelstiltskin is a vile little creature. He spits in people's drinks when they're not looking, masturbates in public, and has been caught urinating into the swimming pool. The Count claims he once saw the diminutive imp sneak into Catwoman's room and sniff her panties.

"I witnessed nothing," Bluebeard says, giving me a look that defies me to challenge him.

Hans Gruber echoes Bluebeard's denial, while Lady Macbeth and Norman Bates shake their heads in silence. Pennywise just lets out another burst of maniacal laughter.

I don't expect anyone to admit they witnessed Mr. Blank's death. As a general rule, villains don't tend to snitch on one another. It's bad form. Plus when you live among dozens of other scoundrels, miscreants, libertines, and evildoers, it doesn't take the intellect of Lex Luthor or Hannibal Lecter to understand that tattletales possess a limited lifespan.

More residents show up to get an eyeful and satisfy their lust, including the Big Bad Wolf and the Queen of Hearts, her hair disheveled and a single stocking bunched up at one ankle. The Wicked Witch of the West watches from behind one of the windows in the grand lounge, refusing to come outside and get anywhere near the swimming pool.

"What happened here?" Moriarty asks over my shoulder as he joins the growing number of rubber-neckers gathered around the swimming pool.

"Someone killed the cubbie," Rumpelstiltskin says with a hint of glee, then repeats it over and over like a nursery rhyme and starts to dance and clap along in rhythm.

"Is that so?" Moriarty takes a puff on his pipe. "Pity."

The ribbon of blood continues to flow out of Mr. Blank's severed throat, twisting through the water like a scarlet snake. A few minutes later, three of Dr. Sinister's henchmen arrive, pushing through the crowd to the edge of the pool.

"All right, all right. Nothing to see here you haven't seen before," one of them says as another readies a grappling hook to retrieve Mr. Blank's lifeless body. "Everyone back inside."

A chorus of complaints rises up from the crowd as it disperses with reluctance, the disappointment palpable. There are more than a few pouty faces.

While death isn't an anomaly at Dr. Sinister's, we don't often get to experience moments such as these that allow us to remember how it felt to vanquish an adversary and stand in triumph over a fallen victim. In a way, we've all become victims, not of each other but of our own nostalgia—wishing for the good old days when we existed in perpetual relevance. Now all we have left to nourish our souls are the memories of our villainous exploits. And the occasional dead body floating in a mixture of blood and chlorinated water.

Moriarty, the Count, and I linger outside the French doors of the grand lounge with a few of the others, soaking up as much of the ambiance as we can.

I glance at Moriarty. "Did you enjoy your afternoon walk?"

He takes another puff on his pipe and gives a single, almost imperceptible, nod. It might just be the light, but he appears to have a twinkle in his eye that wasn't there before.

"Sometimes it's the little things in life," Moriarty says as the henchmen drag Mr. Blank's corpse from the swimming pool.

When the Giant Koi
Returned to San Francisco

Our grandmother used to tell us stories about the way things were when she was a little girl. How the sky was bluer and the air was cleaner and how everything seemed to have more of a shine or a glow.

"Like it was all brand new," she said with this wistful tone and a faraway look in her eyes, as if she'd magically transported her mind back to when she was a little girl while she sat there in her sixty-some-odd-year-old adult body.

My little brother Max looked at the pictures our grandmother showed us of her as a little girl and asked, "If the world was brand new, why was it all in black and white?"

Grandma explained that when she was a little girl, most people still took photos with black and white film.

Molly, Max's twin sister, cocked her head and asked, "What's film?"

"It's how people used to take pictures before digital cameras came along," our grandmother explained.

Whenever we would visit, we would sit down on the floor at our grandmother's feet—criss-cross applesauce or with our arms hugging our legs to our chests—and listen with our mouths and eyes wide open in wonder as she shared the stories of the way the world was before we were born. In addition to film photography, she would tell us how phones used to have dials instead of buttons. Or how there were only four television stations. Or how most people had never heard about computers let alone had one in their home.

"What did they use instead of computers?" Max asked.

"We had typewriters," our grandmother answered.

"Typewriters?" Molly furrowed her forehead the way she always did when she was confused. "What are those?"

"That's what we used instead of keyboards," our grandmother said. "Except they typed words on paper instead of on monitors and they weren't connected to the Internet."

"That sounds lame," I said, chiming in.

As the older sibling, I always felt obligated to proclaim anything that I didn't understand or approve of as either lame or stupid, depending on my mood.

Our grandmother smiled at me. "At the time it was all state of the art."

Grandpa sat in his chair on the other side of the room, the tobacco glowing an angry red in the bowl of his pipe, little halos of smoke rising above his head as he read one of the adults-only hardcover books that he kept on the bookcase nearby. He wouldn't say much while our grandmother was talking, but every now and then he would grunt or snort or let out a harrumph, usually when Grandma told us one of her *'tall tales,'* as he called them.

These *tall tales* usually involved some type of mythological creature or strange animal. Centaurs, leprechauns, and unicorns. Talking crows, magical cats, and rabbits the size of Rottweilers. Sometimes the stories took place in a setting where Grandma lived, while other stories took place in a faraway place or a land we'd never heard of.

There was the story about how every November wild bison would overrun downtown Buffalo, New York. And the one about dolphins that used to leap and play in the canals of Venice, Italy. And the one where every spring, herds of wild mountain goats would overrun a small town in Wales.

Max was always partial to the stories about the leprechauns, mostly because he enjoyed how our grandmother would change her voice and speak in an Irish brogue. Molly, on the other hand, liked the stories about the talking animals and she was always disappointed that none of the dogs or cats we had growing up ever uttered a single human word.

My favorite story our grandmother would tell us was the one about the giant koi that lived in the San Francisco bay back in the 1940s and 50s. "They weren't just the size of dogs or bison," she said. "They were as big as trucks. And not just those small compact, fuel-efficient passenger trucks, but the big commercial flatbeds that haul around farm equipment."

She would describe how the koi liked to swim beneath the Bay Bridge and the Golden Gate Bridge and how every now and then one of them would leap over one of the bridges, scaring the daylights out of the pedestrians on the Golden Gate and causing the occasional traffic accident.

"Sometimes," she said, leaning forward with her elbows on her knees and speaking in an almost conspiratorial whisper, "at high tide, the koi would swim right up to the shoreline where it was deep enough so you could feed them. Some of them would even eat right out of your hand."

Molly would usually gasp when our grandmother said this, while Max would say something like "Uh uh!" or "No way!" until our grandmother convinced him otherwise.

Me? I would imagine what that would be like, to stand on the pedestrian walkway at the Marina Green or on the rocks across from the Golden Gate Yacht Club and have a giant koi eat a loaf of bread or a peeled orange right out of my hand.

I read a lot about koi after hearing my grandmother's stories and learned that koi will eat just about anything. Bugs, insects, plants, algae. They'll even eat people food. Oranges, bread, peas, cantaloupe, and Cheerios are among the variety of treats that koi like to eat. They'll even eat Goldfish crackers.

"But the best part was in the late spring," Grandma said with a smile on her face and a twinkle in her eyes, "when the water was so full of koi that ships and sailboats weren't allowed in the bay because there wasn't any room. If you were of a mind and didn't care about getting your shoes and socks wet, you could walk all the way to Angel Island on their backs."

"Did you ever do that Grandma?" I asked, imagining myself walking across the bay on the backs of a thousand giant koi.

"Your great grandfather wouldn't let me," she said. "But a couple of my friends made it all the way to Alcatraz before they decided that was far enough and turned back."

It was at this point in the story that Grandpa offered up a harrumph, which our grandmother ignored. As did we.

Maybe it was the way Grandma told them or the fact that we were all eager to believe her but at the time, her stories all seemed completely plausible.

As we grew older, we discovered that many of the stories our grandmother told us were indeed tall tales, either partially or completely. This revelation didn't change how much we loved the stories or how important they were in weaving the fabric of our childhood. And we never contradicted our grandmother. It didn't matter that the stories weren't true. What mattered was the experience of hearing her tell them, even after we'd grown into teenagers and then into young adults and were no longer the children who had listened to her tales with open mouths and wide-eyed wonder the way we had all those years ago.

But once the pandemic began to spread and numerous cities and countries across the globe enacted strict lockdowns with people having to shelter in place for several months, we discovered that some of our grandmother's tall tales had more kernels of truth in them than we had come to believe.

As businesses and factories closed, and with the dramatic reduction in the number of cars on the road and boats on the water and planes in the skies, the amount of air and water pollution fell to levels not seen in decades. Just a few weeks after the lockdowns and shelter-in-place orders, satellites orbiting the earth documented a discernable drop in air pollution over China, Italy, and cities from New York to Los Angeles. And with the reduced pollution, traffic, and human activity, nature began to return to places where it was absent for years or generations.

Dolphins have returned to the canals of Venice, frolicking in the empty waterways.

Rare leatherback sea turtles are nesting in Thailand for the first time in years.

Wild boar have been spotted roaming in cities and towns throughout Northern Italy.

Downtown Buffalo, NY, has been overrun by herds of bison that roam the deserted streets day and night.

In Llandudno, Wales, wild Kashmiri mountain goats are running through the streets and devouring flower gardens.

And herds of deer have taken over a housing estate in an East London neighborhood and overrun a shopping area in Nara, Japan.

But the story that caught my attention more than the others—even more than the Rottweiler-sized Continental Giant rabbits that have invaded several country towns in Worcestershire, England—was the most marvelous story of them all.

The giant koi have returned to San Francisco.

I saw the images on my smartphone first, after clicking on a link that Molly sent to me in a text message.

You won't believe this, her text message said.

When I first saw the photos of the giant koi, I thought they were some kind of hoax, another meme meant to amuse or entertain everyone on Twitter and Facebook and Instagram.

The Loch Ness Monster returning to Scotland.

Godzilla seen swimming in the waters off the coast of Japan.

The Furbies spotted in the rainforests of Queensland, Australia.

Then I saw the video from the CBS affiliate in San Francisco, shot from a helicopter flying above the Golden Gate Bridge. But even after watching the un-doctored and verified video footage from

CBS, my inner Doubting Thomas refused to believe it.

So I turned on the television and scanned through the news channels. I searched the Internet for anything relating to 'Giant Koi San Francisco,' watched every video from CNN and FOX and NBC, and found every possible confirmation that the giant koi had, without question, returned to San Francisco.

Then I called my sister.

"When are you leaving?" Molly asked when she answered. No *Hello* or *Can you believe it's true?* Just straight to what we both knew I would be doing.

"I'm on my way as we speak," I said as I drove along Interstate 80, heading west.

I lived in Sacramento, about an hour and a half drive from San Francisco, but there was plenty of time for me to get there before sunset, especially with so few cars on the road compared to the normal commute traffic. And my ex had Delilah for the weekend, so I didn't have to worry about what to do with my six-year-old daughter.

"Are you even allowed to drive to San Francisco?" Molly asked.

"I don't think anyone's going to pull me over and give me a citation for driving on the freeway," I said.

The governor had issued a shelter-in-place order, which meant all residents were supposed to curtail or avoid any non-essential travel until the order was lifted. While driving ninety miles to see what could turn out to be a once-in-a-lifetime phenomenon wasn't considered essential in any official sense, it was essential for me.

"I wish I could go with you," Molly said, her voice filled with longing and disappointment.

Molly lived in Minneapolis, having permanently transplanted there after graduating from the University of Minnesota with a Bachelor's Degree in animal studies. So short of jumping on an airplane and having the travel restrictions lifted, she wasn't making it out to California any time soon.

"I know you do," I said, and then because I knew it was the right thing to say, "I wish you could go with me, too."

The truth was that I didn't want Molly to go with me. The giant koi were my obsession, not hers. But it wasn't just my sister's company I eschewed. I didn't want anyone to go with me. Not even Delilah. This was something I wanted to experience on my own, without any distractions from anyone else. Maybe later I would go see them with Molly, but this first time I wanted to belong all to me.

"Do you think Max has seen the reports?" Molly asked.

"I have no idea."

Max had flown off to Ireland the day after graduating from high school and I hadn't spoken with him more than a handful of times over the past ten years. While Max had never confided in either of us his reasons for moving to The Emerald Isle, Molly and I both knew that our grandmother's stories had played a part in his decision.

"Is he still in Carlingford?" Molly asked.

"As far as I know."

Carlingford is a small coastal village in northeast Ireland, about an hour south of Belfast. Among other things, Carlingford is known for its oyster farms, medieval buildings, and leprechaun sanctuary.

According to our grandmother, a local pub owner in Carlingford claimed he found evidence of a leprechaun in 1989 after hearing a scream near the wishing well on Slieve Foye, the mountain that overlooks Carlingford. When he investigated, he found small bones, a tiny green jacket and pants, and a handful of gold coins surrounded by what appeared to be scorched earth. The discovery sparked an annual hunt on Slieve Foye, with thousands descending on the mountain to search for leprechauns.

Year after year, Max begged our mother and father to take him to Carlingford. He didn't want to catch any leprechauns, he said. He just wanted to see one for himself. Our parents, naturally, declined Max's requests, so eventually he stopped asking.

In 2009, twenty years after the discovery of the leprechaun's remains, the European Union granted official heritage status to the leprechauns who lived in the caverns of Slieve Foye, declaring the mountain and all of its inhabitants, animals, and flora a designated area of protection under the EU's Habitats Directive.

A year later, Max was on his way to Ireland.

"So how's the research going?" I asked, steering the conversation away from our brother.

When it came to discussions about Max, one of us usually took the wheel. Otherwise, we'd end up focusing on him and what he was doing rather than on supporting each other. Inevitably we'd run the conversation right off the road and into a ditch.

"Research is great!" Molly said, her tone brightening. She always enjoyed talking about her work. "We've been making a lot of progress with cat vocalizations, but the dogs are still a challenge to decipher. The crows, of course, are leaps and bounds above the others. A couple of them have even started telling jokes. They're hilarious!"

When it came to our grandmother's stories, Max wasn't the only one affected by them.

Molly's decision to get a degree in animal studies wasn't motivated simply by her love for animals, but by her desire to converse with them. As a kid, she thought animals could talk and it was just a matter of getting them to express themselves in a manner so she could understand them. Whenever she was outside and encountered a crow, a cat, a squirrel, or someone walking their dog, Molly would stop and start chatting up whatever animal happened to be in the vicinity.

Of course, that wasn't enough to satisfy her, so for her tenth birthday our parents got Molly a parakeet, which she named Pete. Molly spent hours conversing with Pete, or at least trying to, but his vocabulary was limited to mimicking Molly's words (and a few choice expressions that Max taught him, such as *Molly Stinks* and *Up Yours Butthead*).

Parakeets aren't known for their stimulating conversational skills.

After Pete passed away due to complications from flying out Molly's bedroom window and into the talons of a barn owl, Molly upgraded to an African Gray named Priscilla. Not only do African Grays boast a vocabulary of more than 1,000 words, but they're also able to learn how to use the words in context to communicate with humans rather than just mimicking them.

With Priscilla as her muse, Molly followed her childhood dream of conversing with animals all the way to an animal studies degree from the University of Minnesota and then to AARF, the Animal Articulation Research Fellowship—a privately funded organization dedicated to the research of animal linguistics. So Molly spends her days talking to cats, dogs, crows, parrots, pigs, squirrels, rats, and the occasional chimpanzee and orangutan. She even spent three weeks at the Dolphin Research Center in Grassy Key, Florida, conversing with dolphins.

"I'm really happy for you, Molly," I said.

What I meant was: *I'm really happy for you but I'm also envious and jealous that you and Max have been able to pursue your passions from our grandmother's childhood stories while I've spent most of the past two decades being disappointed.*

At least now I had the chance to change that narrative.

I finished my conversation with Molly, promising that I would take photos and videos and send them to her, and then I hung up so I could focus on the road, which was hard enough to do considering I was on my way to see something I'd fantasized and dreamt about hundreds of times since I was a child.

At the age of eleven, my parents let me pick out half a dozen goldfish that I put into the fish tank my grandmother had given me for my birthday. After my parents went to bed, I snuck out into the backyard and released all six goldfish into our swimming pool in the hopes that they would grow into giant koi so that I could walk across the pool on their backs. At the time, I didn't realize that goldfish and koi are bred from completely different species of carp. Or that the largest a goldfish can grow is up to one foot. Or that when placed into a swimming pool treated with chlorine, goldfish will die in a matter of hours.

When I came out the next morning to find all six of my goldfish floating lifelessly in the pool, I was devastated—as much from their deaths as from the fact that they hadn't magically transformed into giant koi. My parents didn't allow me to keep any more goldfish after that. And my requests for building a koi pond were met with the repeated mantra "when you're older."

Older turned out to be after I was married but before Delilah was born.

Prevented from having my own koi as a child, I resigned myself to enjoying the koi ponds of the Garden Valley Ranch in Petaluma when we drove out to see the roses bloom in the spring or when visited the Japanese Tea Garden in Golden Gate Park during the summer. Once I was old enough to drive, I would spend my weekends visiting public koi ponds as far away as Newport Beach and Corona del Mar, taking longer trips in the summer to see the koi at the Japanese Garden in Portland and the Flamingo Hilton and Wynn hotels in Las Vegas.

When we started dating, my ex thought my obsession with koi was sweet and humored me when I wanted to plan our holidays to Los Angeles and San Diego so that I could visit the koi ponds at The Disneyland Resort Hotel, the Fairmont Miramar Hotel in Santa Monica, and the Japanese Friendship Gardens in Balboa Park. That humor remained when I wanted to take our honeymoon in Hawaii just so I could see the koi pond at the Ala Moana Mall and Market in Honolulu. After all, who can say *no* to a honeymoon in Hawaii?

But after a few years of vacations that included trips to the Morikami Museum and Japanese Gardens in Delray Beach and the National Arboretum in Washington DC, the humor began to fade. I think the deal breaker was probably when we went to the Gaylord Opryland Resort and Convention Center in Nashville for my twenty-fifth birthday and I spent almost the entire three days in the atrium gardens watching the koi. Either that or it was the Memorial

Day trip I insisted we take to The Houston Zoo and all I cared about were the moats filled with koi that surrounded the habitats.

It was inevitable that my obsession would eventually lead to our break-up.

Without much traffic to speak of, I made it to the turnoff for State Route 37 in less than forty-five minutes. I could have taken Interstate 80 all the way to the Bay Bridge, which was usually the faster route into San Francisco, but 37 was a more scenic drive through the San Pablo Bay National Wildlife Refuge before connecting with 101 south. But the main reason I wanted to approach San Francisco from the north rather than from the east was because it would take me across the Golden Gate Bridge.

Ever since I was a child, I've loved coming into San Francisco across the Golden Gate. I love how the vermilion orange towers loom overhead with such majesty, sometimes contrasted against a deep blue sky and other times partially obscured by the fog—the tops peeking out occasionally through the fog as if playing a game of hide and seek. And if you've ever been on the bridge when a foghorn sounds, the sound resonates all the way to your bones.

As I drove along 37 and on to the ten-mile stretch across the Wildlife Refuge, I kept glancing to my left on the off chance that some of the giant koi might have come all the way up from San Francisco into the San Pablo Bay. Just seeing the bay made me shiver in anticipation at the thought of actually seeing the giant koi. More than once, I thought I glimpsed a flash of color in the water out of the corner of my eye, but it was just my imagination, which wasn't a surprise. When it came to the giant koi, my imagination was all I had to go on.

Prior to the news reports that popped up upon their reappearance, most of what I'd found about the giant koi over the past twenty years was urban legends about how they had come to exist. One theory was that they were fed steroids to win a competition but grew too big and aggressive and were dumped into the bay. Another theory claimed they were created by underwater nuclear explosions.

Our grandmother always changed the origin of the giant koi whenever she would tell the stories about them. One time the giant koi were a government experiment gone wrong and the next time they were genetic mutations that had adapted to live in saltwater. It didn't really matter that the details of the stories changed. I just liked to hear the stories. It was enough for me to believe that the giant koi existed.

Without any information to be found about the giant koi, I used to spend as much of my spare time as possible learning everything I could about domestic koi, including the number of varieties and colors as well as the average lifespan, length, and size. While genetics is the most important factor that determines the size of domestic koi, the dimensions of the pond and the water quality and temperature play a factor in how big they can get, which would help to explain how the giant koi grew much larger in the ocean. But while some domestic koi have been known to survive in colder waters, they live best in water temperatures between 65 and 75 degrees Fahrenheit. Obviously the giant koi had found a way to thrive in the cold waters of the San Francisco Bay, but like most of their existence, how they adapted to the temperature and to the saltwater remained a mystery.

The only mention of the giant koi I ever found in a physical book was during my freshman year in high school while sleuthing through the local history section at the Sacramento Public Library. It was in an obscure book about the marine life of the San Francisco Bay written in 1981, appropriately titled *Marine Life of the San Francisco Bay*.

According to the book, the giant koi were allegedly created after a school of Japanese koi was released into the San Francisco bay in the early 1940s—not because they'd been given steroids and had grown too large and aggressive, but because they'd been dumped in an attempt to dispose of evidence during a raid on illegal exotic wildlife trafficking. But instead of succumbing to the salt water and the colder temperatures, some of the koi thrived and grew to a size that fit their environment, which was reported to be as big as a school bus.

Even though it was another in a long line of uncorroborated stories about the origins of the giant koi, at least it was a more believable story. And it was the one I clung to as I continued my journey from teenager to adult. The problem was that other than some artistic renderings of the giant koi, I was never able to find any actual photos of them no matter where I looked. And my grandmother didn't have any pictures of the giant koi in her albums, so I could only conjure up my own images of them in my dreams and imagination.

When I was younger, that wasn't an issue. The hope that the giant koi existed and that I would someday see them with my own eyes was enough. But as I grew older, the lack of visual evidence began to cause me to doubt their existence. By the time I got divorced, my belief that the giant koi existed beyond my grandmother's stories had faded to the point that it wasn't more than a ghost that haunted my dreams.

When I exited 37 on to highway 101 south, my anticipation and excitement caused my palms to perspire and I had to wipe one hand then the other on my jeans to keep the steering wheel from growing slick. I was just fifteen minutes from the Golden Gate Bridge and had to put the car on cruise control to keep myself from getting a speeding ticket.

Somewhere around Sausalito, my heart started racing and I had to force myself to take deep breaths to calm myself down. When I reached the Robin Williams Tunnel a few minutes later, a chill ran down the back of my neck and caused my entire body to shiver.

My favorite part about driving into the city from the North Bay comes as you're driving through the Robin Williams Tunnel. About halfway through, the Golden Gate Bridge appears beyond the tunnel's exit like an ethereal vision, a glimpse into another world. It's not a coincidence that the opening of a tunnel is called a portal because the moment I exit that tunnel and see the Golden Gate rising up in front of me, I feel as though I've entered a different world.

While I wasn't entering Narnia, I was about to experience something magical.

As I exited the Robin Williams Tunnel and descended toward the Golden Gate—the towers a brilliant orange in the setting sun and streaks of clouds painted across the late spring sky—I thought I caught a glimpse of yellow splashing in the bay.

I told myself it was just the reflection of the setting sun. After all, I wouldn't be able to see the koi from nearly half a mile away. But as I reached the northern edge of the bridge, I caught another glimpse of color splashing in the water off to the left. And then another off to the right. And then another. It took all of my will power and concentration to keep my eyes on the road ahead of me and not stare off into the bay. Besides, I had my dream scenario of how I imagined seeing the giant koi for the first time and it didn't include me crashing into another car while driving across the Golden Gate.

I'd always imagined walking out on to the promenade above Fort Point, looking down at the bay, the Golden Gate Bridge stretching north to Sausalito and the Marin Headlands, and seeing the giant koi splashing in the waters of the bay below me, their colorful bodies stretched out all the way to Sausalito. And in less than five minutes, I would be standing on that very spot, my dream having become a reality.

As soon as I crossed the bridge, I exited to the right and doubled back beneath the bridge to the visitor parking lot at the Golden Gate Bridge Welcome Center, only to find the parking lot closed. I'd completely forgotten that the governor had ordered the closure of all parking lots for beaches and state parks in California, so unless I wanted to risk having my car towed, I wasn't going to get to see the giant koi from the promenade above Fort Point.

The disappointment I felt at not being able to recreate the

scenario I'd dreamt of over the years was drowned out by the panic that ensued when I realized that none of the parking lots near Fort Point or Crissy Field would be open. And with the sun starting to set, I didn't have much time to find a place to park and locate a spot where I could see the giant koi before the light drained from the sky.

I exited the welcome center and turned left onto Lincoln Boulevard, toward the water, looking for any parking options. But the lot above Battery East was closed and there was a gate across the entrance to the road that led down to Fort Point. With no legal street parking or even a narrow shoulder to speak of, I worried that I would have to drive through the Presidio and all the way to the Marina before I would find somewhere to park, until I passed a few street parking spots just before the Crissy Field Overlook and saw that one was open.

I flipped a U-turn, parked, and opened the door to exit my car. In my excitement, I forgot to shut off the engine or unhook my seat belt, so I didn't get very far. My second attempt at exiting my car was more successful and then I was running along the pedestrian path, scanning the bay, scanning the bay for any sign of the giant koi, stopping just before I reached the gated road above Crissy Field.

Even though I was still at least a couple of hundred yards away, I didn't have to wait long before I saw a dozen or so splashes and flashes of color not far from the shore. And when my gaze followed the shoreline along Crissy Field Beach toward downtown, I saw more splashing and flashes of color along the water's surface.

I'd read that when released into the wild, domestic koi will, over several generations, revert to the natural coloration of Amur carp, which is a muddy or rust-colored orange. But I guess that was another urban myth. Or else if it was true, it didn't apply to giant koi.

The flashes of orange I saw were not in the least bit muddy but almost neon bright, like the color of traffic cones. There were also flashes of red, white, yellow, and blue that were so vibrant and luminous it was as if the koi were lit up. And when I stopped and looked out at the bay, I realized that the splashing and flashes of color weren't just off the shore but were spread out across the water from Crissy Field all the way to Angel Island.

Laughter bubbled out of me. I couldn't help it. Or stop it. Once the laughter started, it just kept going. It was the most joyful laughter I could ever remember, or at least that I had experienced since childhood, a laughter unencumbered by the burden of becoming an adult.

And it occurred to me that this was the happiest moment of my life.

The only thing that came close was the birth of my daughter, which is something every parent says, even if they don't mean it. But the birth of Delilah remains one of the happiest and most profound moments of my life. Except this was different. It was like discovering the truth about the creation of the universe. Or finding out that Santa Claus was real.

As I stood there looking out at the giant koi swimming in the iridescent water, their colorful scales breaking the surface and turning the bay into the aquatic equivalent of a laser light show, I tried to get a count of them. But there were too many and they moved past and under and around each other too quickly for me to figure out how many there were. There appeared to be at least a hundred of them. And that was just from what I could see, as the eucalyptus trees to my left limited my view. But when I focused my attention, I was positive that I saw flashes of color in the water all the way to Alcatraz.

Dozens of people were lined up along the beach enjoying the spectacle and I felt a pull to join them, to get closer to the water. Still, part of me wanted to stay where I was so I wouldn't miss a moment. After all, I had a great view. Not as good as from the outlook from above Fort Point, but nearly so. Plus I had it all to myself. But I wanted to get as close to the giant koi as possible.

After one last, long look, I turned and ran around the gate that blocked the entrance to the road that led down to Fort Point and continued along the asphalt toward the water, my view of the bay now obscured by the eucalyptus trees that lined both sides of the two-lane road. As I ran, I kept trying to catch a glimpse of the bay but I couldn't make out anything though the trees. A wave of regret crashed over me for having left my view above Crissy Field and I considered going back. But a few moments later I was clear of the trees, the bay opening up ahead of me, and I saw exactly where I wanted to go.

When I reached the bottom of the road, I cut between the bathrooms and the Warming Hut Café toward the L-shaped wharf that jutted out into the bay. On most days, you could find fishermen standing guard over their fishing poles, their lines cast into the water. But there were no fishermen and only a dozen or so people, so I raced out on to the wharf and didn't stop until I'd reached the end.

Any regrets I had about leaving my original vantage point were washed away as I stood at the edge of the wharf and looked out at the dozens of giant koi swimming in the bay, flashes of blue and orange and red and yellow breaking the surface, the fish rubbing against one another and twitching before diving beneath the surface, only to return moments later. After several minutes, I realized they weren't just swimming. They were spawning.

This time instead of laughing, I started crying. And I had to admit that this was more beautiful than the birth of my daughter.

A loud splash nearby startled me and I stumbled back. When I returned to the edge of the wharf and looked down, I saw two koi swimming in the water not more than ten feet away—one of them white with patches of bright orange and the other a stunning and spectacular golden yellow.

From my proximity to them, the giant koi looked to be about twelve feet in length. Not as big as the truck-sized koi in our grandmother's stories or the bus-sized koi mentioned in the book I'd found, but still four times as big as jumbo koi, which made the prospect of feeding one by hand a little daunting as their mouths would be big enough to take off a human hand. While they don't have teeth, I didn't want to take any chances. Besides, I'd left my bag of Goldfish crackers in the car and I wasn't about to run back to get them.

The two koi cavorted in the water below me for about thirty seconds before they finished their mating dance and swam off.

For the next half an hour, I stood on the end of the pier and watched the giant koi, their colorful bodies visible beneath the surface of the water that looked like liquid gold in the light of the setting sun. But as the daylight waned and the night began to overtake the city, the water turned dark and the colorful bodies of the giant koi faded, almost as if they drew their power from the sunlight. Once the sun finally set and Venus appeared in the sky overhead, the only evidence of the giant koi was the sound of splashing and the occasional glimpse of a dorsal fin breaching the surface of the water.

When I finally turned away from the water, night had fallen fully across the city. The other people I'd run past earlier were all gone and I was alone as I walked along the pier, glancing back at the water in the hopes of catching another glimpse of the koi, but they all seemed to have settled down for the night.

By the time I returned to my car and sat down in the driver's seat, I realized I was starving, so I opened up the bag of Goldfish crackers and shoved a handful into my mouth while I tried to figure out what to do. Driving back home wasn't an option, but I didn't know anyone who lived in San Francisco, or even in a nearby city or town, and all of the hotels were closed up due to the pandemic, which meant I would have to sleep in my car. The idea of spending eight hours crammed into the seat of my Toyota Yaris wasn't at the top of my list of most comfortable places to spend the night, but I hadn't driven this far just to turn around and go home. I had to see the giant koi again in the full light of day.

The signs nearby didn't prohibit overnight parking, so I shifted over into the passenger seat and looked out at the bay, which remained dark and calm, as if the spectacle I'd just witnessed had never happened. But I knew it hadn't been an illusion. It had been real. And much the same as how the birth of my daughter had changed my perspective, I knew my life would never feel the same.

Once you've experienced magic, once you've witnessed a dream come to life in all of its magnificent splendor, there's no going back to the person you were before.

I smiled at the memory of the giant koi spawning in the water ten feet away from me and stared out at the bay, hoping to catch a flash of color or the glimpse of a dorsal fin as I ate handful after handful of Goldfish until the bag was empty. I figured I should probably find something more substantial and healthy to eat since this was the extent of my dinner, but I didn't want to risk leaving and missing anything. So instead, I leaned my head against the window and started out at the bay and the lights of the city.

The thought of sleep seemed like an impossibility and I figured I'd be up all night watching the water, waiting for something to happen. But at some point, I closed my eyes and drifted off to sleep.

I dreamt I was seven years old and my grandmother was alive and walking next to me, my left hand tucked safely in her right hand. She was telling me the story about the giant koi and I was smiling and laughing as we walked through the Palace of Fine Arts, past the lagoon populated by ducks and seagulls, swans and turtles, and night herons perched in the trees. When we came out of the park, we crossed Marina Boulevard and walked past the Little Marina Green, turning right past the St. Francis Yacht Club before continuing along the jetty past the yacht harbor and the Golden Gate Yacht Club, until we reached the Wave Organ at the end of the jetty. There we stood on the rocks above the water, Alcatraz just 1.5 miles away and hundreds of giant koi, their red and orange and yellow bodies covering the surface of the water all the way to the island.

"Are you ready?" my grandmother asked.

I looked up at her and smiled.

"I'm ready," I said.

And then we started to take off our shoes and socks.

When I woke up, the sun had just started to creep up behind the hills of the East Bay, draining most of the night from the sky while leaving San Francisco cloaked in pre-dawn darkness. I opened the passenger door and stepped out on to the pedestrian walkway to stretch out the kinks from sleeping in my car. From my view above Crissy Field, I could already make out the giant koi in the bay, swimming and splashing in the water. And as the sun continued to rise, it didn't take long for me to realize that I had underestimated their number.

There were hundreds of them, spread between Crissy Field and Angel Island and from the Golden Gate Bridge to Alcatraz and beyond. There were so many that I couldn't begin to count them.

For several minutes, I watched their colors shifting and moving in the bay like a surreal kaleidoscope. Then I closed my passenger door, walked around and got in the driver's seat, started up the engine, and pulled out of my parking space. After flipping a U-turn, I drove through the Presidio until I reached Marina Boulevard and took that to Baker Street, where I turned right and parked along the curb by the Palace of Fine Arts.

I didn't bother to retrace the path my grandmother and I took through the park in my dream. Instead, I ran back down Baker Street and across Marina Boulevard, past the Little Marina Green, then turned right at the St. Francis Yacht Club and ran along the jetty past the yacht harbor and the Golden Gate Yacht Club until I finally reached the Wave Organ.

I stood at the end of the jetty with my hands on my knees, trying to catch my breath as the sun peeked over the Berkeley Hills, lighting up the bay and the giant koi, their red and orange and yellow and blue bodies shifting in the water and glistening in the sunrise, a veritable rainbow in the water.

And I couldn't help but think of Max.

I wondered if he was still searching for his elusive leprechauns or if he'd finally found them. Then I thought about Molly and her talking animals and how happy she was and I wondered if this was how she felt all the time. This sense of euphoria at knowing that magic is real, even if sometimes it takes longer for some of us to find it.

The tide must have been in because the koi were swimming right up to the rocks below me, close enough that I could almost reach down and touch them. It occurred to me that I hadn't taken a single photo or video like I'd promised Molly. I'd been so caught up in seeing the giant koi that the idea of taking any pictures hadn't crossed my mind. So I grabbed my phone and took several pictures of the koi, along with a short video, and texted them to Molly with a short message.

Here you go sis. Sorry for not sending sooner. I got distracted.

After a few moments, I texted the photos to my brother.

Hey Max, I don't know if you've seen this on the news, but I thought you might enjoy these pics. Hope you've found your leprechauns.

Two seconds after I hit SEND, Molly texted back.

Oh my gosh! They're amazing! I'm so happy for you! I wish I was there!

I didn't have the heart to tell her I was happy to be experiencing this alone. This was my moment and I didn't want to share it with anyone else. Although there was one person I couldn't wait to share this with.

Delilah was a year younger than I'd been when I first heard Grandma's stories, but I hadn't told her about the giant koi. Once I'd begun to doubt their existence, I just didn't have the enthusiasm. I don't know if the stories will mean as much to my daughter as they did to me, but I can't wait to share them with her and bring her to San Francisco so she can see the giant koi with her very own eyes and know that they're real.

Where are you? Molly texted.

Angel Island was about three miles away as the crow flies. It would take me at least an hour to get there, maybe closer to two hours, not to mention the return trip. That was presuming I didn't fall into the water at some point along the way, but I didn't want to think about that. Instead, I figured I would shoot for Alcatraz, which was about half the distance. Once I'd made it that far, I'd decide what to do next.

I'm about to go for a walk, I texted back.

I put my phone away and looked out at the rainbow path of giant koi that stretched from the edge of the rocks across the water all the way to Angel Island and thought about my grandmother and how much I wished she were here to experience this, to share my wonder as I held her hand in mine. But in a way, she was with me. She always had been.

"I love you, grandma," I said with a smile.

Then I took off my shoes and socks and stepped out into the bay.

Intro to Trademark Infringement at Dunkin' Donuts High

"Applebee's?"

"Here."

"Best Buy?"

"Here."

"eBay?"

"Here!"

eBay answers with her trademark enthusiasm as if trying to make an impression. She's always the first one with her hand in the air whenever Mrs. Archibald asks a question or solicits volunteers. Barely more than one week into my junior year and eBay is already the most annoying kid in my Intro to Trademark Infringement class.

"GrubHub?"

"Here."

"Instagram?"

"Here."

"Johnson & Johnson?"

Several students turn to look at the empty desk behind Instagram. This is the second time since the start of the semester that Johnson & Johnson has missed class with some sort of health problem, which is kind of ironic when you think about it. But when you live in a society where Catholic kids are named Quaker Oats and students named Oracle attend remedial English classes, irony is part of the landscape.

"Krispy Kreme?"

"Here."

"Liberty Mutual?"

"Here."

"McDonald's?"

"Here."

Someone fake coughs and says "Supersized!" at the same time, which is mean since McDonald's is about thirty pounds overweight and one of the biggest girls at school, although she has stiff competition from Burger King and KFC.

That's the double-edged sword of Life Sponsorship discounts and benefits, especially when those benefits involve empty carbs, trans-fats, and an unhealthy amount of sodium. Although there's nothing more onerous than being overweight and having to spend your childhood carrying around the weight of a name like Nationwide.

McDonald's doesn't offer up a retort but just folds her hands in front of her and stares at her desk in an embarrassed silence, her cheeks as red as the background of her sponsor's logo.

Mrs. Archibald scans the classroom over the top of her glasses, her thin lips pursed and her bony hands on her hips, her head shaking back and forth in a display of disapproval as she tries to identify the guilty party before she finally pushes her glasses back up on her nose and goes back to taking roll.

"Old Navy?"

"Here."

"Papa John's?"

"Here."

"Raytheon?"

"Here."

Raytheon cuts an intimidating figure in his black leather jacket, dyed black hair, and perpetual fuck-you scowl. I'm not sure if he's rebelling against his sponsor's military contracts or just going through a phase, but even without the defiant attitude, no one wants to get on Raytheon's shit list since he's sponsored by the world's largest producer of guided missiles.

I always wonder how much of an influence a kid's sponsor has on his or her personality. Had Raytheon been sponsored by Microsoft, would he have brown hair parted on one side while dressed in a blue oxford button-down and khakis? If McDonald's had been sponsored by Adidas, would she be fit and athletic and possess a low LDL cholesterol level?

But it's not as if parents always have a choice when it comes to choosing a Life Sponsor, since most businesses and corporations place a moratorium on the number of sponsorships they offer, so it's kind of a first-come, first-served deal, often leaving parents to take what they can get. That's how you end up with kids named Vaseline and Hot Topic.

Someone behind me giggles. Probably Yahoo! She's always giggling about something. Then Target kicks the back of my chair.

"Starbucks?" Mrs. Archibald calls out as she gives me an exasperated look.

I must have zoned out again.

"Here," I say.

Starbucks is one of the most common names among kids my age. It was a trendy pick when I was born, kind of like Dylan or Brittany back before parents had to start applying for corporate sponsorship in order to raise a family. But I shouldn't complain. After all, I could have been named Jiffy Lube. Or Snap-on.

There are more than two-dozen Starbucks at Dunkin' Donuts High, the most of any sponsor and nearly twice as many as Coca-Cola, followed by Amazon and The Gap. While there's not a Starbucks in every classroom, we're pretty ubiquitous around campus.

I hear it's worse at the high schools in Seattle.

My grandpa says it's not any different from when he attended school with multiple Johns and Jennifers in every class. But at least back then the teacher could call on students by their last names and you could differentiate the two Mikes in your social circle by using nicknames. Now, because of the contract terms of Life Sponsorship, using anything other than the name of our official sponsor is prohibited in public or formal situations. You can use numbers like Netflix #1 and Netflix #2, although invariably someone ends up suffering from feelings of inadequacy. No one wants to be referred to as number two. That kind of thing will stick with you for life.

In order to avoid any favoritism when dealing with students who share the same name, teachers are instructed to number the students in alphabetical order based on their historical family surname. This is supposed to help avoid hurting any of the students' feelings or giving someone delusions of grandeur, which is kind of ridiculous when you're named Roto-Rooter.

"Okay class," Mrs. Archibald says once she's finished roll call, the empty whiteboard looming behind her. "Who can tell me one of the basic elements of trademark infringement?"

eBay's hand is the first up in the air. Go figure. Mrs. Archibald ignores her and surveys the classroom for about five interminable seconds before calling on Twitter.

"Twitter."

"What?" Twitter says.

"Can you answer the question?" Mrs. Archibald asks.

There's a few seconds of silence, followed by a stifled laugh before Twitter responds.

"What was the question again?"

Twitter tends to have a short attention span.

Mrs. Archibald calls on Old Navy, even though eBay still has her hand raised.

"How about you?" Mrs. Archibald asks. "Do you know the answer?"

"Confusion?" Old Navy says.

"Is that an answer or your general state of mind?" Mrs. Archibald asks.

Old Navy looks around as if for help before replying. "An

answer?"

Mrs. Archibald sighs. "Anyone else think they know the answer?"

Nobody in the classroom says anything.

"Okay then," Mrs. Archibald says. "I guess we need to go over the material again. Everyone, open your books to Chapter Two…"

"Hey Starbucks!"

I look across the cafeteria toward the voice, not sure if it's intended for me or for one of the other Starbucks, and see PepsiCo headed my way carrying a tray of food and wearing a big goofy grin.

PepsiCo and I met two years ago in Mr. Taufer's freshman PE class, where we bonded over our sponsors' partnership of ready-to-drink coffee beverages and our mutual contempt for Whole Foods Market. Just because your sponsor exclusively features organic foods free of artificial preservatives, colors, flavors, sweeteners, and hydrogenated fats doesn't make you better than anyone else. More often than not, it makes you a pretentious douchebag.

"What's up?" I say as he sits down across from me with a tray of spaghetti and meatballs.

"Not seven." PepsiCo isn't a fan of Coca-Cola Company products. Big surprise. "Hey, I brought you a present."

He reaches into his backpack and pulls out two cans of Starbucks Mocha Doubleshot Energy, which he slides to me across the table as if we're exchanging illegal contraband. I slip one of the cans into my backpack and pop the tab on the other before I take a swig—the chocolate-flavored coffee filling my mouth. Although it's at room temperature, it tastes like the food of the gods. As far as I'm concerned, Zeus and Apollo never had nectar as good as a Starbucks Mocha Doubleshot.

Other than scoring an occasional cup of coffee at McDonald's,

PepsiCo is my only source of caffeine. My mom won't let me drink any of the free coffee my sponsor provides because she claims the so-called health experts say that caffeine isn't good for children. I can't go into Starbucks and order a mocha or a latte because it would show up on my sponsor discount activity log and my parents would find out. And I can't go into Peet's or Stumptown Coffee Roasters because my contract prohibits me from entering other coffee franchises or consuming their products.

Here I am, a legally bought-and-paid-for living sponsor of the most successful coffeehouse chain in the world, and I'm not allowed to drink a single cup of coffee.

At the table next to us, General Mills watches PepsiCo and me from behind his wire-rimmed glasses with an expression of disapproval.

"What are you looking at, Betty Crocker?" PepsiCo says.

General Mills points to the logo of his sponsor on his T-shirt. "For your information, I'm not Betty Crocker. Betty Crocker is a girl's name. I'm not a girl."

"Whatever, Hamburger Helper," PepsiCo says. "Mind your own Bisquick."

General Mills scoots down toward the other end of the table, where Old Navy and Sears Roebuck are involved in an animated discussion about the latest *Star Wars* movie.

"Why don't you leave General Mills alone?" I say, taking a bite of my hamburger. "He's okay."

"Are you kidding me?" PepsiCo cracks open a Mountain Dew. "That guy's a total Pat."

From the moment you're born into Life Sponsorship, you become a walking billboard for your corporate sponsor, from your proverbial head down to your trademarked toes. You can't even go out in public wearing a generic T-shirt or hoodie without the bare minimum of a two-inch-by-two-inch patch or decal that bears the name and/or logo of your sponsor affixed to your chest or on the back of your clothing.

There's also a morals and behavioral clause in the contract stipulating that drug use, public intoxication, the posting of racial or homophobic slurs on social media, and general unacceptable behavior are grounds for breach of contract. So if you're sponsored by Adidas and caught wearing Nikes or Reeboks, or if you get a DUI or show up on YouTube or Facebook using racially insensitive language, your sponsorship gets cancelled. When that happens, your previous identity as Bridgestone, Pizza Hut, or Abercrombie & Fitch ceases to exist and your name is changed to Pat. It's gender neutral so it works whether you're male, female, trans, or non-binary. But regardless of your sexual identity, the stink of being a Pat follows you around no matter how much you try to wash it off.

"I knew a Pat," I say.

"Seriously?" PepsiCo leans away from me as if I just admitted to having head lice. "You didn't touch him, did you? Or was it a her?" His eyes go wide. "Don't tell me you lost your cherry to a Pat?"

"I didn't lose my cherry to a Pat." I don't admit that I haven't lost my cherry to anyone. Pretending you've had sex is one of the cornerstones of maintaining your high school machismo, even when your parents don't think you're old enough to drink coffee. "It was a guy and he was in my seventh grade Corporate Branding class."

"Sounds like he took that class a little after-the-fact," PepsiCo says and then slurps some spaghetti noodles between his lips.

Pat sat three seats ahead of me, separated alphabetically by Quaker Oats and R.J. Reynolds Tobacco Company. I was smitten with R.J. Reynolds Tobacco, who had this forbidden, tough girl vibe going on that I couldn't resist. We ended up going steady during the last semester of eighth grade, though I never got past first base. Still, it seemed like a match made in sponsorship heaven. Coffee and cigarettes. I thought we were destined to be together. Then she broke up with me over the summer and started dating Johnnie Walker Scotch Whiskey. Told me it wasn't anything personal, but it always is.

PepsiCo and I proceed to eat our lunch in silence, interrupted only by the sounds of our consumption, which takes on a whole new meaning when your entire existence is made possible by a company that profits from the consumption of its products. This makes me think of the Ouroboros, the serpent that eats its own tail, a pagan symbol of the infinite cycle of nature's endless creation and destruction. But it's also a symbol of immortality, since the Ouroboros not only destroys itself and brings itself to life, but also fertilizes itself and gives birth to itself. It's all pretty incestuous if you ask me.

Still, the part about giving birth always resonates with me since Starbucks has given birth to me, figuratively and economically, and by doing so has helped to ensure its own existence. When I'm dead and gone, Starbucks will still be here serving coffee to the masses, having profited from my life in both a commercial and an existential sense.

I spend a lot of time thinking about this stuff. PepsiCo thinks it's all just a bunch of philosophical masturbation, so I tend to keep it to myself.

While we continue to eat our lunch, Nestlé walks past with an entourage of DiGiorno, Häagen-Dazs, Nestea, Stouffer's, Perrier, Arrowhead, Dreyer's, and Lean Cuisine, who could stand to put on a few pounds.

Even though he's just a freshman, Nestlé already has the largest entourage at school. Larger even than Hershey Foods. Nike, however, is the big man on campus and a total jock, while YouTube is easily the most popular girl in school. You'd think the two of them would be an item considering their popularity, but Nike has been dating Reebok since they were freshmen, while YouTube and Facebook are a total power couple.

Following along in the wake of Nestlé's entourage are Subway and Kellogg's.

"What's up homies?" Subway says as he sits down next to PepsiCo.

"Not seven," PepsiCo says.

"That was only funny the first one thousand two times you said it," Subway says.

"Humor is a personal thing," PepsiCo says. "I like to make my own fun."

"Good luck with that," Kellogg's says as she sits down next to me.

Kellogg's is unconventionally hot in a nerdy kind of way, with horn-rimmed glasses and short hair and no real fashion sense. She's wearing baggy, off-brand jeans and a loose-fitting brown T-shirt that says *L'eggo My Eggo*, which works both as an advertising slogan and as a feminist statement against sexual objectification.

"Hey," she says with a small smile.

"Hey," I say back.

That's usually about the extent of our conversation, mostly because I get completely flustered whenever I'm around her, especially when she's sitting close enough for me to catch a whiff of her intoxicating scent, which reminds me of frosted brown sugar cinnamon Pop Tarts. I don't know if it's her shampoo or her perfume or her natural scent, but I can't eat cinnamon toast or Pop Tarts without thinking about her.

"How's the cheeseburger?" Kellogg's asks as I take a bite.

I try to play it cool, but when you're a sixteen-year-old virgin with raging hormones and you're sitting next to a girl who gets you hot and bothered, playing it cool is an exercise in futility.

"It's good!" I say with my mouth full, forgetting my manners. And I have no idea why I said it was good. Or why I said it with such enthusiasm.

"I bet it's not as good as what I have," Subway says.

"Eating fresh as always, I see." PepsiCo nods toward Subway's plastic bag with his sponsor's name and slogan on it. "You got a foot-long in there?"

Subway grabs his crotch. "I've got a foot-long for you right here."

"I hear it's more of a six-inch deal." PepsiCo looks at Kellogg's. "Is that true?"

Kellogg's gives PepsiCo a cool stare from behind her horn-rimmed glasses as she takes a bite of her lasagna. "Do you ever come up with new material? Or is your witty banter switch stuck on repeat?"

"Burn." Subway holds his fist up to bump with Kellogg's, who reciprocates.

I'm not sure what Kellogg's sees in Subway. Not that I think she'd ever be interested in me. It's just that she's so diverse and well rounded that you think she'd be happier with someone like Kraft or Unilever or Procter & Gamble. But sometimes I wonder: if she's so happy with Subway, why does she always sit next to me?

I glance at her thigh barely a foot away from mine, her elbow casually intruding upon my personal space, the fine hair on her arm inches from my cafeteria tray. When I inhale, her intoxicating scent permeates every molecule of air.

Kellogg's catches me looking at her, so I look away and pretend to be engrossed in eating the rest of my cheeseburger. At the table across from us, YouTube and Facebook are sucking on each other's faces, all lips and tongues and pheromones, which isn't helping my state of mind. So I shift my attention to McDonald's sitting by herself at another table, her tray piled with obesity, diabetes, and high cholesterol, and that seems to do the trick.

"Hey," PepsiCo says, nodding toward the front of the cafeteria. "Here come Gucci and Prada."

Gucci is a gorgeous blonde goddess with high cheekbones and long legs who could rival Venus for the title of Miss Universe, while Prada is an exotic brunette with dark eyes and a full-bodied figure that shouldn't be legal on a high school campus. Just because I prefer Kellogg's style of packaging doesn't mean I don't appreciate the consumer appeal of Gucci and Prada.

The two designer deities glide through the cafeteria in tight vintage jeans, red leather, and knowing smiles as all heads and eyes turn to follow them.

"Man," PepsiCo says. "Sometimes I wish I was made out of Italian leather."

"Or vintage denim," Subway says and fist bumps PepsiCo.

"You two are disgusting," Kellogg's says.

"We're not disgusting," PepsiCo says. "We're just boys."

"Same thing," Kellogg's says.

As Gucci and Prada saunter past our table, I find my gaze lingering not on the shape of their asses in their thousand-dollar designer jeans, but on the slope of Kellogg's neck and the line of her jaw and the way her hair sits tucked behind her ear. I imagine what it would be like to kiss her on the neck just below her earlobe, to inhale the scent of her sweat and shampoo, to lose myself in her brown sugar cinnamon aroma.

The longer I stare at her neck, the more I feel caught up in her gravitational pull. I'm like a dead moon orbiting a vibrant planet, her tidal forces opening up cracks and fissures beneath my surface, shifting my tectonic plates, creating quakes in the depths of my soul. It's all I can do to keep from falling out of orbit and burning up in her atmosphere, breaking into thousands of pieces as I plummet to a fiery and spectacular death.

Before Kellogg's can catch me staring at her again, I force myself to look at Gucci and Prada, who have sat down at the table at the far end of the cafeteria with Louis Vuitton, Ralph Lauren, Burberry, and Hermès, who looks enough like a Greek god to get invited to a party on Mount Olympus. I don't see Armani or Tiffany & Co., but chances are they'll show up soon.

When it comes to cliques, Dunkin' Donuts High has them in spades, diamonds, hearts, and clubs. The difference is that in the old days where you used to have jocks, rah rahs, stoners, slackers, punks, preppies, skaters, gamers, band geeks, and nerds, now your high school social status is determined not by your athletic or academic prowess or by your extracurricular proclivities, but by your corporate sponsorship. And your corporate sponsorship is determined by your parents' financial status.

Students from upper middle-class families get sponsored by companies like Gucci, Prada, Rolex, Louis Vuitton, Dolce & Gabbana, Versace, Cartier, Tiffany & Co., Emirates, American Express, Goldman Sachs, Mercedes Benz, Rolls Royce, Four Seasons, and Vera Wang, which is an unfortunate moniker whether you're a boy or a girl.

At Dunkin' Donuts High, this exclusive group is known as The Untouchables.

Just below The Untouchables in the teenage pecking order are The Blue Chips. These are the kids who come from solid, middle-class stock and who are sponsored by companies such as Microsoft, Sony, Apple, Verizon, Google, Nike, Hasbro, Amazon, Toyota, Goodyear, Best Buy, Time Warner, The Gap, Footlocker, and Victoria's Secret, the last of whom are always female and, not surprisingly, some of the most popular girls in school.

At the bottom of the proverbial corporate sponsorship totem pole are kids from the lower middle-class, sponsored by the likes of Target, Walmart, Staples, McDonald's, Carl's Jr., Buffalo Wild Wings, Denny's, Old Navy, Round Table Pizza, Kraft, Subway, Kellogg's, Starbucks, PepsiCo, and Dr. Pepper Snapple Group. Any food related company gives you away as coming from a lower middle-income family.

We're collectively known as The Wannabes.

Other than Pats, the only social group that's lower than The Wannabees are kids from lower class families who are prohibited from applying for Life Sponsorship. Poor kids are considered too much of a risk by corporations, especially when it comes to the morals and behavioral clauses in the sponsorship contracts since everyone knows that the impoverished are more likely to engage in criminal behavior.

Kids from unsponsored lower class families are known as The Unwashed.

It seems to me that if corporations sponsored kids from needy families, it would allow them to be not so needy and help them to live more fulfilling lives. But I'm just a horny sixteen-year-old Wannabe with a 2.7 GPA. What do I know?

"How is it that they can be so hot?" PepsiCo asks, still drooling over Gucci and Prada. "Do you think they're naturally born that way? Or are they genetically engineered?"

"Genetically engineered," Kellogg's says, taking a bite of her lasagna. "Nobody can look that good without help."

While PepsiCo and Subway debate the benefits of genetic engineering, I glance at Kellogg's again and can't help but smile. When she reciprocates my glance *and* my smile, my heart starts racing. It's more like the hundred-yard-dash than a half marathon but I'm just as flushed from the adrenaline rush.

I return to my cheeseburger and tater tots, my mind wandering to thoughts of Kellogg's and me walking together hand-in-hand, staring into one another's eyes, maybe even kissing. I'm so absorbed in my daydream that I become oblivious to my surroundings, so I don't notice that the cafeteria has grown silent until PepsiCo kicks me under the table.

"Ow!" I say, my exclamation reverberating throughout the silent cafeteria.

PepsiCo doesn't explain why he kicked me. He just motions with his head toward the front of the cafeteria where a boy and a girl stand by themselves with their lunch trays as everyone stares at them. The reason the two are the center of attention is because neither one is wearing any corporate sponsored apparel, patches, or flair. Not a belt or a necklace or a button. Instead, they're dressed in plain navy blue pants, unadorned light blue oxford shirts, and logo-free white tennis shoes.

The uniform of The Unwashed.

"Holy Jesus," Subway says, his mouth full of meatball and marinara. "A Mary and Joseph."

Subway isn't Catholic. He's not making a blasphemous interjection of surprise. Well, except maybe for the *Holy Jesus* part.

But the *Mary and Joseph* part refers to The Unwashed boy and girl standing at the front of the cafeteria.

In the United States, kids whose parents don't get corporate sponsorship for the naming rights of their children all end up being named Mary or Joseph. In Mexico, it's María and José, while in Canada they're named Noah and Ruth. All non-sponsored Western European children are named Adam and Eve. In Asia and Africa, they're all called Mohammed and Maryam.

For some reason all default names for low-income children who don't qualify for Life Sponsorship are based on the Bible. I guess in a way that means they're all sponsored by God.

"You ever meet a Mary or a Joseph?" PepsiCo whispers.

I shake my head.

We'd all heard that a Mary and a Joseph had enrolled as freshmen, but since we're juniors, we couldn't be bothered to show any interest. Especially in Unwashed underclassmen. Still, that didn't mean I wasn't curious. I'd snuck glances in the hallways and in the courtyard since the start of school to see if I might catch a glimpse of them, but they'd remained a rumor until their inaugural appearance in the school cafeteria.

I'm guessing they weren't expecting a warm welcome.

When the Mary and the Joseph start walking down the aisles looking for somewhere to sit, everyone's heads turn to follow them. But unlike with Gucci and Prada, the faces aren't filled with expressions of envy or lust but with sneers of disdain and disgust.

It's not that the Mary and the Joseph are obese or have faces covered with acne. They both have clear skin, average builds, and brown hair—his short and neat, hers long and pulled back in a ponytail. But in this paradigm of lifetime corporate sponsorships, the two of them are outliers. Anomalies in a promotional world. Oddities in a corporate age. And at Dunkin' Donuts High, where your sponsorship status defines you and separates you from the other cliques based on financial status and social hierarchy, we are all united in our shared superiority over The Unwashed.

The Mary and the Joseph continue past the other tables dressed in the uniform of the disadvantaged and the disavowed, their lowly status a fetid cloud of shame, whispers and laughter following along behind them like flies.

As they approach our table, Kellogg's scoots a little further away from me while Subway mirrors her, putting a little more distance between himself and PepsiCo. At the other end of the table, General Mills, Sears Roebuck, and Old Navy spread out, sending the message loud and clear: these seats are taken.

While PepsiCo and the others at our table ignore the Mary and the Joseph, I can't help but look. I've never been this close to an Unwashed before and have only seen one on rare occasions outside of school from a distance. Marys and Josephs don't tend to run in the same social circles as Life Sponsors.

The Joseph looks straight ahead, avoiding my gaze, while the Mary gives a quick turn of her head, making eye contact with me for the briefest of moments, but it's long enough to notice that her eyes are green. Then they continue past us and sit down at the end of a table occupied by Monsanto and Dow Chemical, both of whom get up and move to another table.

"That was close," Subway says. "I thought for sure they were going to sit down next to us."

"Admit it," PepsiCo says. "You wanted that Mary to sit down next to you so you could show her your six-inch meatball sub."

"Did you get a good look at their clothes?" Kellogg's says as she scoots back next to me, an inch or two closer than before. I'm not sure if it's on purpose or by accident but I'm not about to complain. "They're so plain and ordinary. I'd feel so exposed without any logos or slogans. Almost like I was naked."

The image of Kellogg's without any clothes on makes it difficult for me to maintain any sense of focus or contribute to the conversation, so I just smile and nod.

"They look like security guards," Subway says, glancing over his shoulder.

Kellogg's nods. "That's probably what they'll grow up to be."

"Either that or prison inmates," PepsiCo says.

While PepsiCo, Subway, and Kellogg's continue to gossip about the Unwashed and a steady stream of murmurs flows from the kids at the other tables, my mind wanders from thoughts of Kellogg's in her birthday suit to the Mary and the Joseph and the other kids who are born without sponsors.

I wonder what it's like to be them, to have to deal with the constant stares and whispers and laughter, always feeling like an outsider. As if they don't belong. As if they're less than the rest of us. It must be a difficult life, being so ordinary and poor.

"I hear that the Josephs are sold into slavery when they turn eighteen," Subway says.

"I hear that the Marys are sterilized at birth so that they can't reproduce," Kellogg's whispers.

When I look over at the Mary and the Joseph, I expect to see them consuming their lunch in a brooding, joyless silence. Eating more as a process of biological necessity than anything that provides them with any sense of pleasure, hoping to get out of here as soon as possible. Instead, they're having what appears to be a leisurely meal filled with normal conversation. While they're too far away for me to hear what they're talking about, whatever the Joseph says causes the Mary to laugh.

The idea that they could be happy, that they could smile and laugh and act like normal kids, isn't something I've ever considered. I always presumed the lives of the Unwashed were cold and dreary, an endless winter without sunshine or blue skies or the promise of Christmas. But this Mary and Joseph, in their plain clothes and drab, sponsor-less lives, appear to be enjoying themselves.

The longer I watch them, the more I think about what their lives are like compared to mine. And the more I think about them, the more I wonder if they're happier not being owned by corporations. While it's true that their opportunities are limited by their inferior social status and their parents' annual after-tax income, it occurs to me that, in a way, they might have more freedom than I do. Without the constraints of a Life Sponsorship contract, they're free to do and say what they want. To make mistakes in public and act inappropriately. To get caught in compromising positions without fear of losing their sponsorship. To just be average, ordinary, normal kids.

My mom tells me that I think too much, that I should embrace my place in society and not worry about anyone else, about what they do or don't have, but I can't help it. It's just the way my mind works. When it starts to wander off the well-traveled path, it discovers thoughts and ideas buried under years of educational undergrowth and hidden beneath brambles of repetitious programming.

"Earth to Starbucks. Earth to Starbucks." PepsiCo leans forward across the table, snapping his fingers in front of my face. "Come in Starbucks."

"What?" I ask.

"You're not daydreaming about boning that Mary, are you?" PepsiCo says.

"Don't be ridiculous," I say, avoiding eye contact while taking a bite of my cheeseburger. "I just feel sorry for them, that's all."

"Aww, that's so sweet," Kellogg's says, reaching out and placing her hand on my arm. "You're so empathetic."

"Emphasis on *pathetic*," Subway says.

Kellogg's hand lingers on my arm. I don't know if it's on purpose or if it's just my imagination running off into fantasyland, but I like the warmth of her hand against my skin and I don't want the moment to end.

"Go choke on your foot-long," I say to Subway.

PepsiCo snorts laughter, spraying Mountain Dew across the table and splattering Kellogg's, who screams in a combination of disgust and laughter, simultaneously removing her hand from my arm to wipe away the stray droplets. Oh well. Nothing lasts forever.

After a few moments, things settle back down, with the

conversation shifting from gossip and derogatory comments about the Mary and the Joseph to more mundane topics—like class schedules, least favorite teachers, and what everyone's doing for the upcoming Walt Disney Company Labor Day Weekend.

Throughout the conversation and the rest of lunch, my gaze continues to wander and linger. But instead of settling on Kellogg's and the slope of her neck or the allure of her unblemished skin, my gaze wanders to the Mary and the Joseph and to the austerity of their attire, lingering on the intrigue of their unsponsored souls.

Inside the Monsters Studio

(*Note: The following is a partial transcript of a recent episode from *Inside the Monsters Studio*, hosted by James Lipton, with his guest the Flying Spaghetti Monster.)

James Lipton: We begin, as always, at the beginning. Where were you born?

Flying Spaghetti Monster: On top of spaghetti, all covered with cheese. That's what I've been told, anyway. I don't actually recall my birth. That's just what my dad always said whenever I asked him.

JL: Tell us about your father.

FSM: We had a difficult relationship from the beginning. As far back as I can remember. No matter what I did I couldn't please him and he couldn't accept the fact that I would never be like him.

JL: Your father was a lasagna.

FSP: Yes. As you can imagine we never saw noodle to noodle. He wanted a son he could relate to. A son who understood the beauty of alternating layers. I think he always considered me his greatest disappointment.

JL: And you never knew your mother?

FSM: She left me and my father for a manicotti before my meatballs descended.

JL: That must have been difficult for your father.

FSM: It was. I don't think he ever recovered from the fact that my mother chose large, ridged tubes over my father's wide, flat noodles.

JL: One of the traditions of this series has to do with tattoos. Anyone who has watched this show knows I'm not allowed to have one. You have a tattoo, do you not?

FSM: I have two of them.

JL: And where are they?

FSM: On my meatballs.

JL: That must have been rather painful.

FSM: You have no idea.

JL: And what do the tattoos say?

FSM: The one on the left says Starch and the one on the right says Gluten.

JL: The two major components of pasta.

FSM: They're essential to a properly manufactured pasta and play a big role in maintaining the consistency and texture of the mixture of flour and water. The last thing you want is to end up as a rigid piece of wheat with a whitish color. I've known others who turned out that way. It's sad to see. But it happens.

JL: What about gluten-free pasta?

FSM: Gluten-free pasta is for pussies.

JL: You're also a big proponent of durum wheat flour.

FSM: Anything but durum wheat is an abomination. In Italy, the use of common wheat flour in manufacturing pasta is considered fraudulent and against the law.

JL: They take their pasta very seriously.

FSM: As they should.

JL: An entire religion has been built up around you: The Church of the Flying Spaghetti Monster. A parody faith created to challenge the teaching of intelligent design in public schools and to satirize creationism.

FSM: And my father told me I'd never amount to anything more than Aglio e Olio.

JL: How does it feel to be deified?

FSM: It's flattering, but I'm still not used to people coming up to me and asking for my autograph. I never know how to react.

JL: Your followers are called Pastafarians.

FSM: Apparently.

JL: Many of these Pastafarians wear T-shirts and other paraphernalia with your image on it with the claim that they have been "touched by your noodly appendage."

FSM: They wouldn't be the first.

JL: Yes. You're apparently quite the ladies' man.

FSM: I've never seen the point in settling down. Seems kind of antithetical to my existence. The whole idea of monogamy just baffles me.

JL: So you've never thought about raising a family.

FSM: That's too much responsibility for me. But I wouldn't be surprised if I had some little spaghettinis running around out there.

JL: One of the central beliefs of Pastafarianism is that you created the universe after a night of heavy drinking.

FSM: Sounds like something I'd forget doing.

JL: Another central belief is that you have the ability to become invisible.

FSM: Only when it comes time to pay the bill.

JL: You were introduced to drugs and alcohol at an early age.

FSM: It was the culture I grew up in. Mushrooms were encouraged and wine and pasta go together like pancakes and syrup.

JL: Or like spaghetti and meatballs.

FSM: Precisely. So I lived that way for years, indulging my appetite for mind-altering substances. But after a while, you realize you can't keep living like that forever.

JL: So you've given up the lifestyle.

FSM: Not entirely. I incorporate mushrooms into myself every now and then, but I'm not as much of a drinker anymore. Too many calories. And my metabolism isn't what it used to be. There's nothing more unattractive than a middle-aged flying spaghetti monster with a muffin top. Though I do still enjoy an occasional glass of Chianti.

JL: In Pastafarian heaven there is a beer volcano and a stripper factory. In hell, the beer is stale and the strippers have sexually transmitted diseases.

FSM: Sounds about right to me.

JL: Would you add anything to either of these versions of heaven or hell?

FSM: Heaven would have whole wheels of fresh Parmigiano Reggiano cheese that you had to grate by hand and hell would have the pre-grated imitation crap that comes in plastic, sixteen-ounce containers with Flavor Lock caps.

JL: Are you the creator of the universe?

FSM: Not that I'm aware of. But then I suppose that's the whole point, isn't it? That I created the universe in a drunken stupor. So I don't know. Maybe I did. To be honest, it's not something I'd really want to take credit for. I'd like to think I would have done a better job than what we ended up with.

JL: What is it like to fly?

FSM: It's like dropping acid and then going into a transcendent meditative state. Nothing can compare to it. Except maybe tantric sex.

JL: We had Mothra on the show not long ago and when I asked her the same question, she described flying as communicating with the molecules of the wind and the air until you all speak the same language, then floating along on a shared psychic journey.

FSM: Sounds like her. She's absolutely brilliant, you know. An IQ of something around two-hundred-and-twenty. She scored a perfect sixteen-hundred on her SATs. And she has these crazy psychic powers. She always knows what you're thinking, so playing poker with her is pointless. Unless it's strip poker and you don't mind losing.

JL: You two dated for a while.

FSM: It wasn't anything serious. Neither one of us wanted a relationship, so we did the friends-with-benefits thing for a while until it got a little too weird.

JL: One of you began to develop feelings for the other?

FSM: No, no, no. Nothing like that. It was those twin miniature priestesses who accompanied her everywhere. I can never remember what they're called.

JL: The Shobijin.

FSM: Yeah. Initially I thought they were kind of cute, but then they started to get on my nerves. Always hanging around, chanting and singing at all hours, talking in unison. Plus they had this strange, telepathic connection to Mothra that creeped me out. But what eventually ended it was that I couldn't deal with the fact that whenever Mothra and I felt like playing hide the meatballs, those two wanted to watch.

JL: You and Mothra are still friends.

FSM: Absolutely. She's the sweetest monster you'll ever meet. Kind and benevolent, always protecting Earth. Talk about divine. Plus she has the whole metamorphosis thing going on, from larvae to pupa to imago, with her death coinciding with the hatching of her own larvae. It's very heavy on the resurrection theme. You want a monster to build a religion around, she's it.

JL: How did you meet Godzilla?

FSM: We both went to Oxford while studying abroad and we ended up taking a class together on Japanese culture. He sat behind me in class and would always ask me questions about the previous day's assignment or look over my shoulder during tests.

JL: He wasn't a diligent student.

FSM: Not at all. He spent most of his nights going out and getting drunk and destroying small towns. Eventually he got busted and ended up doing community service.

JL: You didn't become friends right away.

FSM: It took a while. Not only did he constantly cheat off me, he had horrible breath. Sometimes I could barely make it through class without dry heaving or passing out.

JL: I can only imagine.

FSM: And he's a mouth breather, which made it even worse.

JL: What event precipitated your eventual friendship?

FSM: I was hanging out in Soho one night, looking to score some shrooms and maybe find a nice Cockney prostitute to noodle, when Ghidorah and Megalon showed up and started busting my chops. I've never been much of a fighter, so I was just trying to get out of there before things got out of control, but they had me cornered. Just as things were about to get ugly, Godzilla came stumbling around the corner and beat the crap out of both of them. He was drunk, of course, and it was all I could do to keep from gagging on his breath, but we ended up going out for drinks and by the end of the night we were the best of friends.

JL: He credits you for getting him through college.

FSM: That's because I let him cheat off me the rest of the year.

JL: He also said that you're responsible for introducing him to his eventual wife.

FSM: Yeah, well, he wasn't particularly lucky with the ladies until I bought him some Altoids.

JL: Your friendship wasn't always an easy one.

FSM: For a long time Godzilla had a lot of hostility toward the human race, which started off as a simple misunderstanding and then got blown *way* out of proportion. It didn't help that he let the whole "King of the Monsters" thing go to his head. He should have hired a publicist but he thought he could handle things on his own.

JL: You tried to reach out to him.

FSM: Of course I did. We all did. But he was so full of anger he wouldn't listen. Even after King Kong kicked his ass he didn't come around. But after the Mothra debacle he hit rock bottom and realized he needed some help. So he got into therapy, started taking Lorazepam, and eventually ended up becoming the kinder, gentler Godzilla that everyone came to know and love.

JL: And from there he went on to become a legend.

FSM: The biggest.

JM: You never achieved the fame of Godzilla, Mothra, or even

King Kong. Was there ever any jealousy?

FSM: From me? No. I mean, sure, every now and then I wondered what it might have been like had things been different, but I'm pretty happy with the way my life turned out. After all, how many monsters can say they've had an entire religion devoted to them?

JL: Has your own recent brush with celebrity affected any of your relationships?

FSM: Not the ones that matter. But after this whole thing came out about me being the creator of the universe, a lot of monsters I haven't talked to in years suddenly started friending me on Facebook. Eventually I had to block them.

JL: We end this portion of our program as always with the questionnaire that was invented by Proust and brought to perfection by my hero, Bernard Pivot: What is your favorite word?

FSM: Bolognese. It just rolls off the tongue.

JL: What is your least favorite word?

FSM: Fusilli. It's a long story.

JL: What turns you on?

FSM: Capelli d'angelo. If you've never been with an angel hair pasta, you don't know what you're missing.

JL: What turns you off?

FSM: When someone tries to keep pasta noodles from sticking together by rinsing the cooked pasta in cold water. Just add salt to the water before it boils. Or drizzle some extra-virgin olive oil over the pasta once it's cooked. But never cold water. That's just a cry for help.

JL: What sound or noise do you love?

FSM: Godzilla's roar. First time I heard it I was blown away. It still gives me chills.

JL: What sound or noise do you hate?

FSM: The high-pitched giggles of Mothra's twin little pixies. Especially when they're stoned.

JL: What is your favorite curse word?

FSM: Cazzo. That's *fuck* in Italian.

JL: What profession, other than your own, would you like to attempt?

FSM: I'd like to be a game show host. Or maybe a judge on *American Idol.*

JL: What profession would you *not* like to participate in under any circumstances?

FSM: Politics. You ask me, they're all a bunch of self-serving cunts.

JL: If Heaven exists, what would you like to hear God say when you arrive at the Pearly Gates?

FSM: You were always my favorite.

Remedial English for Reanimated Corpses

"Aaaaaay," Professor Warner says, drawing out the noun so that he sounds like Fonzie from *Happy Days*.

A chorus of *Uuuuunhs* fills the classroom as the twenty-nine students attempt to emulate the sound. I do my best to emit a sexy, full-throated groan, but even though I was a soprano before I died, just about any sound that comes out of me now is more Louis Armstrong than Billie Holiday. Not that I could sing like Lady Day, but spin some ABBA or Cyndi Lauper and I was a karaoke goddess.

"Eeeeeee," the professor says, overemphasizing his teeth in an attempt to get his point across. They're nice teeth: straight and white and perfect. I wish I still had teeth like that. But it's all I can do to keep mine from rotting and falling out. I probably should have flossed more while I was alive.

"Uuuuunh," the students respond.

"Almost," Professor Warner says without a trace of sarcasm. It's an endearing attitude when you consider that he's teaching a classroom full of speech-challenged corpses who invite ridicule. But that's just one of Professor Warner's many attractive qualities.

We're only halfway through the first week of the semester and I'm already in love with my English professor.

"Iiiiiii," he croons to the class.

"Uuuuunh."

In my head I hear the vowels clearly and know how to say them. Just because I'm undead doesn't mean I've forgotten the rudimentary mechanics of speech. But there's a disconnect somewhere between my liquefying brain and decaying vocal cords that makes everything I say come out sounding like an uninspired orgasm, which is something at which I've had plenty of practice. Let's just say that when it came to sex, most of the men I dated practiced the Andy Warhol Method: their sexual fame lasted about fifteen minutes and then they were done.

I look around at the faces of the other students to see if any of them mirror my frustration at being unable to utter simple vowels, but it's hard to tell from the preponderance of slack-jawed expressions.

"Okay." Professor Warner takes a drink from his water bottle, then wipes a couple of stray drops from his plump, blood-filled lips that look good enough to chew on. I'd never admit to anyone that I'd like to eat his face, of course, because that would just perpetuate the stereotype.

"Let's see how you do with this one," he says. "Ooooooh,"

"Uuuuunh."

"Great!" Professor Warner says with genuine enthusiasm.

This is followed by a general sense of accomplishment among the students, many of whom manage to contort their faces into something approximating smiles. A few raise their palms to high-five their fellow students, which seems like a good idea until someone's hand falls off.

While it's not uncommon for zombies to lose an occasional limb, it's never convenient and always embarrassing. Especially when you're interviewing for a job or out on a first date.

Professor Warner spends the rest of the class teaching us basic vowel enunciation, which is what we've been working on all week. None of us have made any noticeable progress, but this doesn't deter the professor from giving everyone encouragement and praise.

By the time class is over, it's apparent that I'm not the only reanimated coed who has a crush on Professor Warner.

After my Remedial English class, I attend Basic Cognition with Professor Brooks, who spends the entire class lecturing us on object permanence and causality as if we're all infants in the sensorimotor stage of development. While I suppose it's important for zombies to have a good foundation and some basic building blocks before jumping into the concrete operational stage, most of us are ready to tackle intuitive problem solving. So more than a few students zone out during class. It doesn't help that Professor Brooks has a droning quality to his voice that tends to stimulate our salivary glands, so there's a lot of open-mouthed drooling going on.

Once the tedium of Basic Cognition has ended, Peter, Grant, Beverly, and I shamble over to the Bela Lugosi University Center to grab a bite to eat.

Now before anyone goes and gets all judgmental or starts spouting pro-vegan, anti-meat evangelism as if you're somehow superior because of your dietary habits and lifestyle, let's get one thing perfectly clear: not all zombies are cannibalistic ghouls. That's just the reputation we've been given courtesy of Hollywood propaganda. Most of us prefer a good plate of spaghetti and meatballs or a Cobb salad.

Zombies, by nature, are omnivorous. Bananas, hummus, and deep fried mozzarella sticks are just a few of the staples of our diet. And while most of us don't perpetuate zombie mythology by devouring people, we do enjoy a good burger. Bacon is especially popular among zombies. It's the Tofurkey of human flesh.

All in all, the majority of zombies aren't discriminating when it comes to the food pyramid. Cockroaches. Garbage. Cigarettes. Any port in storm. We're kind of like Great White sharks. We'll eat just about anything that's put in front of us. It helps that our taste buds are pretty much useless, so quality isn't really a factor. It's more a texture thing, which is why I still refuse to eat tofu.

Once we reach the University Center, Peter, Grant, Beverly, and I slowly make our way down the steps to The Rathskeller. It's not easy to negotiate a narrow flight of stairs when your legs are stiff and your vision is impaired with the onset of post-mortem cataracts. Good luck renewing your driver's license. It's tough enough walking down the street without getting hit by a car, let alone getting behind the wheel of one.

Halfway down the stairs, Beverly loses her balance and stumbles into Grant, who topples forward and lands awkwardly on the bottom step with an audible *snap* just before Beverly falls on top of him.

"Uunh ech gak," Peter says from behind me.

I nod my agreement.

The university needs to install a ramp to make places like The Rathskeller more accessible for zombies. It's not as if the issue hasn't come up before. For years, the Zombie Leadership Council has been pushing the university to adopt standard ADA guidelines, but the administration has historically dragged its feet, claiming that zombies aren't technically disabled since we all lack the basic motor skills of other monsters.

If you ask me, it's a classic case of passive-aggressive discrimination. Just because we're rotting corpses doesn't mean we shouldn't be allowed access to establishments that serve food. After all, they let werewolves in The Rathskeller and they have more fleas than Europe during the Black Death.

When Peter and I help Grant to his feet, we notice that his radial bone is sticking out of his rotting flesh just above his left elbow. Peter shoves the bone back inside while Beverly takes an Ace bandage out of her backpack and wraps Grant's arm. Zombies always need to be prepared for situations such as these, so it's good to keep some gauze and Ace bandages and a spare girdle handy. You never know when a body cavity might burst open and you have to perform emergency triage to keep your intestines from falling out.

It happens more often than you'd think.

Once we get Grant patched up, we shamble into The Rathskeller, where a succubus with a Goth complex stands behind the host station with a petulant demeanor that says *I don't want to be here but I don't want to be anywhere else, either.* Typical succubus attitude. She gives the four of us a look of disgust accompanied by a wrinkled nose and a faux gag reflex before reluctantly showing us to a corner table as far away from the kitchen and the front door as possible.

We open the menus and pretend we don't care that we're treated like second-class monsters, but it's just another check mark in the long list of indignities we have to deal with on a daily basis.

Two mummies sit a few tables away, whispering and casting furtive glances, while a trio of ghouls shakes their heads and gives us condescending stares. Like they have any room to talk. On the other side of the restaurant, a pack of werewolves sits at another table, laughing and drinking beers and tearing into a deer carcass, all of them sporting their varsity letterman jackets in case anyone didn't get the memo that they were on the football team.

Werewolves are the jocks of monsters: full of testosterone and sprouting hair everywhere; all rage and bulging muscles; bursting through their jerseys and baying at the moon. More often than not you'll find them roving around the campus, making obscene comments or gestures to succubi, pulling wings off mothmen, and unwrapping mummies. When they've been drinking, they're even worse.

Werewolves are total dicks.

The ego of a lycanthrope is second only to that of a vampire, so naturally they don't believe the rules apply to them. And to a large extent, that's true.

While the other students at Bela Lugosi University have to attend classes like Basic Cognition, Principles of Mummification, and Advanced Blood Sucking, werewolves skate by on their scholarships and take paper classes such as Grooming 101, Introduction to Howling, and Silver Screen Shape Shifters, which requires them to sit and watch werewolf movies in order to get a passing grade.

Just because they can throw a fifty-yard spiral or hit a ninety-five mile-per-hour fastball doesn't mean they should receive preferential treatment. But that's the way things have always been, so why try to fight it?

After a few minutes, a golem comes over to our table. The golem doesn't speak but just stands at attention and writes down our lunch order, which we make by pointing to the menu since most golems don't understand zombie. Peter and Grant both order bacon cheeseburgers with fries, while Beverly sticks to her Paleolithic diet and opts for the pork ribs, substituting a salad for the mashed potatoes. I can't make up my mind between the veggie wrap and the mac and cheese, so I end up ordering both. I can always take the leftovers back to my dorm room.

After the golem walks away, one of the werewolves addresses his flea-infested buddies. "Hey, do you guys smell something?"

"Like what?" one of the other werewolves asks, this one with a dimwitted expression and a toothy grin.

The first fleabag inhales, then wrinkles his nose. "Like something died."

His buddies make a theatrical show of sniffing at the air, attempting to locate the source of the smell, but it's all for show. They know exactly what they're doing.

Werewolves really are assholes.

The one who started it all, a lycanthrope with a backwards sloping forehead and a pronounced under bite, gets up from the table and pads around the restaurant on all fours until he stops six feet from our table.

"Hey you guys, I think I found it!" He takes another step toward us and sniffs once more. "It's this group of decomposing fucktards!"

We get called a lot of names. Decomposing fucktards. Shambling shitheads. Maggot-infested, brain-dead abortions. Most of the time it's just sticks-and-stones, but sometimes you can't help but take it personally when someone calls you brain-dead.

"Argh splck," Peter says.

Grant nods and lets out a guttural "Uuuuunnnnhh!"

I know Grant means to sound assertive, but it comes across more like he's struggling with a bowel movement.

"What's that?" the alpha werewolf says, holding one paw up to his ear. "You'd like to take a bath?"

At first I think he's just making another joke about the way we smell, until he turns to one side and lifts his leg.

Before we have a chance to move, he sprays us with urine.

Peter and Grant, who are sitting on the outside of the table, take most of the spray, though Beverly and I don't escape unscathed. I can feel a few stray drops in my hair and on the back of my neck. Fortunately I turned away in time and didn't get any on my face, but it's tough enough just getting the smell of formaldehyde out of your hair with shampoo and Pine-Sol, which means I'll probably have to buy some Nature's Miracle.

The pack of werewolves howls and whoops it up, clinking their beer bottles together and giving each other high-fives as their leader struts back to the table, Mr. Big Shot Conquering Hero.

Where's a gun loaded with silver bullets when you need one?

"What the hell is going on out here?" yells the manager, an ogre with a nasty disposition and an unwashed purple suit that's one size too small.

The alpha werewolf points an accusing paw in our direction. "Those decomposing freaks are stinking up the place!"

"Is that so?" The ogre turns to us—drool spilling over his lower lip and down his chin. He takes a single whiff and waves a hand in front of his face. "Christ, who let them in here? Lilith!"

The succubus looks up from her iPhone with a bored expression. "What?" she says, as if the act of answering a question is a monumental inconvenience.

"Don't give me that tone," the manager says, strands of saliva flying from his lips and a runner of mucous dripping out of one nostril. "Did you let these disgusting creatures in here?"

Irony is wasted on ogres.

"No," the succubus says with disdain, as if the idea that she would have seated us is preposterous. "They must have let themselves in when I wasn't looking."

Bitch. Never trust a succubus. They'll throw you under the proverbial bus without a second thought.

"Okay maggot monkeys." The ogre leans down on our table with his hairy palms, every word he speaks a shower of saliva and mucous. "Time for you to shamble."

"Ehng ochh unsplr," I say.

"I don't care what happened," the manager says. "Get the fuck out of my restaurant."

While many ogres are multi-lingual, that doesn't change the fact that most of them are narrow-minded, obstinate, baby-eating racists.

The four of us get up from the table and shuffle out the door to the sound of laughter and howling from the table of werewolves as the mummies and ghouls applaud our departure. No one stands up for us. No one comes to our defense. We're the unclean and unwanted. Outcasts among our own kind. Untouchables in the kingdom of monsters.

"And don't come back!" the succubus shouts. Backstabbing whore.

With the fiasco of The Rathskeller casting a familiar pall over our afternoon and our stomachs grumbling, we shamble across campus to Raimi Dining Hall—the zombie cafeteria that caters to the indiscriminate palates of the reanimated dead—but by the time we get there, the dining hall is closed. So we head to Peter and Grant's room in Romero House to share some leftovers before our two o'clock classes.

Romero House is one of two zombie dorms, the other being Fulci House—where Beverly and I live—which sits right next door. Naturally, there's a bit of a rivalry between the two dorms but it's a friendly competition, with students from both houses attempting to academically outdo the other. At the end of each semester, we get together for move night and watch *Night of the Living Dead* or

Zombi 2, depending on which house has earned the best combined GPA. Though to be honest, neither dorm helps to bring up the school average.

The residents of Romero and Fulci Houses affectionately call the two dorms Zombie Towers, which are located downwind from the main campus and a good half a block from Karloff Hall, the nearest residential housing, where the mummies live.

You'd think zombies and mummies would share a little common ground. After all, we're both living corpses brought back from the dead. But mummies make a point of distancing themselves from zombies, claiming that having a doomed love for a mortal woman somehow makes them more romantic and empathetic. Plus they're cursed rather than being created by some kind of a virus, which is apparently a status thing. Mummies are big on status, pointing out that all respectable mummies are former pharaohs, high priests, or members of the upper class, making them far superior to the proletariat zombies.

Mummies are a bunch of stuck-up rolls of Charmin.

The four of us sit down to eat in Peter and Grant's dorm room, which they share with a third zombie, Ricardo, so their room is larger than most of the others and as such has enough space for a dining table. Zombies are big on communal eating and pot lucks, so we do our lunch family style.

Beverly shares some leftover salt pork and roasted Brussels sprouts, while I contribute a dead squirrel that I found out behind the Lon Chaney Jr. Dining Hall. Peter makes a tuna sandwich on whole wheat bread that he cuts into quarters and Grant brings out four cans of Budweiser, which I accept with grace, though I'm really more of a Guinness girl.

None of us talks about the fiasco at The Rathskeller. Instead, we eat in silence and avoid eye contact, doing our best to pretend that nothing happened. It's one of our defense mechanisms. A coping tactic we use to deal with the fact that no matter what we do, we're not going to be treated as equals. Not even by ghouls, golems, or ghosts. So most of the time we avoid dealing with the problem and wait for it to go away. But it's kind of difficult to ignore the truth when we all smell like werewolf urine.

Just as we're preparing to wash down the last of the dead squirrel and Brussels sprouts, Ricardo staggers in through the front door looking as if he's seen the bogeyman, which is more than likely considering the bogeyman has been a student at Bela Lugosi for the past five years.

A lot of us are on the five-or-six-year plan. Most monsters aren't in a big hurry to step out into the real world. It's scary out there.

Ricardo waves his right hand in the air while pointing at the empty shoulder socket where his left arm used to be. "Mmgur slbbb unnnh goff!"

Ricardo has an accent, so sometimes I have a hard time understanding him, but I'm pretty sure he said that three fraternity pledges stole his left arm. Since there's only one fraternity on campus, it's not as if we don't know who he's talking about.

Sigma Beta Nu.

According to some translations, *Sigma* means 'lord of the dead' and *Beta* refers to 'the demonic challenger of God,' while *Nu* is often associated with 'nighttime and the underworld.' So it's no surprise who belongs to the only fraternity on campus. When you think about it, it makes sense. Vampires are total frat boys. Always primping and preening and full of themselves; all charm and seduction and Jell-O shots; trying to get you into bed so they can drink your blood and then brag about it to their buddies.

I wouldn't be caught dead dating a vampire, but I know some banshees and succubi who were lured in by the old neck-nibbler charm and thought they were in a monogamous relationship, only to find out that the asshole they were dating was sucking someone else's blood.

You can't really trust a monster who walks around pretending to be human.

Some of the most famous graduates of Bela Lugosi University were members of Sigma Beta Nu, which boasts a prestigious list of alumni that reads like a roll call of single-name celebrities.

Dracula. Lestat. Barnabas.

I never met any of them, as they were all students here long before my time, but it's not as if I feel like I missed out on anything. Most of the vampires I've interacted with are major douche bags.

For obvious reasons—including the misguided value placed on immortality and the fact that the university's biggest donors are all alumni of Sigma Beta Nu—the fraternity is held in high esteem by the administration and as such, its members are afforded more perks and disciplinary loopholes than any of the other monsters, including werewolves. Even their fraternity occupies a more prominent position at the university, as Sigma Beta Nu sits on top of Nosferatu Knoll, the highest geographical point on campus.

Out of all the monsters, vampires are the creepiest. Not in an eerie or ghoulish kind of way, but more in an ex-boyfriend-who-keeps-texting-you-and-showing-up-at-your-home-and-wanting-you-to-invite-him-in kind of way. Every vampire I've ever met has Future Restraining Order written all over him.

Vampires are total stalkers.

And apparently, they've also stolen Ricardo's left arm.

"Mmrt uunnh blln," Ricardo says, then sits down on the couch and starts to cry, covering his eyes with his lone remaining hand.

Beverly and I sit down on either side of Ricardo and do what we can to try and comfort him, while Peter and Grant stand around looking awkward, clearing their throats, and glancing at the ceiling. Men. Even in undeath, they don't know how to deal with their emotions when they see another grown man cry.

Once we manage to get Ricardo calmed down a bit and offer him the last of the dead squirrel and a Budweiser, he explains what happened.

He was shambling from the library to his one o'clock Fundamentals of Formaldehyde class, where zombies are taught how to delay decomposition by consuming household items. Toothpaste, mouthwash, deodorant, antiperspirant, bubble bath, shampoo, fingernail polish, lipstick, and most cosmetics all contain trace amounts of formaldehyde. You'd be amazed at how much formaldehyde you can consume from a single bottle of liquid foundation. Cover Girl is especially nourishing.

Ricardo was running late for his class (zombies are always running late) when three bats flew out of a tree and started dive-bombing him, circling around his head and scaring him. Ricardo apparently had a fear of bats when he was alive and even though we're monsters, our phobias follow us into undeath.

The truth is, zombies aren't much different than we were before we died. Yes, we're slowly decomposing and we have to deal with sloughage and the occasional emotional fallout of a rapidly digesting pancreas. But we still enjoy listening to Top 40 music and watching reality television. We still crave security, companionship, and love. We still laugh and cry and feel emotional pain.

Just because our hearts have stopped beating doesn't mean they can't ache.

Startled by the bats, Ricardo stumbled away from them, looking for somewhere to hide, paying more attention to the bats than to where he was going, and ended up falling over his own feet and into a manzanita shrub.

We zombies aren't known for our dexterity.

Moments later, the bats transmogrified into three pale, smug vampires wearing Sigma Beta Nu pledge pins. Before Ricardo had a chance to call out for help, the three pledges tore his left arm from his socket and flew off laughing.

Members of Sigma Beta Nu have been sending their pledges on scavenger hunts for years, stealing wings from mothmen, bandages from mummies, and shems from golems. There's nothing more pathetic than an anthropomorphic creature made from mud having its magic inscription stolen and then turning to dust.

But stealing appendages from zombies is something new.

While we've all heard stories about horrible things that happen to zombies in other cities or towns—being dismembered or immolated or donated to medical science—this is the first time something like this has happened to someone we know. In the grand cosmic scheme of things, who the victim is shouldn't matter. We're all creatures of the earth, interconnected by the simple fact of our existence, so our empathy should extend in equal measure to friends and strangers.

But sitting here on the couch in Peter and Grant's dorm room, holding Ricardo's decomposing remaining hand and attempting to comfort him while he leans his head on my shoulder and sobs, grieving over the loss of his left arm and spilling his Budweiser in his lap, I can't help but take what happened to Ricardo personally.

"Wwlg hllt unht smmtg," I say.

Translation: We have to do something.

For several moments, no one says anything and my declaration of action hangs in the air like a slowly deflating balloon.

Eventually, Grant breaks the silence. "Urlk wrt?"

Translation: Like what?

He says this with a tone that indicates his belief in the futility of any course of action we might choose to take.

Although Grant's an attractive enough zombie with whom I could see myself having a one-night stand or two just for kicks, he's not my idea of boyfriend material. I prefer someone with a little more backbone and initiative and Grant never seems to have much of either. Plus he has this nasty habit of picking at his decomposing flesh.

Peter's not much better, but at least he occasionally offers up constructive ideas and shows a willingness to take action. But at the moment, both he and Grant appear to be useless on both counts.

"Wwrl slld wunh dunh?" Peter asks.

I don't *know* what we should do. But sitting here in this dorm room feeling sorry for Ricardo and lamenting our place in the monster hierarchy isn't going to prevent someone else from having one of their appendages stolen.

Several more moments of awkward silence pass before I stand up and walk out of the room. At first I'm not sure where I'm going. I just need to move. But soon I find myself walking down to the end of the hallway and knocking on the last door. No one answers but that doesn't deter me. I knock on another door. And another. And another, working my way back up the hallway. At this time of day most of the students are in class or scavenging for lunch, but about every third door I knock on opens. When the vacant face of a fellow zombie appears, I simply say "Clhm unh."

Translation: Come on.

It's a simple directive and one that you might not think would have much of an impact, but most zombies don't possess an abundance of functioning gray matter, especially those of us who weren't embalmed prior to reanimating. Even though reanimation slows down the process of decomposition, brains tend to go pretty fast. The bacteria that forms in the mouth after death chews through the palate. Since the brain is soft, it liquefies quickly and pours out the ears and bubbles out the mouth.

This is one of the reasons why zombies have a reputation for craving brains. In a way, I guess you could say we're kind of like scarecrows trying to find our way back to Oz.

But even though some of us still have some meat left in our craniums, zombies are the lemmings of monsters and as such are highly suggestible creatures. So it doesn't take much to convince the reanimated corpses in Romero House to follow me. By the time we get to Fulci House, Grant, Peter, and Beverly are all following my lead, knocking on doors and taking up my rallying cry. However, once we leave Zombie Towers and head en masse toward the center of campus, I'm the one out in front with more than five-dozen zombies staggering along behind me.

I'm just a sophomore, not even a week out of my freshman diapers, so there are dozens of upperclassmen who have more experience than I do in dealing with the university administration and campus politics. But in the twelve months and change that I've been attending Bela Lugosi University, I have yet to see any of our so-called leaders do anything more than talk about the problems we zombies face. So far, the extent of their action has involved lodging complaints or filing petitions with the administration, which has proven to be about as effective a plan for change as Don't Ask, Don't Tell.

When we reach the Quonset huts where the majority of the reanimated corpse curriculum takes place, I walk into the one o'clock Basic Cognition class and interrupt Professor Brooks in the middle of his lecture on object permanence, talking to his students as if they're all infants and can't grasp the concept that objects exist even if they can't see or smell them.

"Clhm unh," I say.

The students all turn around in their desks and stare at me.

"Can I help you?" Professor Brooks asks in a tone that indicates I must be either lost or brain dead.

No. He can't help me. But it's time we all helped ourselves.

I glance out the classroom door to the horde of living dead shuffling around outside the Quonset hut. While they've followed me this far, I'm not sure how my fellow zombies are going to feel about the idea of a revolution. It's kind of difficult to gauge the mood of your audience when the majority of them wear emotionless, open-mouthed expressions.

I turn back to the students in the classroom.

"Clhm unh," I say again.

At first nobody moves. Then a female zombie named Claire stands up and starts shambling my way. A couple of other zombies she passes follow her lead and in a matter of seconds, all of the other students stand up and start moving toward the door.

It's the law of reanimated kinetic energy on full display. And here I thought my zombie science classes were all a big waste of time.

"Where are you going?" Professor Brooks says, raising his voice above the murmur of *Uuuuunhs* that resonate throughout the classroom like zombie purrs. No one pays any attention to the professor's protestations. Instead, they follow me out the door to join the growing army of reanimated corpses.

We hit the other Quonset huts, putting a premature end to Zombie Biology, Fundamentals of Formaldehyde, and How to Survive a Human Apocalypse. The last stop is Remedial English with Professor Warner.

"Hello Miss Knox," he says as I enter the classroom. "Back for more?"

His disarming smile and the fact that he knows my name makes my undead heart flutter, but I can't allow a professor crush to cause me to lose focus. Still, I'm too flustered to answer him, so I just shake my head and say "Llss gunh."

Translation: Let's go.

"Very good!" the professor says as a dozen of his students rise up from their desks. "This is what I'm talking about, class. If you apply yourself like Miss Knox here, you'll be speaking clear, intelligible sentences in no time."

Professor Warner doesn't appear to be concerned that his class is gradually filing out the door, although zombies aren't the most adept when it comes to merging or taking turns, so there's a bit of a pile up getting out of the classroom.

This is one of the reasons why we have a hard time being taken seriously.

By the time we leave the Quonset huts, our numbers have grown to over two hundred and we've attracted an audience. Mummies and mothmen, witches and werewolves, golems and ghouls, succubi, ogres, chimeras, and banshees watch us shamble across the campus. Some watch in wonder while others, mostly werewolves and ogres, point at us and laugh.

Zombies have routinely been the butt of pranks and jokes, treated like second-class monsters, and are always the last ones to get picked for dodgeball. There was a time when I thought I lacked some inherent quality that had relegated me to this status, that I was a lesser creature simply because I was a zombie.

When you're constantly denigrated and made fun of and told that you're of a lower class than the other monsters, eventually you start to believe it.

But in spite of our physical and mental disadvantages, zombies have something to offer that the other monsters don't, especially vampires and werewolves. And that something is authenticity.

Unlike vampires and werewolves, zombies don't have any ulterior motives. We don't try to impress anyone with our immortality or our castles or the fact that we're the starting quarterback on the varsity football team. We don't walk around pretending to be something we're not, living among humans while sneaking into their bedrooms at night to drink their blood or waiting for a full moon to reveal our true nature. We're honest about who we are and what we want in a relationship. We wear our decomposing hearts on our sleeves and aren't ashamed to say, "I'm a zombie and I want to eat your brains."

Well, some of us anyway. Personally, I've never been a big fan of brains, which aren't as easy to get to as Hollywood depicts. The idea that we can crack open a human skull with our teeth is just preposterous. It's tough enough to bite into an apple without losing an incisor, which is why zombies eat a lot of applesauce and mashed potatoes. But every now and then, you just have to go with the flow and embrace the stereotype.

A collective groan rises up from our undead horde. "Uuuuunh!"

Translation: Brains!

I add my voice to the rallying cry of my reanimated brothers and sisters as we shamble up Nosferatu Knoll and swarm around Sigma Beta Nu.

The Time Traveler's
Guide to Insomnia

The bottle of Johnnie Walker Black lay on its side on the coffee table amid an assortment of empty beer bottles that stood upright like sentinels, guarding their fallen comrade. June lay on the couch and stared at the nearly empty bottle of Scotch—the last couple of swallows pooled along the side of the bottle like blood settling in a dead body.

Nothing like imagining blood pooling in corpses to start the day, she thought. *That's one way to keep from finishing off the bottle.*

Considering all of the empty beer bottles and the slow, dull throbbing in her head, it was probably a good thing she didn't feel compelled to finish off the Johnnie Walker. The prudent or wise decision, as her mother always liked to say. But *prudent* and *wise* weren't two words that described June, especially when it came to her drinking.

You're not twenty-two anymore, June. That ship sailed a good decade ago.

The voice was hers but it might as well have been her mother's, which almost made June reach for the bottle in spite of her burgeoning hangover. The thought of turning into her mother was enough to drive anyone to drink, especially when the mother in question was April Johnson.

In June's family, there was an unspoken tradition of naming daughters after months of the year. It had started with January

Chandler (Jan for short), who had been named by her parents after the month in which she'd been born. Jan had gone into labor on Mother's Day and named her daughter May, who, in turn gave birth to June's mother two days after filing her taxes, checking April off the list. June, meanwhile, had come into the world just after midnight on the first Monday of June.

When she was a little girl, June had wondered what she would name her daughter since there weren't any months left that worked other than August, and she wasn't fond of the name Augustine. Her mother had told her maybe she'd have a boy instead of a girl. At the time, June thought boys were weird and yucky. Her mother had assured her there would come a time when her perspective would change. Hadn't that been the truth. But in spite of all of her boyfriends and other male companions over the years, she'd never had to decide on a name for her child since she'd never reached the 'let's have a kid' stage of any relationship. And, contrary to her mother's predictions, she'd never ended up tin roof rusted.

June stared at the bottle of Johnnie Walker a few moments longer, contemplating various excuses that would justify drinking the last of the Scotch. There was nothing like chasing a couple of Advil with a shot of Johnnie Walker to help blunt the sharp edge of a hangover. But any thought of drinking went out the proverbial window as soon as she sat up.

The world started spinning and her stomach joined the party as a sickening warmth washed over her, causing her forehead and the back of her neck to break out in a slick sweat. She'd read once that women didn't sweat. They glowed. Cows sweated, men perspired, and women glowed. She didn't know if that was some scientific classification or just a bunch of euphemistic bullshit, but she didn't feel like she was glowing. She was sweating. And Johnnie Walker Black was oozing out of her pores.

The bathroom was less than twenty feet down the hallway but it might as well have been on the other side of the planet, which meant she was going to vomit on the couch, the carpet, or her lap.

Or all three. Fortunately, someone had the foresight to place a small plastic garbage can next to the couch in case of emergency. June didn't know if that someone had been her, her boyfriend, or the hangover fairy, but she was grateful for the courtesy.

In a single motion, she grabbed the garbage can, brought it between her thighs, and leaned forward. There wasn't much food to speak of, mostly just Johnnie Walker Black and some stomach bile. Reverse drinking is what they used to call it. Maybe somewhere they still did. But right there, sitting on the couch in the living room of the one-bedroom apartment she shared with Luke—her stomach clenching and her mouth opening in silent dry heaves over a white plastic garbage can held between her thighs—June thought it felt more like stomach pumping. Or at least how she imagined that would feel. For all of her drinking escapades since she'd first discovered the highs and lows of alcohol as a sixteen-year-old, she'd never had her stomach pumped.

Well, that's a surprise, her mother's voice said in her head.

Once the dry heaves tapered off, June carefully stood up and walked down the hall to the bathroom, taking the garbage can with her. She emptied the contents of the garbage can into the toilet, then rinsed the garbage can out with water and her mouth out with mouthwash before she chased a couple of Advil with some water, starting the process of getting back to normal. After splashing cold water on her face, she pulled her hair back in a ponytail, added a couple of drops of Visine to each eye, pinched her cheeks to get some color in them, then looked in the mirror and tried on a small smile.

"June Johnson, reporting for duty."

Less than ten minutes after waking up with a hangover and emptying the contents of her stomach into a garbage can, she looked fresh from a sober night's sleep. It was one of her talents. No matter how much she'd had to drink the night before or how hung over she felt the next morning or how much time she'd spent with her head hovered over a toilet bowl, she always managed to look like a million dollars. Or at least half a million.

She'd been blessed with good genes that included natural blonde hair and high cheekbones, both of which she'd inherited from her mother's Nordic ancestry. Because of her bone structure and low-register voice that bordered on what some might call husky, most people, especially men, usually added five years to her age. When she was a teenager that had been both a blessing and a curse. Now, halfway through her thirties, she found it to be more of the latter.

The bloating from all that booze doesn't help, honey.

"Shut up, Mom."

June returned to the living room and found a half-smoked joint on the coffee table among the empty beer bottles. She didn't remember getting high last night and she wasn't a big beer drinker, so either Luke had knocked back a couple and left her on the couch to sleep it off or she'd had some guests over and they'd gone home at some point after she'd passed out. Or maybe before. It was hard to know. She didn't remember passing out. To be honest, she didn't remember much of anything about last night. It had been a while since she'd blacked out, which usually only happened when she mixed alcohol or smoked pot. So maybe all of the empties on the coffee table belonged to her.

She waited for her mother's nagging voice to chime in, to say something about her addictive personality or lack of self-control. Before her mother's voice could chime in, June grabbed the joint, found a lighter, and sat back down on the couch.

She didn't smoke pot very often. Once or twice a week tops. More often than not, it was just a couple of hits to take the edge off. Hair of the dog was fine on the weekend, but going into work with alcohol on your breath was asking for trouble. People could generally tell if you'd had a couple of shots of booze for breakfast. They could smell it on your breath. But your average person didn't suspect that the co-worker in the next cubicle had taken a couple of hits from a joint. Of course if your boss discovered you'd been coming into work stoned, that would be worse than getting caught clocking in on an Egg McMuffin and Johnnie Walker breakfast.

The fact that the country continued to condemn marijuana use while running beer ads during sporting events and on prime time network television was the epitome of hypocrisy, at least as far as June was concerned. And it had even spilled over into the Presidential election. Just last month, Bill Clinton had admitted to experimenting with marijuana when he'd been a student at Oxford. While he'd claimed he hadn't inhaled, the press had blown the story up into a big character-issue thing. June thought Clinton's story was a load of crap. Of course he'd inhaled. He was in college. Everyone partied in college. If he was still smoking pot while running for the President of the United States, she could understand how that might be a problem. But twenty years ago? In England? Who gave a shit?

She didn't understand why everyone was making such a big fuss over it. But knowing the electorate's predilection for being convinced that they should place importance on stories that didn't matter, Clinton's pot smoking admission would probably be the final nail in the coffin of his bid for the Democratic Presidential nomination.

June flicked the wheel on the lighter and held it up to the half-smoked joint, the cherry glowing red as she inhaled. She didn't need much, just enough to help settle her stomach, but since it was the weekend, she took a second hit before she turned on CNN to see what was happening in the world.

As she was taking a third hit on the joint and contemplating washing down the last of the Johnnie Walker with a plate of scrambled eggs and some bacon to help soak up the booze, Luke appeared dressed in khakis and a light blue button-down oxford with a yellow patterned tie.

"What are you all dressed up for?" June asked as CNN news anchor Deborah Marchini discussed business on the television. "Going to church?"

She said this with a laugh, in part because the idea of Luke going to church was funny and in part because she was a little stoned.

"I'm going to work," Luke said, as if his appearance was self-explanatory.

"On a Sunday?"

"It's Monday." Luke looked over the empty bottles littering the coffee table and June sitting on the couch with a joint in her hand, the disappointment evident in his sanctimonious expression. "You're going to lose your job again."

"I'm not going to lose my job. It's Sunday, asshole. Stop fucking around." June took another hit on the joint. "And what do you mean *again*?"

On CNN, Deborah Marchini passed things over to Cathy Marshall, who offered a look ahead to the stories on Daybreak.

"I don't want to get into this with you right now," Luke said.

"Get into what?" June asked. "I didn't realize we were getting into anything."

The post-hangover-pot-smoking high was beginning to kick in and June wanted to coast along on the mellow vibe and relax on the couch and enjoy her Sunday morning, not fight about whatever shit her boyfriend was pulling. But Luke didn't seem to be in the mood to play along.

"Do you even remember what happened last night?" he asked.

"Sure I do."

"Really? Well then why don't you share your version of events?"

On CNN, Cathy Marshall was giving an update about unusual activity in Waco, Texas, outside the compound of a cult leader named David Koresh.

"David Koresh?" June said, diverting the flow of conversation away from her apparent blackout and the fight she didn't want to have. "Who the hell is David Koresh?"

"Are you going to answer my question?" Luke asked.

June continued to ignore Luke. "Eventually, but who is David

Koresh?"

"You're kidding, right?"

June didn't answer but just gave Luke a look that said he was being an ass.

"CNN and every other news channel has been covering this 24/7 for the past two months," he said. "The Attorney General nominated by your hick president has turned this into a huge fucking quagmire."

June didn't know what the hell Luke was talking about and she didn't feel much like listening to him. So she turned up the volume on the television to drown him out as Cathy Marshall continued to talk over the shaky video image of multiple two and three-story buildings bunched together.

"Some of those reports are saying that they have entered one building of the compound. We also had reports throughout the morning of tanks gathering outside the complex. There's also been a report that a tank has knocked out a window at the complex. We're hearing all different things coming. But the activity is definitely more than we've seen in the past weeks. We're now in week eight of the standoff, day fifty-one that is. We'll have more coming up on CNN right after this."

June muted the television. "How has this been going on for eight weeks and this is the first I've heard of it?"

Luke straightened his tie in the hallway mirror. "Probably because you've been living inside a bottle for the past two months."

"Fuck you, asshole."

"Sticks and stones."

June glanced back at the television, the sound muted, trying to understand how she could have missed eight weeks of news about a siege on a compound of a cult leader that apparently was being covered around the clock by CNN and every other cable news station. That's when she saw the chyron graphics on the screen beneath Deborah Marchini as she sat at her desk, pretending to look busy:

CNNBUSINESSday

June stared at the television and rubbed her eyes, thinking that she was seeing things. But the graphics on the television continued to insist that it was a year later than it was when she went to bed last night.

"What the hell is this?" June said, more under her breath and to herself than as a question to Luke.

"I'll tell you what this is." Luke walked around until he was standing between June and the television. "This is me being a grown up and getting ready to go work and earn an income so I can pay my bills, while you stay home and get stoned and sit on your ass and watch TV."

June stared at Luke, mostly because he was in the way. She didn't know why she was still with him. Probably because it was easier to maintain the status quo and be miserable than to try something new and risk happiness. Human beings had a predisposition for stupidity and June had engaged in her own share of bad decisions for as long as she could remember. But she was trying to make sense of what she'd just seen and heard on the television, not count her regrets about her bad life choices.

"What day is it?" she asked.

"I told you. It's Monday."

"Not the day," June said, even though she knew it was Sunday, not Monday, but she wasn't going to argue the point. "The date."

"April 19," Luke said. "And if you think you're going to smoke pot all day tomorrow, too, forget about it."

June stared at him and blinked her eyes, another question forming in her head. A ridiculous question, one that you didn't ask unless you were in a science fiction movie and had just crawled out of a cryogenic freezing tube. Or woke up hung over after a night of heavy drinking that you didn't remember while CNN posted a chyron copyright date a year later than it had been the last time you looked.

"What year is it?" June asked.

Luke picked up the bottle of Johnnie Walker and shook his head in disgust. "Did you finish off the bottle on your own or did your friends help?"

At least that was one mystery solved. But the bigger question remained unanswered.

"What year is it?" she repeated. Not in anger or frustration. She just wanted to know.

"I don't have time for whatever this is that you're doing." Luke set the bottle down. "Now get off your ass and get dressed and get to work. I don't earn enough to cover your share of expenses if you get fired."

Luke turned and walked away. A few moments later, the front door to the apartment slammed shut. Meanwhile on CNN, a muted Bill Clinton stood behind a podium talking to a bunch of reporters. The podium had the State Seal of the President of the United States on it. And behind him was an oval emblem of the White House. June unmuted the television and listened as Clinton fielded questions from different members of the press, each one addressing him as Mr. President.

Yesterday Clinton had been dealing with the aftermath of pot smoking allegations as the Governor of Arkansas and trying to win the Democratic Primary against Jerry Brown. When had he become President of the United States?

Probably while you were smashed out of your mind on booze, her mother's voice said.

June stared at the television and watched President Clinton field questions from the White House press corps as she tried to figure out how she could have missed his election and inauguration and an entire year of her life.

How much did I have to drink last night?

On that matter, her mother remained silent.

The next morning, June woke up naked in bed with Luke spooning her from behind, one arm draped around her waist, their bedroom still bathed in pre-dawn darkness.

She let out a sigh and closed her eyes, taking several deep breaths to fight back the tears of relief. After the fight they'd had last night, she'd expected to wake up on the couch or at a friend's place. Or maybe alone in a motel room.

Luke had come home from work to find June in tears, babbling about President Clinton and Waco and the bombing of the World Trade Center. She'd spent the entire day watching the news and learning that she'd somehow slept through an entire year. At least that's what it seemed like. How else could she have gone to sleep on April 18, 1992, and woken up on April 19, 1993? Had she been in an accident and lost her memory? Spent a year in a coma? Suffered some kind of head injury? These were a few of the questions she'd assaulted Luke with as soon as he'd walked in the door.

Instead of listening to June and trying to understand her, Luke had assumed she'd spent the day drinking herself into an incoherent mess. While it was true that she'd finished off the last of the Johnnie Walker and the remnants of some Jack Daniels, June had not been incoherent or drunk. A mess? Yes. Who wouldn't be a mess after discovering that they'd lost a year of their life? The incoherence had been a result not of the whiskey but of her growing hysteria at having spent eight hours coming to the realization that her reality had become unmoored.

But no matter how much she tried to explain what had happened, Luke attributed her hysteria and confusion to drinking and told her he'd had enough. He was done. Past done. His reserves of patience and understanding had been drained and depleted to the point that there was no chance of refilling them. She had until the end of the week to pack up all of her crap and find another place to live and someone else to deal with her bullshit.

She'd spent the rest of the evening pleading with Luke, begging him to believe her. And June was not a begging woman. But she wanted him to believe her. She needed him to believe her. But he'd refused to even entertain the possibility that she was anything other than delusional. So she'd done the only thing she could think of, reacted the way she usually did when confronted with a crisis: she'd gone to the nearest liquor store, bought a bottle of Johnnie Walker Black, then took it back to the apartment, where she'd spent the rest of the night drinking and crying while packing up her belongings.

So when she woke up in bed with Luke instead of alone on the couch, June figured she'd somehow managed to convince him she was telling the truth. She didn't remember the conversation or crawling into bed naked with him or the inevitable drunk make-up sex, but it didn't matter. She was just grateful that she and Luke had reconciled. So after allowing herself a smile of hope, she closed her eyes, snuggled up against him, and fell back asleep.

When the alarm clock went off at 7:00am, June opened her eyes, half-expecting Luke to be gone and a note to be sitting on the bedside table reminding her that she had until the end of the week to pack her shit and get out. But Luke remained curled up against her and there was no note on the bedside table. That was the good news. The bad news was that there wasn't a bedside table.

June blinked her eyes several times, hoping that the bedside table would magically materialize out of her morning hangover fog. It wouldn't be the first time she'd woken up in the aftermath of a night of drinking and imagined furniture missing or stumbled out of bed and run into furniture that she hadn't expected to be in her way.

But the space next to the bed remained empty. That's when June noticed that the wall was further away from the bed than she remembered. It should have been just three feet away but was instead a good six feet from the bed. And the print of Dali's *The Persistence of Memory* that had hung on the wall for the past two years had been removed, leaving the wall blank. As her eyes adjusted to the morning light, June realized that the wall wasn't a wall but a closet with two sliding doors.

"Good morning," Luke said from behind her before kissing her on the neck.

Except the voice wasn't Luke's. It was softer and deeper, with a hint of an accent that reminded June of an old boyfriend who was from South Carolina.

June rolled away and out from under the arm draped across her waist as if it had been a scalding hot iron before she stood up next to the bed. When she turned around, it wasn't Luke in bed or her old boyfriend from South Carolina. It was someone she'd never seen before.

"Who the fuck are you?" she asked, backing up against the closet that should have been a wall.

The stranger, who had dark hair and a sculpted chest, laughed and sat up in bed. "Is this another role-playing game? Because if it is, I think I need a new safe word."

June stared at him for several moments, trying to jog her memory as she looked from his unfamiliar face to the unfamiliar room and tried to piece together what she'd done last night. After the run to the liquor store, she'd gone back to the apartment and started packing, throwing her belongings into her suitcase and duffel bag. Anything that hadn't fit into those she'd stuffed into several plastic garbage bags. The entire time, she'd alternated between drinking from the bottle of whiskey and sobbing into her knees. That she remembered with absolute clarity. But after that, her memory grew hazy. She had no idea where she was or how she'd ended up there.

"Hey, are you okay?" the man asked, his playful smile morphing into an expression of concern.

She looked back at his face. It was a kind face, soft and forgiving. Not like Luke's, which had always been hard and accusatory, as if he was always waiting for an excuse to yell at her.

"How did I get here?" she asked.

"How did you...?" he said, then he let out another laugh, the smile returning. "You're fucking with me, right?"

June shook her head. "What happened last night?"

"Okay, I'll play along," he said. "We went out for drinks and a movie with Doug and Kim."

Doug and Kim? Who the hell were Doug and Kim?

"A movie?"

"*Four Weddings and a Funeral*," he said. "You loved it. You said no one should get married. They should just agree to live happily ever after."

She stared at him with no recollection of what he was talking about.

"You seriously don't remember?" he asked.

June looked around the room again, an uncomfortable sense of déjà vu washing over her. "What day is it?"

"It's Wednesday," he said.

Yesterday had been Monday, she was pretty sure. At least the yesterday she remembered.

"What's the date?" she asked.

"April 20. Why? Oh, I get it. This is a pot joke, isn't it?"

June shook her head, in part because this wasn't a joke but mostly because she didn't want to believe it had happened to her again. "What year is it?"

He laughed again then stopped, the smile falling from his lips. "You're serious?"

June nodded.

"How much did you drink last night?" he asked.

Luke had asked her that same question on a regular basis, at least a few times each month. The same question so many of her boyfriends had asked her over the years.

How much did you drink last night?

"What year is it?" she asked again.

"It's 1994." He climbed out of bed and put on a pair of boxers.

"What's this all about?"

June looked around the bedroom, a foreign landscape with unfamiliar markings and she was a traveler from another planet suffering from a severe case of jet lag. Her eyes settled on the stranger standing at the side of the bed in his boxers. "Who are you?"

June awoke naked in bed, curled up on her side beneath the covers, and stared at the nightstand, where a half empty bottle of Johnnie Walker Red stood next to a couple of shot glasses, one of which contained the roach of a joint. Next to the shot glasses, a torn and empty condom wrapper sat on the table like a discarded promise.

At least there was a nightstand this time, but she didn't recognize the shot glasses or anything else in the bedroom other than the bottle of Johnnie Walker Red, which was like seeing an old friend. As for the rest of her surroundings, she didn't know if she lived here or was just passing through. But that wasn't anything new. Each of the three mornings prior to this one, she'd woken up some place different with no idea of where she was or how she'd arrived there.

The rational part of June kept trying to convince her to seek out medical attention, or at least talk to someone who might be able to help her make some sense of what was happening to her. But the cynical part of her insisted that anyone who heard her story would think she was drunk or suffering from some form of alcohol or drug-induced delusion that required her to be institutionalized. As usual, the cynical part of June won the argument.

So instead of seeking medical attention, she'd stayed up all night drinking, which had done the trick. At least for one day. But voluntary insomnia wasn't a permanent solution, especially when your drug of choice was alcohol and not cocaine. So eventually, June had succumbed to exhaustion and passed out. Now here she was again in an unfamiliar room with an unfamiliar bedmate.

Behind her came the clearing of a throat, followed by shifting beneath the covers. June continued to stare at the bottle of Johnnie Walker, not wanting to turn around, wondering if the whiskey had been her idea or that of whoever was moving around beneath the covers next to her. If she were giving odds, she'd lay ten to one the idea had been hers.

It usually is, her mother's voice said in her head.

Like the bottle of whiskey, her mother's voice remained a constant in her new reality. As much as she appreciated the company of Johnnie Walker, she wished the voice of April Johnson would shut the fuck up.

A moment later, a naked body spooned her and a hairy, tattooed arm snaked over her side, reaching down to cup one of her breasts.

"Good morning," a deep voice murmured behind her ear, a blast of warm breath washing over her, scented with onions and garlic and whiskey.

She didn't respond but remained on her side, her gaze lingering on the bottle of Johnnie Walker before shifting to the shot glasses and the roach and the torn condom wrapper. After a few moments, her attention fell on the tattoo on the forearm of the man spooning her. She could only see part of the tattoo but it appeared to be a Celtic cross that ran from just inside his elbow to the wrist. On a banner beneath the crossbar, she could read the first three letters of a word:

FAI

With her brain still in a whiskey-induced haze, June tried to figure out what the word might be. Fair. Faith. Fairy. Her memory was useless in conjuring up an image of the entire tattoo, so if she had to guess, she put her money on Faith.

Or Failure, her mother's voice said. *But that would be your tattoo, wouldn't it, dear?*

A pair of lips kissed her on the neck and behind her ear. She didn't recognize the lips or the voice or the hand that continued to fondle her breast. If she rolled over, she probably wouldn't recognize the face or the rest of the body that went along with everything else, which was the main reason she stayed curled up on her side looking at the bottle of whiskey and the shot glasses. Those at least made sense to her. But the longer she avoided turning around, the longer she could put off the awkward moment when she would have to admit that she didn't know the name of the man in bed with her or remember anything about him.

Ever since the morning when she'd woken up to discover that the last eight months of 1992 and the first four months of 1993 had elapsed during a single implausible night, June had experienced what to her were a series of drunken one-night stands. She would wake up with another man in a strange house or apartment or hotel room with no memory of what had happened the night before. But as she soon discovered, it wasn't just the night before that was a complete blank. It was the entire year. And what seemed to June like three days of one-night stands was actually three years of serial relationships that had taken her from 1993 to 1996.

The morning after waking up to discover that she'd been in a six-month relationship with Aaron (the dark-haired stranger with the sculpted chest and slight South Carolina drawl), June had woken up in a hotel room in St. Petersburg with Joshua, her boyfriend of three months. The morning after that she'd found herself in a studio apartment in Sarasota with a struggling artist named Peter. Apparently, she and Peter had been a hot item for a little over a month.

That had been April 22, 1996. Now here she was on boyfriend number four, or at least the most recent boyfriend she'd slept with last night or early this morning, which, according to the calendar in her head, should have been April 23, 1992. But based on recent history, at least the history she remembered, the calendar had more than likely slipped forward another three-hundred-and-sixty-five days and it was 1997 and time for another round of sexual Clue.

It's Colonel Erection with a one-night stand in a two-bedroom apartment.

Only instead of Professor Plum or Mr. Green or Colonel Mustard, she kept waking up next to men named Peter and Joshua and Aaron. June didn't know if there was any significance to the fact that all of the men were named after Biblical characters, but it was becoming a habit. And it had all started with Luke, a proselytizer of personal responsibility who also happened to share the name of a major player in the New Testament.

Maybe on some deeper level she was searching for salvation, a subconscious attempt to redeem herself before it was too late. But considering five years had passed in what to June had taken less than a week, *too late* had apparently come and gone.

The most frustrating part was that she couldn't remember anything. Her head should have been filled with the experiences and memories of the life she'd lived and the people she'd shared it with. Instead, there existed a blank void, an empty chasm that stretched out as far as she could see, and the longer she stared into it the more she began to lose her balance and feel as if she was about to fall into it. So she kept trying to fill the emptiness with whiskey and pot and sex. Avoidance was her coping mechanism of choice. That was the only way she knew how to deal with what was happening to her: to pretend it wasn't happening. To pretend it wasn't real.

Sooner or later, she was going to have to face reality. But at the moment, reality would have to wait.

The hand caressing her breast grew more aggressive, the lips kissing her neck and her ear occasionally using teeth, and the breathing behind her grew harder along with the cock pressed against her ass. June closed her eyes and tried to conjure up some sort of memory of the man in bed with her, the smallest hint of who he was or why she had chosen to be with him: his demeanor or his confidence or his sense of humor. But there was nothing. No memories. No emotions. No feelings of love or friendship or passion. It was the same story day after day, year after year: naked stranger after naked stranger; a stray hand cupping one of her breasts, massaging it or squeezing it or pinching her nipple; a morning erection pressing up against her like a persistent solicitor knocking on the door, asking for a few minutes of her time.

The only memories she had of the years she'd missed were the days she'd woken up in between them. But they weren't enough for her to figure out what was happening to her. Or how to make it stop, other than never going to sleep.

June glanced at the Celtic tattoo on the forearm of the man in bed with her who was doing everything he could to get her to spread her legs. She still couldn't see more than the first three letters of the word on the banner on his arm, but she chose to believe that the letters spelled out FAITH. She didn't know if that was because she needed to have faith in herself or in the idea that she would figure out what was happening to her but right now, it was the only thing she could hold on to.

After another thirty seconds, June gave up on the futility of trying to remember anything about the naked stranger in bed behind her and turned around to lose herself in the moment.

⌚ ⌚ ⌚

The stranger who June had woken up in bed with on April 23, 1997, was named Matthew and he was a construction worker who June had been dating for three weeks. That brought her total number of boyfriends with Biblical names to five, two of whom were named after the canonical gospels. If things kept going the way they were, she figured she would get Mark and John crossed off the list in a couple of more days and wrap up the New Testament by 1999.

But on the morning of April 24, 1998, June didn't wake up next to anyone named Mark or John. Or next to an Adam or Isaac or Saul. For the first time since she'd awoken on the couch in the living room of the apartment she'd shared with Luke five years ago, June woke up alone.

Technically, she was never alone because her constant companion, a half-empty bottle of Johnnie Walker Red, sat on the floor next to the mattress. But no one shared the mattress or the room with her. And, as far as she could tell through the haze of her hangover, the building.

She was in a house that was either condemned, abandoned, or under construction—although from the empty beer cans and used condoms and the graffiti that decorated the walls, she guessed it was either abandoned or condemned. And just like each time she'd awoken over the previous four mornings (years), she had no idea where she was or how she'd gotten there.

How is that different from any other day in your adult life?

Her mother's voice, always there to remind June of her failings. While she would have preferred some words of encouragement rather than her mother's perpetual criticisms, at least it was something familiar.

The bottle of Johnnie Walker sat next to a battered backpack that June presumed belonged to her. On the wall behind the bottle of whiskey, someone had painted the word SCAB in bold, red letters. Next to that was a poorly drawn black outline of a door and the words NO EXIT written above it.

"Well that's comforting," June said, her voice sounding as if someone had gone to work on her vocal cords with sandpaper.

Just in case, June glanced around to verify that the room did indeed have an exit. While there weren't any windows, the room had a door, or at least a doorframe. Any door that might have once existed was long gone, the hinges broken and rusted. The room also had a dirty skylight in the ceiling above the mattress that offered a glimpse of the world outside.

Through the skylight, June could see a patch of clear blue sky in the otherwise pallid ceiling. She tried to conjure up any memory of where she was and how she'd ended up here, but the last thing she remembered was getting drunk with Matthew and going to a tattoo parlor.

It had started, as it so often did, with whiskey. They'd been at a bar in Sarasota, which one she couldn't recall, but she'd asked Matthew about his tattoos, of which he had several, including a Celtic knot armband on one bicep and a compass on one shoulder.

"The Celtic knot is about no beginnings or endings, the timeless nature of the spirit," he'd said. "The compass is a reminder to maintain my direction and remain focused on my goals."

"What about that one?" June had asked, taking his right hand and turning it over to display the Celtic cross on his forearm.

"That one," he'd said, with a little smile that would have melted her heart under normal circumstances. "Is a reminder of my Irish heritage and to believe in myself, which is why I had FAITH tattooed on the banner beneath the crossbeam."

June had traced the words on his forearm without looking up.

"I could use a little faith," she had said, though she hadn't confessed why or tried to explain to Matthew what was happening to her. From her previous experiences with Luke and her other biblical boyfriends, she knew that wouldn't make for a fun night. Instead, she had answered *yes* without hesitation when Matthew asked her if she wanted to get a tattoo.

June lifted her left arm and pulled up the sleeve of her shirt to reveal a one-inch wide Celtic knot armband around her bicep. It looked like a rope made up of multiple knots, done in black ink, with the word FAITH spelled out in the white of her skin inside the rope. She vaguely recalled the parlor and how much getting the tattoo had hurt. What she remembered most about the experience was Matthew holding her hand with a combination of tenderness and firmness that was both comforting and terrifying at the same time.

She stared at the tattoo another moment before she pulled her sleeve back down. She'd hoped that by getting the tattoo it would help to remind her to have faith that she would figure out why this was happening to her and give her something to hold on to each day. But after waking up on a dirty mattress in an abandoned house littered with empty beer cans and used condoms, June didn't have faith in much of anything, let alone in herself.

After staring at the NO EXIT door drawn on the wall for another minute, June sat up on the mattress, stretched and took a deep breath, which she immediately regretted. The room smelled of stale urine and something else that conjured images of rotten fruit or sour milk. Whatever it was it nearly made her gag, so she grabbed the tattered backpack and half-empty bottle of Johnnie Walker and left the room.

It didn't take long to find her way out, as the building only had the one room plus a small kitchen, a bathroom, and what appeared to be an office with its windows boarded up. She considered making use of the bathroom but the smell in there was worse than in the bedroom, so she made her way out the back door that had been pried open and knocked off its hinges.

When she emerged into the morning light, June found herself standing in an open yard with empty beer cans, discarded fast-food wrappers, and other assorted paraphernalia scattered around. The yard stretched more than a hundred feet to some kind of warehouse. One side of the yard was lined with numerous palms and other varieties of trees, while on the opposite side was another warehouse, separated from the yard by a dirt road.

From the palm trees and the humidity that was already causing her head to swim, she guessed she was still in Florida, probably Sarasota, where she had lived for most of her adult life.

June had moved out of her mother's house in Fort Pierce the day she'd turned eighteen and moved in with her high school boyfriend, which had turned out to be the first of many mistakes.

Four years later, after adding a few more mistakes to her résumé, she threw her clothes and personal belongings in her car and drove west to put as much distance between her and Fort Pierce as possible. Once she reached the Gulf, she'd intended to take Interstate 75 north to Interstate 10 west all the way to New Orleans. But she'd decided to stay in Sarasota for a few weeks to earn some money before starting her new life in The Big Easy. The rest, as they say, is history. Or was history. The way things had turned out, June didn't know anything about her own history once she'd started time travelling.

That was how she'd come to think of what was happening to her. She was travelling forward one year at a time. At least some version of her was time travelling and remembering one day each year. Considering that she had woken up next to a new boyfriend each of the previous five years, she figured some other version of herself was living her life the other 364 days of the year. She didn't pretend to understand what was happening to her but whatever it was, she needed a drink. And not the kind that came in a shot glass or served on the rocks.

That's a surprise. Are you sure you're feeling well, honey?

"Fuck you, Mom," June said and then unzipped her backpack to take stock of her personal possessions.

There was a water bottle, half-full or half-empty depending on your point of view. June took the pessimistic POV and gulped down the rest of the water before she turned her attention to the backpack's remaining contents. In addition to the now empty water bottle and the half-full bottle of Johnnie Walker, she found a pair of sunglasses, a small wallet containing a Florida identification card along with $217, a bag of beef jerky, one orange, a first-aid kit, two ball-point pens, a composition book, a battered copy of *Slaughterhouse-Five*, a bottle of sunscreen, three tampons, a Zip-Lock bag with a toothbrush and a tube of toothpaste, a rolled-up rain poncho, a pair of jeans, two T-shirts, a pair of shorts, two pairs of socks, and three pairs of underwear.

After taking inventory, she ate the orange. She hadn't realized how hungry she was until she'd found it, so she sat down on the overgrown grass in the back of the boarded up building and peeled the orange, eating one segment after another and savoring the flavor and the juice that filled her mouth. Once she was done with the orange, she took out a piece of beef jerky and devoured that in three bites, regretting that she'd already finished off the water.

The urge to urinate reintroduced itself. Lacking any other options and not wanting to brave the stench of the bathroom inside the abandoned home, June went to the nearest corner of the yard where the house met the line of trees, pulled down her pants and underwear, and squatted. Although she didn't have any memory of peeing in the yards of abandoned homes, she had a feeling this wasn't the first time she'd done this.

After she'd emptied her bladder, June found a clean area of the yard, sat down, and flipped through the battered copy of *Slaughterhouse-Five* before she picked up the composition book, rubbing her thumbs over the soft, marbled black and white cover. It was made by the Ampad Corporation out of Holyoke, Massachusetts, and, according to the cover, contained eighty wide-ruled sheets. On the white square in the center, beneath the words Composition Book, were two lines on which was written:

The Time Traveler's Guide to Insomnia
April 27, 1997 –

It was definitely her handwriting, but she had no memory of buying the composition book, let alone writing anything on or in it. The absence of an end date made her wonder if she'd forgotten to add a final entry or if this was supposed to be an ongoing journal that had started four days after her last and only memory from 1997.

When she'd first opened the backpack, she'd hoped its contents might provide some clue as to what she'd been doing for the past twelve months. At least she presumed it had been twelve months since she'd gotten the tattoo on her arm with Matthew, who had apparently grown tired of her like all of her other boyfriends. But now that she held the composition book in her hand, she was afraid to open it.

What if there were truths in there she didn't want to know about? What if she'd done something horrible? Or what if something horrible had happened to her?

The fact that she'd woken up on a dirty mattress in an abandoned building that reeked of human waste was horrible enough, so June figured that whatever she found inside the composition book couldn't be worse than not knowing how she'd ended up here. But still she hesitated, apprehensive of what she might find.

Oh stop being such a baby and open the damn thing.

After a few moments, June listened to her mother, opened the composition book, and started to read.

April 27, 1997

Here it is. My attempt to chronicle my life so that I'll have some record of it. Not that my life is special in any way or worth chronicling, but if things continue the way they've been going, this is the only record I'll have of my memories.

The problem is I was never good at keeping a diary or a journal so I'm not sure what to write. I'd say I have time to figure that out, except time and I aren't exactly on the best of terms lately. But then I guess you know that better than I do. I'm also guessing you won't remember any of this because I never have. If that makes any sense.

Oh, and I decided to sober up to see if that helps me to stop time travelling. For all I know I've tried this before but I'm guessing that it never stuck. I can understand why.

The headaches and shakes started on the first day, with the nausea and night sweats joining forces on day two. That was a lot of fun. On day three, the insomnia kicked in, along with the occasional hallucination. No pink elephants, but shadowy figures keep showing up in my peripheral vision before ducking out of sight. There goes one now!

I don't know how long I can keep this up. It's all I can do to keep from driving to the liquor store to pick up a bottle of Johnnie Walker.

April 30, 1997

While the night sweats and shakes have finally begun to subside and the phantom figures have decided to haunt someone else, the headaches have stuck around for the ride with the insomnia riding shotgun.

Before, or at least the memories I have of before, booze made it easier for me to fall asleep, although I guess it was less like sleep and more like alcohol-induced oblivion. But now I lie awake in bed, my mind racing and shifting from one thought to the next: my mom, Luke, the boyfriends I barely remember, my cat Sam who got out one day when I was a kid and who was found three days later dead on the side of the road.

My brain is a regular funhouse.

But mostly, especially late at night, I think about closing my eyes and waking up in 1998 with no memory of what happened to me over the course of a year. If that's not enough to give anyone insomnia, I don't know what is. Hey, there's an idea. Maybe if I never fall asleep, I'll finally stop time travelling. As far as horrible ideas go, that's right up there with New Coke.

May 1, 1997

Today marks one week of sobriety. I have no idea how I made it one week without a drink. I'd mark the occasion by celebrating, but right now even a glass of sparkling cider seems like a slippery slope.

May 3, 1997

Since I can't sleep, I figured I might as well do something constructive with my time, so I've started working nights at reception at the Lido Beach Resort. I'm not what you would call a "people person." I'm more of a "go fuck yourself" person. Not the best fit for working reception, but they didn't have any openings in management. At least the work keeps me out of trouble, which seems to find me even when I'm not looking for it. But I'm trying.

May 5, 1997

I've been sober for eleven days now, which is a personal best, at least as far as I know. I'm not sure if I should be proud of that or embarrassed, but I'm shooting for the former. At least most of the withdrawal symptoms have abated, although I'm still having trouble sleeping. And every now and then, my left hand shakes uncontrollably. Plus the cravings cause my stomach to cramp up. But other than that, I feel great. (Please note the sarcasm.)

I'm not attending any AA meetings, just trying to do this on my own. It would probably help to have someone to go through this with, but there are too many references to God in AA and we both know our relationship with God isn't any better than it is with Mom.

Is it weird that I'm writing this as if I'm talking to someone else? I guess in a way I am, since I'm talking to my future self who probably won't have any memory of me writing this. So in a way, we're complete strangers, you and I. Either that or I'm slowly losing my mind.

May 9, 1997

I meant to write an entry every day but obviously, that hasn't happened. The whole idea was to document my life so that if I wake up in 1998 without any memory of what happened, I'll be able to read this and see how I ended up wherever I ended up and with whomever I ended up with.

By the way, Matthew is gone. He didn't last long after he asked me what I was writing about and I told him I was a time traveler and my journal entries were to help me remember my life when I woke up in 1998. Probably not a good idea to share that information early in the relationship. Need to build up to that. First the damaged childhood, then the alcoholism, then the time traveling. At least I have this nice tattoo as a reminder of our time together.

May 12, 1997

A tornado touched down today in Miami. It swept through downtown, bypassing the city's skyscrapers, touching down briefly in Miami Beach and flipping over a car before eventually dissipating over Biscayne Bay. It didn't do much damage, and it didn't have any impact on Sarasota since we're on the other side of the state, but I feel as if I can relate to what it would be like to be caught in a tornado. It's as if I'm stuck in some kind of swirling vortex, unable to control what's happening to me. I wish I knew how to make it stop. One of these days (or years) I'm afraid that, like a tornado, eventually I'm going to just dissipate and disappear, as if I never existed.

May 13, 1997

Wow. That last entry should win a prize for being maudlin.

May 17, 1997

The insomnia is starting to catch up to me. I keep spacing out at work, sending messages to the wrong room, and forgetting to close out guest accounts after they check out. One of my co-workers, Josh, keeps covering for me. He's made it clear that he's interested in me for more than just my reception skills. I told him if his name was Mark or John I might consider sleeping with him, but I already had a Joshua on my Bible Gospel Bingo card.

May 23, 1997

I lost my job. On top of the fact that I kept sleepwalking through my shifts, one of the guests complained that I was condescending to her. Actually more than one guest filed that particular complaint. I think the total number was somewhere north of six. But I can't help it that people are stupid or that they don't know how to behave. It's amazing to me how often people with money have absolutely no manners.

May 25, 1997

So much for sobriety. But at least I finally got a good night's sleep.

May 31, 1997

I met someone at a bar. Big surprise. His name is David (another biblical name) and he likes to drink, too, which has its pros and cons. Right now, I'm mostly trying to focus on the pros and not think about the fact that I couldn't make it a full month without drinking.

June 3, 1997

Happy birthday to me. Never thought this is where I'd be when I turned 40 but I guess that's what happens when your best friend is a bottle of Scotch and your memory is reduced to sixteen hours of consciousness once a year.

June 17, 1997

Testing, testing...one, two, three. Hey, is this thing on?

Speaking of on: after more than three weeks of dating Mr. Walker, I'm on the wagon again, which has always struck me as an odd expression. It seems that if you were on the wagon, you'd be drinking and laughing it up and having a great time, while anyone who was off the wagon would stand and watch as you went by, wishing they were on the wagon with you. Two days sober so far. We'll see how long this time lasts.

June 23, 1997

I had to break up with David because his alcohol consumption wasn't conducive to my sobriety. Oh well. There are plenty of fish in the sea. And men on the Gulf of Mexico.

July 1, 1997

Landed a new job, this one with less exposure to

unpleasant, rich people. It's at the Barnes & Noble on South Tamiami Trail. It's nice and relaxing, though I don't know as much about modern literature as I should. I asked Philip, my manager, if he recommended any books on time travel, specifically ones where the main character jumps forward in time, and he suggested *Slaughterhouse-Five*, so I guess I'll give that one a shot, see if it might help me to understand what's happening to me.

July 4, 1997

Happy Independence Day!

July 10, 1997

Finished *Slaughterhouse-Five*. Pretty good book. Never read any Vonnegut before. Will probably read it again. Have adopted "So it goes" as my new personal mantra.

July 15, 1997

One month of sobriety. That's a new record, at least this time around. I can't be sure of the other times since I don't have any memories from the past five years. At least now I'll have a record that I can look back on and know for sure. I just wish I would've thought to do this sooner.

Most of the time I manage to get along without my memories, but then someone brings up some topic on pop culture or technology or some major world event that I should know or have heard of and I have no idea what they're talking about.

July 22, 1997

The air conditioner died on my car. Driving around with the windows down to keep from suffocating in Florida during July is like having a mobile sauna. When I get to work, I'm literally dripping wet. I can't wait for the summer to be over.

August 5, 1997

The job at Barnes & Noble didn't work out due to the fact that I didn't show up for work for three days after falling off the wagon again. I'm also late on my rent, which makes two months in a row. At this point, I'm not sure where the money's going to come from. I need to find another job. So it goes.

August 10, 1997

I met another guy, this one named Mark, which means I just have to find a John to complete my Bible Gospel Bingo card. Apparently, the only time I meet men is when I'm drinking. I guess when I'm sober the idea of sex and relationships has no appeal, which seems fucked up. But at least Mark and I have a good time together. And he paid my rent, which gives me another three weeks to scrape together next month's rent.

August 16, 1997

The more time that has passed since I woke up in bed with Matthew, the less likely it seems as if I've been jumping forward in time. I keep waking up day after day the way I'm supposed to, the way normal people do, and my brain tries to convince me that the time traveling I've been doing was just a dream. But even if something inexplicable did happen, even if I'm willing to believe that, I find myself starting to believe that it won't happen again. Every day I wake up and it's the next day, not the next year, I wonder if I've just been so drunk that I've blacked out entire years of my life.

Being crazy is fun!

August 26, 1997

I'm going to be late with my rent again. I'd ask Mark for help but we broke up. Story of my life. So it goes.

September 7, 1997

My car died. The car that I drove across Florida when I left home 18 years ago. It's like having to say goodbye to an old friend. I can't afford to get it fixed, so I sold it for scrap. $250. At least it'll help me to cover my rent. And I don't have to worry about paying insurance or registration. Always look on the bright side, right?

September 18, 1997

Got a part-time job at Stop N' Shop. Just twenty hours a week. It's not much but it's better than nothing. Taking public transportation is as bad as it sounds.

October 1, 1997

Late with my rent again. To raise some money, I've sold off anything I have of any value, including my car. At least I still have my Johnnie Walker.

October 14, 1997

It occurs to me that my Bible Gospel Bingo card is already filled as I've had an on-again, off-again relationship with a John for the past twenty years. Sometimes he's a redhead, sometimes he's a brunette, sometimes he's more than I can handle and not the best of listeners or much into cuddling or pillow talk, but he's always there when I need him. And right now, I need him more than ever.

October 30, 1997

Lost my job at Stop N' Shop. Looks like I'm not going to make rent. So it goes.

November 9, 1997

I received an official Notice of Eviction for Failure to Pay Rent from my landlord. I have three days to pay my rent or else I have to vacate the premises. At this point, I don't have the money or anywhere else to go, so I figure I might as well ride this out and see what happens.

So it goes.

November 15, 1997

My landlord filed a summons to gain possession of the property. So it goes.

November 27, 1997

I sat down to write a list of things I'm thankful for, thinking that might be good for me to do. Build up some optimism. That was a mistake. Although I'm thankful that I still have a roof over my head, that won't last much longer. Not really sure what I'm going to do.

December 8, 1997

Nothing to see here. Move along.

December 25, 1997

Merry Christmas.

That was the last entry. The rest of the pages were blank, not even a scribble or a doodle.

June looked up from the composition book at the blue sky. It didn't feel like December. Or even January. It felt more like spring. And since she'd woken up on consecutive days in April for the past five years, June guessed that the date was probably April 24, 1998. If that were true, and if she had lost her apartment sometime in December, that meant she'd been homeless for the past four months. She wondered if the mattress in the Hotel Stench was her permanent bed or just the previous night's accommodations. At this point, she didn't know which was worse.

June closed up the composition book and stared at the contents of her backpack spread out on the ground, the sum total of her possessions amounting to not much more than four square feet. Before she could stop herself, she covered her face with both hands and started sobbing.

Oh get a hold of yourself, June. Self-pity never solved anyone's problems.

Her mother's voice coming in loud and clear from 150 miles away. Most of the time June told the voice to shut up or to leave her alone. This time she heeded her mother's admonition.

After taking a few deep breaths and wiping her eyes and nose on her sleeve, June shoved her belongings into her backpack and zipped it up. She thought about leaving the bottle of Johnnie Walker—or smashing the bottle to resist any temptation of coming back for it—but she couldn't bring herself to part with her lover just yet. So she shoved the bottle into her backpack and took the dirt road around to the front of the abandoned home. Across the street was the Midco Petroleum Company, where half a dozen large white gasoline tanks sat behind a chain link fence. To the right, the street dead-ended at some railroad tracks, while across the street next to the Midco Petroleum Company, a yellow sign advertised REAL ESTATE ONLY FOR SALE in red letters with the name Sarasota Realty beneath it. So at least she was in the right place.

Don't kid yourself. This isn't the right place, not by a long sight.

June looked up into the sky. From the position of the sun, she guessed it was early morning, maybe eight or nine. In spite of the orange and the beef jerky, she thought she could use some breakfast. And some water. And a shower.

There were public showers and locker rooms at Lido Beach, so June put on her sunglasses and walked down the street until she reached the intersection of 6th and North Lime. She had no idea where that was in Sarasota, but the commercial properties had given way to residential homes. There wasn't any traffic to speak of and no one around to ask directions, so after consulting the position of the sun to get her bearings she turned right and headed in the direction she thought would take her toward the beach.

At the next intersection, June stopped in front of a church across the street from the Colonial Village Shopping Center that boasted a laundromat, a Check 'n Go, a Family Dollar store, a Western Union, and a Save-A-Lot. At the corner of the shopping center, beneath the shade of an umbrella, a woman sat in a chair behind a small round table covered with a gold-colored cloth. A few feet away, a white plastic A-frame sign read:

Madame Queenie – Psychic
Fortunes and Palm Readings – $5.00
Your Destiny Awaits!!!

Dressed in a black and gold striped blouse, black skirt, and a gold sash wrapped around her head, Madame Queenie looked like a carnival psychic who had been swept up in a tornado and deposited on the corner in front of the shopping center. As June stared, Madame Queenie waved to her. Not wanting to be rude, June waved back. Then Madame Queenie gestured for her to come over.

June didn't intend to fork over five dollars to hear someone tell her that she was destined to go on a journey and meet a mysterious stranger who would change her life, but she figured it couldn't hurt to talk to the psychic. At the very least, June figured she could get the date out of her without having to pay anything.

Madame Queenie smiled at June as she approached. On both of her wrists, the psychic wore half a dozen bangles of gold and black, while gold earrings that looked like miniature chandeliers dangled from her ears. Around her neck hung a gold chain with a gold scarab beetle pendant that appeared to be clinging to her ample bosom. In front of her on top of the gold silk cloth, in the center of the table, sat a crystal ball about the size of a softball.

From a distance, June had guessed Madame Queenie to be in her mid-forties. But up close, she looked at least a decade younger. When Madame Queenie spoke, she had more than a hint of an Eastern European accent.

"Good morning," she said, the charm flowing off her like over-applied perfume. She gestured to the unoccupied chair across from her. "Please to take seat."

"I'm just passing by," June said, not wanting to sit down and feel obligated.

"Everyone is just passing by," Madame Queenie said with a dismissive wave of her hand. "So is good to stop and have conversation. Maybe make new friend."

June looked at the chair. She hadn't come over here to make a new friend or have her fortune read so she didn't want to give Madame Queenie any false impressions.

"Is okay," Madame Queenie said. "I won't bite."

June hesitated a moment before she finally decided to sit down.

"I am Madame Queenie," the psychic said and then sat there wearing an expectant smile until June realized it was her turn.

"June," she said. "My name is June."

"And here is only April," Madame Queenie said with another smile. "Is small joke."

June wasn't in much of a joking mood, but she faked a smile.

At least she knew she was still in the right month.

"Now, what brings you to Madame Queenie?"

June almost said something about an alcoholic fugue state that had sent her one year into a homeless future but decided that would just complicate things.

"I didn't come over here to have my fortune read," June said. "Or to learn about my destiny."

"No?" Madame Queenie said with a small smile. "Then why did you come over?"

She started to explain that she'd just come over to find out today's date and that she couldn't afford the five dollars, but admitting that she was broke and unemployed made her feel ashamed and embarrassed. The truth was she wished she had more money so she could afford to give five dollars to Madame Queenie. Not because she thought the psychic could tell June her destiny. She just wanted someone to give her some good news. Or at least something she could look forward to, even if it was just a hot meal or a warm bed.

"You just want to hear good news," Madame Queenie said.

June stared at Madame Queenie, who smiled back. Maybe it was a lucky guess. Or maybe it was something the psychic said to everyone. But the possibility that Madame Queenie might have actually read her thoughts was enough to convince June to reconsider the idea of parting with five dollars. It wasn't the most practical or sensible thing to do, but as June's mother would say, *When did that ever stop you?*

Before she could talk herself into changing her mind, June reached into her backpack and removed her wallet, took out a five-dollar bill, and handed over the money, which Madame Queenie tucked between her breasts.

"So how does this work?" June asked, feeling more than a bit foolish.

"Please," Madame Queenie said. "Place hands on table, palms up."

June placed both of her hands on the table as instructed. Madame Queenie lifted June's hands lightly and studied them for several moments.

"I see great mystery for you," Madame Queenie finally said.

"A mystery?" June asked, feeling more foolish by the second. "What kind of mystery?"

"Is difficult to say. That is why is mystery." Madame Queenie closed her eyes while continuing to hold June's hands. "But I sense it involves unexpected journey."

"An unexpected journey?" June tried to maintain a façade of interest but this was already turning out to be a waste of money. "Where am I going?"

Madame Queenie didn't respond right away, which June figured was because she was trying to come up with some exotic or distant location like Jamaica or Paris or maybe the Lost City of Atlantis.

"You are not going anywhere," Madame Queenie said, her eyes still closed. "Is journey you are already on."

That might have been a lucky guess, but it was more likely a generalization about a personal journey of self-discovery.

"How is this journey related to my destiny?" June asked.

"I see building," Madame Queenie said.

"What kind of a building?"

Madame Queenie shook her head. "I do not know. But I sense someone is waiting for you."

In spite of her skepticism, June found herself intrigued by the psychic's words.

"You must go there." Madame Queenie opened her eyes and let go of June's hands. "Is only way to fix what is broken."

"Is that where I'll find my destiny?"

"You cannot find destiny," Madame Queenie said. "Destiny finds you."

"Okay," June said. "So where is this building?"

Madame Queenie placed her hands on the crystal ball and

closed her eyes, appearing to go into a brief trance. "I see numbers."

"What numbers?"

"Please not to interrupt." Madame Queenie's lips moved in some sort of silent mantra. "Fifty-four."

"Fifty-four?" June said. "What is that supposed to mean?"

The psychic didn't answer but continued her silent mantra, her eyes moving back and forth beneath her eyelids.

"Fifteen," Madame Queenie said.

"Wait," June said. "Are these lottery numbers?"

"I see sign," Madame Queenie said.

June nearly burst out laughing. If this wasn't some kind of elaborate carny trick, then she was the Queen of France.

"A sign?" June tried her best not to sound skeptical and annoyed. "What kind of sign."

"A street sign," Madame Queenie said. Ten seconds passed before she continued. "G."

"G?" June said. "As in G Street?"

"Street name begins with G," Madame Queenie said.

"Well that narrows it down," June said, no longer hiding her exasperation.

Madame Queenie opened her eyes. "You do not believe Madame Queenie?"

"I believe you're very convincing," June said. "And I believe I just gave you five dollars to tell me some mumbo jumbo about mysteries and journeys and buildings that don't exist."

"Madame Queenie does not deal in mumbo jumbo."

"So you have a street name for me?" June asked. "Or do I need to search every street in Sarasota that starts with a G?"

"I have name," Madame Queenie said, then gave a little smile. "But maybe you have five more dollars?"

"I already gave you five dollars more than I can afford," June said. "So I think I'm going to go get something to eat and then try to figure out where I'm going to sleep tonight so I don't have to book another room at The Hotel Stench."

"I do not understand."

"You're not supposed to." June stood up. "Thanks for the life lesson."

June walked away and across the shopping center parking lot, more annoyed with herself for wasting five dollars on Madame Queenie's scam than she was with the psychic for taking advantage of her. A fool and her money, she thought.

Well, at least that's five less dollars you can spend on booze.

"Shut up, Mom."

June went into Save-A-Lot and bought a banana, two bottles of water, a raisin bagel, a pack of granola bars, and some string cheese. Then she sat down outside on a bench and ate her breakfast, which consisted of the bagel, the banana, and one of the granola bars. She didn't know how long it had been since she'd eaten a regular meal, but her breakfast tasted like a gourmet meal at a four-star resort.

While eating her breakfast, June looked over at the corner where Madame Queenie had set her trap and saw that the psychic had apparently packed up and moved on to another location.

"Serves me right." June finished off the banana and wiped her mouth with the back of her sleeve. "It looks like I was the sucker born during that particular minute."

She waited for her mother's voice to agree, or to disparage her in some manner, but her mother didn't have anything to add.

June finished her breakfast, then took the composition book out of her backpack, along with one of the pens, and opened the book to the first blank page.

"Excuse me?" she asked a young bearded man in a black tank top and blue jeans who approached the Save-A-Lot entrance. "What's the date today?"

"April 24," the man said.

"1998 right?"

The man looked at her as if she'd asked him if he had a heart and a pair of lungs. "Yeah."

"Thank you," June said and started writing:

April 24, 1998

Woke up on a stained mattress this morning in a boarded up hovel replete with human waste and used condoms without any idea of how I'd gotten there. Mom would be proud. She still talks to me in my head. Or at me. We don't really have what you would call conversations.

I'm apparently homeless. All I have left are the clothes I'm wearing, a half-empty bottle of Johnnie Walker Red (or half-full if I want to take the positive point of view), and a backpack of simple bare necessities (although as the song goes, I can't say I've forgotten about my worries and my strife).

I ate breakfast outside of a Save-A-Lot in the Colonial Village Shopping Center. This was after getting hustled by a psychic named Madame Queenie who told me I was on a journey of mystery and needed to go to some building on a street that started with the letter G where someone was waiting to help me fix my broken destiny. The cost of gullibility these days is $5. Am now in search of a shower. Nothing else matters. Any answers I'm searching for will have to wait.

She was about to put the cap back on her pen, then decided to honor the version of herself who had experienced the past year.

So it goes.

June closed the composition book then shoved the book, pen, and the rest of her groceries into her backpack. After she slipped her arms through the straps, she bent down to tie her shoes. When she stood up, Madame Queenie was standing in front of her holding a folded piece of paper and a five-dollar bill.

"Here," the psychic said, handing the money and the piece of paper to June. "You take."

"Why are you giving me my money back?" June asked.

"Because you need more than I do," Madame Queenie said. "And because you should not be sleeping in this Hotel Stench."

June laughed. She couldn't help herself. "Thank you."

"You must go to address," Madame Queenie said, pointing to the piece of paper in June's hand. "Is very important."

June unfolded the piece of paper and read the address:

5415 Georgia Street

"Why is it so important that I go to this address?" June asked.

"Because is your destiny."

June stared at the psychic, who stared back at her without any trace of humor. "You're serious?"

"I am always serious," Madame Queenie said without a trace of a smile. "And if you tell anyone I gave you money back, I will put curse on you."

With that, Madame Queenie turned and walked across the parking lot to her car, climbed in behind the steering wheel, and drove off without looking back. It wasn't until she was gone that June thought to ask her for a ride.

That's my June. Always a day late and a dollar short.

"Put a sock in it, Mom," June said.

She folded up the piece of paper and stuck it in her front pocket, then walked out of the shopping center, continuing south until she reached Fruitville Road, where she walked west along the sidewalk with her thumb out, hoping someone would give her a lift to Lido Beach so she could take a shower. After that, maybe she'd find someone to give her a ride to 5415 Georgia Street.

June sat on the beach at Siesta Key, her bare feet dug into the white sand that was like fine sugar, the turquoise water as clear as the sky growing darker by the minute. The sun would be setting in less than an hour, the sky turning orange and gold and peach before the sun vanished beyond the Gulf.

Her trusty backpack lay on the sand next to her, the brand new composition book on top with a pen clipped to the cover, inviting her to write down the memory as she was experiencing it so that she wouldn't leave anything out. But even though she knew that she wouldn't remember the feel of the sand between her toes or the changing colors of the sky, June wanted to soak up as much of the moment as possible, experience it without transcribing it. Her journal entry could wait.

It was five years to the day since she'd made her first journal entry on April 27, 1997. Over those five years, she'd accumulated more than a dozen composition books. She'd become more diligent about writing each day and making the entries as long and as detailed as possible, often including historical events and popular culture. They were a chronicle of her life and the only proof she had that the years she'd lost had ever existed.

But the journals weren't just to help her keep track of the time and the memories that she'd lost. They were part of the process of trying to fix her life and figure out what she needed to do to make the days and the months and the years slow down.

Except the years hadn't slowed down. They had just kept coming, one almost literally right after the other. Ten years ago, she had fallen asleep on April 18, 1992, only to wake up in 1993 to discover that Bill Clinton was President and the world as she had known it had passed her by, taking her memories with it.

For June, it didn't feel like ten years. It felt like ten days. But her life had become a manifestation of that Pink Floyd song about time. So she had run to try to catch up with the sun but it was always sinking before she could reach it, racing around to come up behind her again, over and over, ad infinitum. And tonight was her time travelling anniversary, as she had come to think of it—the night before everything jumped forward and she woke up without any memories of the previous year.

But in spite of her unusual existence, she had grown used to her time travelling, to her strange and frustrating life, and had learned to accept it because to do otherwise would have likely meant that she would have continued her toxic relationship with Johnnie Walker in all of his various colors. So instead, she had accepted what was happening to her and tried to deal with it as best as she could. And by taking steps to fix the parts of her life that needed fixing, starting with her drinking.

She'd come a long way since that April morning in 1998 when she'd woken up jobless and homeless on a dirty mattress in an abandoned hovel that she still thought of as Hotel Stench. After using the public showers at the Lido Beach Resort, she had managed to make herself presentable enough to land a job waiting tables at Denny's. It helped that she had good genes and the manager interviewing her was a man about her age. That was something that had worked to June's advantage throughout her life. Men were always more willing than women to give her a chance, regardless of their age. Probably because men always thought there was a chance they might get laid.

She'd found a room at a halfway house near the Denny's and, other than attending AA meetings and picking up groceries, she did nothing but go from her room to work and back again for nearly six months. That was about the only way she figured she could stay out of trouble. After another year and a half, she'd been promoted to shift manager, which allowed her to move into her own studio apartment. She'd even bought a car. Not a new car but it had four tires and less than 100,000 miles and it hadn't broken down on her. Not yet, anyway.

More important than the car of the job or the apartment was the fact that she'd been sober for the past four years. Or for most of them. She'd had a few setbacks, the last one at the turn of the new millennium when everyone thought the world might implode due to something called Y2K. But none of her setbacks ended up with her broke and homeless in a condemned house.

According to her journals, she'd been on the proverbial wagon since January 2, 2000, which put her just shy of twenty-nine months from the date of her last sip of booze.

But it hadn't been easy journey to get to this point. Even now, as she watched the sun slide closer to the horizon, the sky turning into a celebration of colors, June could feel the ghost of a bottle in her hand. But the ghost was more of a reminder of who she used to be rather than a memory that haunted her. Of course, none of her memories haunted her anymore. They just existed on the pages of her journals.

Once the sun had set and June had returned to her apartment, she commemorated her ten-year anniversary and the impending loss of her memories by lighting a vanilla candle and cracking open a bottle of Martinelli's Sparkling Apple Cider, a ritual she'd started three years earlier. She found it helped to mark the occasion by striking a positive note rather than a sour one. She'd even bought a plastic champagne glass to make things more festive.

"To the memory of my memories," she said, toasting the candle and downing half of her glass.

After she finished off the last of the Martinelli's, June wrote down the memory of the evening in her journal, trying to recall as many details as possible in the hopes that it might help her future self to remember. Then she meditated for twenty minutes before she blew out her candle and crawled into bed a few minutes shy of midnight.

When she drifted off to sleep, her last waking thoughts were of the sand between her toes and the peach-colored sky before the sun vanished beyond the blue waters of the Gulf.

June woke up to the early morning sunlight pouring through the windows on the east side of her studio apartment, coming in at just the right angle so that she could see beams of light cutting through the air. Several of the more religious members of her AA group might attribute the phenomenon to God or some sort of heavenly hocus pocus, but June knew it was just the sunlight bouncing off the dust particles, which meant it was time to clean her apartment.

June sat up in bed with a start, her eyes wide, looking around the room as if she'd never seen it before. But she had lived in the same place, alone, for the past three years and recognized every aspect of it. So it wasn't that anything was unfamiliar or out of place. Just the opposite. Everything was where it should have been. Or at least where it had been last night when she had toasted her memories. She could remember the scent of the vanilla candle filling the room and the taste of Martinelli's, sharp and sweet on her tongue. And that wasn't something she had ever woken up remembering.

She grabbed her composition book and opened it to her last journal entry. This was part of her annual ritual, the only days she remembered from each of the years she'd missed: reading her journals so that she could catch up on the twelve-month gap where her memories should have been. But she didn't need to read the description of the peach-colored sunset or the cool, white, powdery sand between her toes to remember the sense of peace she'd felt sitting on the beach and watching the sunset.

June let out a single burst of laughter and then covered her mouth, as if letting the laughter out would somehow break the spell and her memories would spill out along with her laughter and she wouldn't be able to put them back. But she couldn't stop from laughing.

As her smile widened and the laughter spilled out between her fingers, June watched the dust swirl in the beams of sunlight and thought back to her memories of yesterday morning, and then to the day before that, and then to the day before that, going in reverse day by day, week by week, and month by month.

She remembered cheering on the U.S. athletes during the Winter Olympics and ringing in the New Year with Dick Clark. She remembered crying when George Harrison died from lung cancer and watching in horror as the airplanes crashed into the World Trade Center. She remembered spending the Fourth of July at a co-worker's home on Longboat Key and celebrating her forty-forth birthday at the Salvador Dalí Museum in St. Petersburg. She remembered everything that had happened over the past twelve months until she finally reached April 27, 2001, her last anniversary, when she had woken up in this very same apartment without any memories from the previous year.

When June took her hand away from her mouth, the smile and laughter had dried up and tears were spilling down her cheeks. She didn't know when she'd started crying. It was at some point after the New Year but before September 11. It might have been during Halloween when she'd dressed up as Fiona from *Shrek*. Or maybe it was in August when she'd encountered the stray cat who had reminded her of her childhood cat Sam. Or maybe the tears had started right away and she just hadn't noticed them because she'd been too busy reminiscing to focus on what was happening in the present. But it didn't matter when they had started. The tears were here now, and they weren't about to stop.

The tears soon turned to sobs that doubled June over, her face pressed against the comforter, her breath coming in great big hitches, crying so hard that at several points she thought she might pass out. It was as if ten years of joy, sorrow, relief, and grief were pouring out of her, all at the same time. But she welcomed the tears just as she had welcomed the laughter.

Once the sobs abated and the tears dried up, June sat up and took several deep breaths as she thought about what she should do. The obvious answer was to celebrate. Maybe spend the day on Longboat Key. Or take a drive up to St. Pete. Or get out on a boat and go parasailing, something fun and momentous to mark the occasion.

Instead, she spent the rest of the day in bed reading her journal, starting with the entry from April 27, 2001 and working her way forward. Although she'd spent each of her past four anniversaries doing the exact same thing, this time instead of filling in the blanks of her life, she wanted to verify that what she remembered had actually happened. She wanted to know, without any doubts, that her time travelling had finally come to an end.

⌚ ⌚ ⌚

June drove south along Route 1, palm trees and mangroves and lush Florida vegetation growing wild along either side of the four-lane highway, the greenery broken up by the occasional billboard or strip mall or fast food restaurant. The sky above remained gray and bleak, the rain having made good on its threat earlier, leaving the highway wet and treacherous and reminding June that she needed to get replacement blades for her windshield wipers. At least she had new tires so she didn't have to worry about hydroplaning and sliding across the grassy median into oncoming traffic.

That's a pleasant thought. Maybe you can conjure up a category five hurricane while you're at it.

The voice was June's rather than her mother's, and had been for most of the past two years, offering words of support and encouragement more often than not, which was a refreshing respite from her mother's constant rebukes and criticisms. But that didn't prevent June from calling herself out when she needed to.

While it wasn't hurricane season, the inclement weather had caused June to question the wisdom of what she was doing and where she was going. She wasn't big on portents or harbingers of doom, but a cheery blue sky with some fluffy white clouds and plenty of warm sunshine would have helped to set a better mood than the gloomy skies and foul weather that had followed her for most of the past ninety minutes.

The weather gods are trying to tell you something, June. You should listen to them and turn around, go back to your original plan.

June's original plan had been to drive north along the Gulf Coast and then eventually head west until she ended up in New Orleans, like she'd planned to do more than twenty-two years ago. She still couldn't fathom the idea that she'd lived in Sarasota for half of her life. It didn't seem possible. The fact that she'd wasted most of that time at the bottom of a bottle was the main driving force behind her decision to go to New Orleans. She wanted to follow some of her dreams and see where they led rather than imagining what might have happened and wishing she'd done something more with her life.

Considering her history and relationship with alcohol, going to a city that was renowned for drinking and partying probably wasn't the best idea. But after living in Sarasota for more than two decades, June had decided she needed a change of scenery.

Two weeks after waking up to discover that her time travelling had stopped and after making it halfway through May without her memories fading or suddenly disappearing, June had given notice at work and to her landlord. A little over two weeks later, and two days before her forty-fifth birthday, June packed up what few personal possessions she had, filled her gas tank, and drove out of Sarasota without so much as a tearful goodbye.

She headed out of town on Highway 41 before taking the Skyway Bridge over Tampa Bay into St. Pete. From there she planned to follow Highway 19 north to Highway 98, which would take her nearly all the way to Tallahassee before turning east along the coast of the Panhandle to Pensacola, where she would meet up with Interstate 10 and take that the rest of the way to New Orleans. That had been the plan.

She'd made it as far as Clearwater before she'd turned off of Highway 19 and headed east on State Road 60. It had almost been a subconscious decision, an action she'd taken without thinking. But somewhere in the back of June's mind, she'd known all along that this was where she needed to go even if she didn't want to go there.

It'll be fine. You might not believe it right now, but this was the right decision. You can do this.

A little over four hours after leaving Sarasota, she reached Vero Beach and was heading south on Route 1. She could have taken the Florida Turnpike or Interstate 95 to shorten the drive, but as much as she knew this was what she needed to do, she wasn't in any hurry to get there.

As she drove past St. Lucie Village, which you would miss if you blinked, June kept glancing to her left. She hadn't been back to the east coast of Florida in more than two decades and she'd forgotten how much she used to love to go out to the Jetty Park and stare out across the Atlantic, imagining herself living in Morocco or Portugal or one of the other foreign and exotic countries on the other side of the ocean. But that's all she'd ever done: imagined it. She'd never been across the Atlantic, or even out of the state of Florida.

When June pulled into Fort Pierce just after three in the afternoon, she had an overwhelming urge to keep heading south until she reached Key West. Maybe from there she could catch a flight or charter a boat to The Bahamas as an alternative to New Orleans. Instead, she turned off Route 1 on to Georgia Avenue and drove for thirteen blocks before she pulled on to the shoulder of the road by the white mailbox with the numbers 1554 glued on one side.

June reached over to the passenger seat and picked up her tattered and taped together copy of *Slaughterhouse-Five*. Other than the journals, most of the personal possessions June had owned or acquired since she'd started time traveling had been lost, stolen, or sold. But the one other item she'd held on to was the copy of *Slaughterhouse-Five* she had bought during her short stint at Barnes & Noble. Every now and then, she would walk past a bookstore and think about going inside and buying a new copy, but she couldn't bring herself to part with the tattered book she'd carried around with her for the past five years. She thought of it as a kind of talisman that had helped her to find her way. She couldn't replace it with another copy any more than she could turn in her liver for a new one.

Tucked inside the cover of the book was a folded piece of paper. June removed the piece of paper, then unfolded it and stared at the address that Madame Queenie had given to her a little over four years ago.

5415 Georgia Street

After receiving the address from Madame Queenie, it hadn't taken June long to determine that Georgia Street in Sarasota was just a half block of auto repair shops with addresses that started at 8400, not at 5400. And while there was a Georgia Drive with a dozen or so homes lining the horseshoe shaped street, none of them were a match.

She'd checked Siesta and Longboat Key, and had gone as far south as Venice and as far north as Bradenton, but she hadn't found her destiny or a building where anyone waited for her. So June had given up and stopped looking for the address because she figured it was just a red herring or a snipe hunt. Or else because Madame Queenie had given her the wrong street name or address.

It took June nearly two years to realize that Madame Queenie had flipped the numbers of the address. And that Georgia Street was Georgia Avenue.

1554 Georgia Avenue was a single story house, painted baby blue, with a narrow, concrete sidewalk that led past a couple of twenty foot palm trees and a lawn that was more dirt than grass.

The sidewalk ended at a three-step concrete stoop. At the top of the stoop was the entrance to a screened in porch. Several neglected shrubs grew on either side of the stoop, while a forty-foot oak tree and a smaller one behind it loomed over the house.

You must go there. Is only way to fix what is broken.

June stared at the house from the safety of her car, remembering Madame Queenie's words, thinking she could still change her mind as long as she didn't turn off the engine. But she didn't really have a choice. This was part of what she needed to do to fix her life. If she gave up on this now, none of the other work she'd done over the past four years would matter.

She pulled up the sleeve on her left arm to reveal the black Celtic knot tattoo on her bicep, the word FAITH spelled out inside the knot on her pale skin. Then she folded up the piece of paper, returned it to the pages of *Slaughterhouse-Five*, turned off the engine, and stepped out of the car into the wet afternoon heat. After a few more moments of hesitation, she took a deep breath, wished herself luck, then walked along the sidewalk and up the three steps, where she hesitated before she opened the screen door and stepped on to the porch. It was barely two strides to the front door but to June it might as well have been two miles. Or two hundred miles. Or however many miles was the equivalent of twenty-seven years.

She took another deep breath, took two steps across the porch and across all of those lost years, and knocked on the front door. Nearly a minute passed without an answer. June was about to knock again when the front door opened.

For several moments, no one said a word. The two just stared at each other in the thick Florida humidity until June finally found her voice.

"Hi Mom."

The Curse of the Amazing Colossal Thing from Outer Space

Reeb takes a deep drag on the half-smoked joint, the cherry glowing bright orange in the waning twilight like our own little personal sun, then he passes the joint to me and exhales. For a moment, the cloud of smoke lingers above us, as if Reeb's soul has escaped the confines of his body for a breath of fresh air. I wouldn't blame it. If I were Reeb's soul, I'd sure as hell want to step out every now and then, maybe take a bubble bath. Then the smoke drifts away, leaving Reeb a husk of human detritus without a soul.

Or maybe that's just the pot talking.

"You ever think about the end of the world?" Reeb asks, his eyes fixed on the western sky.

Reeb and I are sitting on a couple of sun-bleached lawn chairs in the bed of my Dodge truck, sharing a joint and a twelve-pack of Olympia and watching the stars come out. We do this every now and then: park off-road a couple miles north of Route 95 outside of Tonopah, hoping to catch sight of a UFO or a flying saucer while avoiding the crowds that flock to the Extraterrestrial Highway around Rachel and Area 51. We've never seen anything other than a few shooting stars and a couple of jackrabbits humping, but we don't really care. The pot and the beer are the main attractions.

"Think about it how?" I say, and take a hit.

Reeb finishes off his beer. "Like what you would do if it happened."

I empty my lungs in little puffs of smoke that drift up toward the indigo sky littered with the discarded light from a million dead stars. Or maybe it's a billion. It's hard to keep count. I pass the joint back to Reeb. "I hadn't really given it much thought. Why?"

"Just something that seemed worth thinking about," Reeb says, one hand digging around in the ice chest, his gaze fixed on a point in the sky about three beer cans above the glowing horizon.

Reeb doesn't usually think anything's worth thinking about unless it's beer, pot, or pussy, so I follow his gaze until I see a star so bright it has to be a planet. Except the longer I look, the brighter it grows.

"Is that a satellite?" I say.

Reeb shakes his head. "Don't think so."

We sit in silence and watch it grow bigger, now nearly twice as bright as any other star in the sky, and it's definitely descending.

"It looks like it's coming right for us," I say.

"Yep," Reeb says, matter-of-fact, like it's nothing more than a tumbleweed.

I don't know if it's the pot, the beer, or Reeb's contagious nonchalance, but I don't feel any sense of urgency to get out of the way.

"Hey Mur?"

"Yeah," I say as the celestial object races toward us, dark and red, like a blood moon plummeting toward the earth.

I expect Reeb to give some kind of sentimental affirmation of our friendship. Or maybe a confession, like he killed someone or he was gay. Then he says, "We're almost out of beer."

Five seconds later the meteor roars past about twenty stories up and directly overhead—the heat blasting us like someone opened the door to a cosmic furnace. We stand up in unison and turn to watch the red ball of fire slam into the earth about a mile away, burrowing through the desert for maybe another quarter mile before finally coming to a stop.

We both turn to look at each other, neither one of us able to find the words to describe what we just witnessed.

"That was fucking awesome!" Reeb says.

I stand corrected. *Fucking awesome* pretty much captures the moment, so I just nod my silent agreement.

"Let's go check it out!" Reeb says, like a kid on Christmas morning.

Reeb climbs behind the wheel of my truck, so I give him my keys and we drive east to the impact point, the Dodge's brights lighting up the way. When we get there we find the earth scorched by a black scar a good ten feet wide and four feet deep that runs more than a quarter mile through the dirt and sagebrush, while several cactus lay broken and scattered to the sides like the bodies of dead soldiers.

Along the edges of the scar, strange formations have sprouted up. Once we get out of the truck we realize they're crystallized glass sculptures, each one standing about three feet high on a single two-inch thick column and topped by what looks like half a dozen or so withered fronds. In the wash of the truck's headlights, they look like miniature, frozen, un-watered palm trees lining the dead road to an apocalyptic oasis.

Or maybe I'm just really stoned.

"It's meteor art," Reeb says, running an appreciative hand along one of the formations like he's caressing a woman's thigh.

"*Meteorite* art," I say. "A meteor is what it's called before it hits the earth."

"Meteor art sounds better," Reeb says. "Hey, do you think that's copyrighted?"

Reeb and I walk along the edge of the scar until we reach the meteorite's final resting spot, which is a couple of feet below us beneath a cactus tree with a dozen spires that serve as the crater's headstone.

"That what a meteorite's supposed to look like?" Reeb asks.

I shake my head. "I don't think so."

Instead of an irregular shaped piece of space debris, the meteorite is smooth and white and appears perfectly round like a giant, luminous cue ball. Almost as if the moon had been sanded, buffed, and polished to a high shine before being loaded into a cannon and fired at the earth. Except the moon is sitting three-quarters full just above the mountains in the east.

"What do you think it is?" Reeb takes out the joint and sparks it back up.

I shrug. "Your guess is as good as mine."

We stare down at the round, white, glowing orb half-buried in the scorched desert as we pass the joint back and forth. Sobering up was probably the smarter course of action, but when you encounter a giant cue ball from outer space, getting stoned seems like the thing to do.

As I take a drag on the joint, something cracks and hisses and I jump away from the edge of the scar, half-expecting the cue ball to split open and some alien creature to come clambering out. Then I realize it's just Reeb opening the last can of Oly.

"Hey, how hot do you think that thing is?" Reeb asks.

While it's not smoking or giving off any steam, it did create a quarter-mile long skid mark of charred desert.

"Probably pretty hot," I say.

Reeb takes a drink of his beer, then he gets this raised-eyebrow, crooked-grin expression he always gets whenever he comes up with an idea.

"What?" I say.

Still wearing his crooked grin, Reeb walks around the edge of the crater until he reaches the cactus tree.

"What are you doing?" I ask.

"I want to see how hot it is." He leans forward with one outstretched hand and tips the can of Oly until some beer trickles out and drops into the crater, landing on the scorched earth a foot from the meteorite.

"Shit, hold on," Reeb says, as if I'm waiting on him for something.

He tests one of the spires of cactus for support, muttering

"ouch" three times in succession before he finally takes off his sweatshirt and wraps it around his hand. Then he leans out again, pouring the beer into the crater.

As soon as the beer hits the cue ball, the liquid crystallizes and turns to glass, shooting up toward the beer can. Just before the crystalized beer reaches his hand, Reeb lets go of the can and the column of glass flares out at the top like a frozen Fourth of July fireworks display.

"Holy shit!" Reeb says.

While the single column of frozen beer is less than half the width of the other glass sculptures, the top reminds me of the dead palm trees that line the quarter mile of scorched desert. Except rather than withered palm fronds, these look like tentacles.

Off to the south, more than half a dozen sets of headlights appear in the growing darkness headed our way. Maybe lookie-loos. Maybe military. Maybe men in black. Whoever they are, they're closing fast.

"Reeb, we've got company."

"Just a second," he says and unzips his pants.

"What the fuck are you doing?"

"Taking a piss," he says with a drunken grin.

I glance down at the white glowing orb and the frozen beer sculpture with the tentacles, then I glance back along the blackened desert at all of the other sculptures lining the scar.

"Hey Reeb, I don't think that's a good idea."

"Why not?"

Reeb doesn't give me a chance to elaborate before he releases his bladder.

The urine hits the giant cue ball and immediately crystallizes at the point of impact, turning to glass as it races back along the stream of urine toward Reeb. I know without him saying so that he thinks he can shut off the stream before the frozen urine reaches him, but good timing has never been Reeb's strong suit.

Reeb's playful expression turns to wide-eyed shock as the

crystallized urine shoots into his urethra. He opens his mouth to scream but before any sound comes out, he turns to glass and freezes, one hand still holding his pecker like a pornographic Greek statue. Pan caught in a moment of orgiastic self-gratification. Dionysus giving a golden shower.

"Holy shit," I say, taking a tentative step toward him. "Reeb? Hey Reeb?"

He doesn't respond and I don't know what to do, but when your best friend turns into a statue after crystallized urine shoots into his pecker through his pee hole, you have to at least make an effort.

I take a couple more steps forward, not all that sure I want to get any closer, just in case what happened to Reeb is contagious. The thought of jumping into my truck and getting the hell out of there waves its hands in my face, trying to get my attention, but I can't just abandon Reeb. We've known each other since we were kids. He's my best friend. Plus he has the keys to the Dodge in his front pocket.

"Reeb, you in there?"

The approaching headlights are less than half a mile away. From the silhouettes of the vehicles racing along behind the headlights, I'm pretty sure they're not lookie-loos. Even if I could make a break for it I wouldn't get far before they caught up to me, so I take one last hit on the joint and toss it into the crater before popping a breath mint.

A few moments later, a dozen military vehicles arrive in a cloud of dust and humorless efficiency. Barricades are set up and a perimeter established with guards carrying intimidating guns. Floodlights are turned on to light up the impact point, while half a dozen figures in white decontamination suits and blue particle masks and black rubber elbow gloves climb down into the scar and start collecting samples.

Three uniformed figures approach, two of them armed and flanking the third, who doesn't look happy to see me. I get the feeling he never looks happy to see anyone.

"What happened here?" he says, confrontational and accusatory, like all of this is somehow my fault.

I used to get the same kind of attitude from my mom.

It seems pretty obvious what happened here, but it's probably not a good idea to point that out to Colonel Dickhead, so I keep it simple.

"We were just drinking some beer and checking out the meteorite," I say, motioning toward Reeb's frozen figure while trying to sound sober. "Then my friend pissed on it and turned into a glass sculpture."

"How long ago was this?" Colonel Dickhead asks.

"A few minutes ago," I say.

He turns to one of the men in decontamination suits who are standing at the top of the crater near Reeb. "Disconnect him."

"Are you sure, Colonel?" the man says from behind his blue heavy-duty particle mask.

"Don't question me," the colonel says. "Just do it."

"Yes sir." The man in the decontamination suit walks up to Reeb, then takes out a small hammer and what looks like a two-foot long chisel, which he places on the frozen stream of urine a couple of inches from the end of Reeb's dong. He gives the chisel a single whack and the frozen stream of urine shatters and falls into the crater, taking an inch of Reeb's manhood along with it.

"Man, that's not cool," I say.

Colonel Dickhead gives me a cold, appraising glance, then turns to his minions. "Get him out of here."

"Hey," I shout as the two guards escort me away from the crater. "Aren't you going to do anything to help him?"

Colonel Dickhead doesn't respond but just turns his back on me.

I glance at Reeb, his mouth open in an un-birthed scream and his hand holding what's left of his pecker. For a second I think I see his face twitch, like a wink or a muscle spasm, but then it's gone. Or maybe it was just my imagination.

When we reach the military truck, one of my two escorts pulls out a pair of plastic restraints and zips my wrists together in front of me while the other guard opens the passenger door. Before they can pack me into the passenger seat, there's a loud *crack* from the crater and someone shouts, "Something's happening!"

Colonel Dickhead starts barking out orders as armed guards run toward the crater while the men in decontamination suits run in the opposite direction. My armed escorts and I are nearly a hundred feet behind the crater so I don't see anything at first and I think that this time maybe the crack I heard *was* the giant cue ball splitting open. Then I see movement along the top of the cactus, like a snake curling around one of the spires. When a spotlight turns on the cactus, I realize it's not a snake but a tentacle.

"Stay inside!" one of my escorts shouts before he shoves me into the truck and closes the door, then he runs off toward the crater with his buddy, their guns drawn.

When authority figures tell me to do something, I usually do the opposite. A lesson I learned from my father. But when the authority figures have large semi-automatic guns, I'm likely to make an exception. Except I can't just leave Reeb out there. I don't know what's going on or what I can do to help him, but I have to try.

I grab the handle with my cuffed hands and open the door. Lots of voices are shouting, a mixture of authoritative commands and barely controlled panic. More floodlights turn toward Reeb and the cactus, lighting them up like a movie premiere as I step out of the truck and look around for a sharp edge to cut away my wrist restraints.

There's another *crack* and a second tentacle appears, waving in the air beside the cactus. Whatever is coming out of the cue ball must be huge because those tentacles are at least twenty feet long and look like they can do some serious damage. And Reeb is at ground zero.

I'm trying to figure out if I can make it across a hundred feet of desert to Reeb before the tentacles crush him or knock off more of his body parts when I realize the tentacles aren't coming out of the giant cue ball. They're coming out of Reeb, one on either side of him.

I freeze next to the truck and stare at my best friend, struggling to believe what I'm seeing. It doesn't seem possible. Just half an hour ago, the two of us were sitting in the back of my Dodge, watching the sunset and getting stoned. Now I'm under military arrest and Reeb is a glass statue with tentacles sprouting from his arms.

Colonel Dickhead shouts out commands and draws his revolver, which he aims at Reeb, while a dozen soldiers take up positions in a perimeter around my best friend, a few of them wearing what appear to be canisters on their backs.

I can't see Reeb's face and for that I'm thankful, because the next moment the back of his head splits open with another loud crack and a third tentacle slips out, wraps around the base of the cactus tree, rips it out of the ground, and swings it at Colonel Dickhead like a cleanup hitter unloading on a 3-and-0 fastball down the middle of the plate.

Colonel Dickhead flies more than fifty feet in the air before crashing into one of the floodlights, knocking it and the Colonel out of commission, while the other tentacles dispatch half a dozen nearby soldiers with a couple of flicks and snaps.

All of this takes place in a matter of seconds.

Gunfire erupts as three more tentacles sprout out of what remains of Reeb and joins the others, silencing the guns and extinguishing another floodlight. The tentacle with the cactus swings again, this time connecting with a trio of soldiers wearing canisters. One of the soldiers depresses his trigger before impact and flies through the air like a human comet, a trail of fire tracing his path before he lands at the edge of the barricade and goes up in a fiery *whump*.

Another soldier stands in a jeep behind a mounted machine gun and starts firing. One of the tentacles whips out, grabs hold of the jeep, and flings it into the air in a single motion. The jeep flies into the night sky, the soldier screaming as he tumbles out of the vehicle and plummets to his death, landing head first twenty feet away from me with an audible *snap*. When I look up, the jeep is coming right at me.

I run and dive to the ground an instant before the jeep slams into the truck, metal and glass crunching and exploding behind me. When I get to my feet, there's only one remaining floodlight and it's hard for me to see what's happening, just the occasional highlighted tentacle swinging through the air and the silhouettes of the other tentacles wreaking havoc.

A round of gunfire erupts, then another, but it's less like a counter attack and more like the death throes of the last un-popped kernels of Jiffy Pop popcorn. Another flamethrower shoots out a jet of flame and gets snuffed out, along with the last remaining floodlight.

Somewhere in the darkness, someone is screaming for Jesus.

When the attack finally comes to and end less than a minute after it began, the only light remaining other than the three-quarter moon is the high beams of my Dodge lighting up the crater where half a dozen tentacles the size of trees wave back and forth where Reeb used to be.

An alarm goes off in my head, flashing red, telling me to run but I just stand there, waiting to see what happens next. I've never been good at probability and statistics, but I figure when you're staring at a giant tentacled creature from another planet that just wiped out at least three dozen armed military troops in less than a minute, drawing attention to yourself isn't the best way to improve your chances of survival.

The tentacles continue to wave back and forth in the air until one of them stops and points west. Two of the others follow suit, almost as if they're communicating with one another. A fourth tentacle disappears from view and returns a moment later with the giant cue ball held protectively in its grasp.

When the creature starts moving, I expect it to glide along the desert like some kind of terrestrial squid or octopus. Instead, it walks away on some form of appendages. Not exactly legs, but more like a pair of enormous, flexible tubes. From where I'm standing, the creature appears to be at least three stories tall.

It's hard to believe something that big came out of Reeb.

Once the creature is far enough away, I walk over to the edge of the crater and, in the wash of the headlights from my truck, I look for any remaining signs of Reeb, hoping that he's somehow still alive; hoping that I'll find him in a pool of extraterrestrial ectoplasm or cosmic afterbirth. But all I find is a bunch of shattered glass, one crystallized foot, and the frozen, disembodied inch of Reeb's dong.

"I told you it wasn't a good idea," I say.

I walk back to my truck and use the edge of the front bumper to cut away my wrist restraints, then I reach into the ice chest for a beer until I remember that Reeb drank the last one. He also had the rest of the pot in his back pocket. Hopefully one of the military trucks still has the keys in the ignition or else I'm going to have a long, sober walk back home.

Nearly a mile away and following the same line as the extraterrestrial skid mark, the silhouette of the creature moves along the desert. Several of its tentacles wave in the air as it heads west toward the Monte Cristo Mountains, retracing the path the giant cue ball took when it entered our atmosphere as if following some kind of invisible, cosmic trail of breadcrumbs. Either that or it's on its way to meet a spaceship that will take it back home.

"Water," a voice says from behind me.

I turn and see one of the men in the white decontamination suits standing on the other side of the crater, his suit torn and his particle mask gone, though he's still wearing one of the black elbow gloves.

"Sorry," I say. "I don't have any water. And Reeb drank the last beer."

"That's where it's headed," he says. "It's looking for water. For the orb."

"For the orb?" I say. "You mean the giant cue ball?"

He nods. "That's how it reproduces."

"No shit," I say.

I look back at the creature and decide if that's the case, it might be a good idea for me to go as far and as fast as possible in the opposite direction. After all, if the orb can create just one of those things from a single stream of Reeb's urine, imagine how many it can create with a swimming pool. Or a lake. Or an ocean.

"Hey," I say to the guy in the decontamination suit. "This isn't the end of the world, is it?"

He looks at me, then turns to follow the path of the creature. "It might be."

"That's a bummer."

I guess I should have listened to Reeb and given more thought to what I would do if the world ended. But it's not as if you ever expect your best friend to piss on a meteorite and cause Armageddon.

The sound of a steady *thwup thwup thwup* turns my attention to the sky, where several helicopters approach, searchlights playing across broken vehicles and dead bodies and the empty crater. The guy in the decontamination suit waves his hands over his head and gestures west. The helicopters hesitate a moment, then turn and follow the creature toward the Monte Cristo Mountains, toward Mono Lake and California and the San Francisco Bay Area.

Toward the Pacific Ocean.

All of the Lost
Creatures are Found

Bucky and I stand in the middle of the multi-purpose gymnasium with scores of other soon-to-be sixth graders, all of us milling around as we wait for the John Venn Middle School Job Fair and Orientation to start.

"I don't like this," Bucky says. "This seems too much like being an adult."

"I think that's the point," I say.

More than three-dozen tables are set up around the perimeter of the gym, each table manned by two adults with a laptop connected to a compact printer. An identifying sign hangs on the wall behind each table so no one ends up getting in the wrong line.

While most of the other kids seem excited to be here, laughing and animated and exuding enthusiasm, I'm more somber and silent and oozing dread, my demeanor better suited for a funeral. Or a prison sentencing.

"There must be a thousand kids here." Bucky stands on his toes for a better look, as if that's going to help him with an accurate head count.

"A thousand at least," I say, not needing to stand on my toes.

At five-feet and seven inches, I'm taller than most of the other kids here. If I were a boy that wouldn't be such a big deal. But the fact that I'm a girl makes me that much more of an anomaly. And when you're eleven going on twelve, no one wants to be considered odd or quirky or incongruous. You just want to look like everyone else and not stand out in a crowd.

It's awkward enough having to make the transition from fifth grade to sixth: changing schools, getting thrown into a pool of unfamiliar students, and losing all of the social cachet you built up from kindergarten through fifth grade. Now not only do we have to figure out our new status in an unfamiliar and intimidating social dynamic, but we're also thrust into a stress-filled process that will determine what careers we'll have for the remainder of our lives.

That's a lot of responsibility and upheaval for eleven-year-olds to process. On top of that, puberty has started to kick in and adolescence is right around the proverbial corner. It's a wonder there aren't more emotional breakdowns, temper tantrums, or bomb threats.

"Do you think this building is supposed to hold a thousand kids?" Bucky asks. "I bet that's against fire code."

"Totally against fire code," I say.

There aren't actually a thousand kids in the gym, but Bucky and I are often on the same wavelength when it comes to things like irony and the fine art of exaggeration.

"Do you see anyone from Descartes?" I ask.

Descartes is the elementary school Bucky and I attended. We studied, therefore we learned. At least in theory.

"I see Felicia," Bucky says, pointing. "And Milo."

I spot Felicia and Milo talking with two other students near the Performing Arts table, which seems like wishful thinking. Students from Descartes Elementary aren't known for their acumen in theater, singing, dancing, songwriting, choreography, or stand-up comedy. Most of the students who end up waiting in line for Performing Arts are from schools like Stanislavski Elementary, Baryshnikov Grammar, or Cole Porter Prep, while the majority of the magicians and circus performers come from Harry Houdini Elementary or The Ringling Academy.

After another minute or so, Felicia wanders off into the mass of students. Milo looks around, spots me towering above the crowd, and waves his hand emphatically as if he's experiencing an epileptic seizure before he starts walking our way.

"Here comes Milo," I warn Bucky, who responds with a roll of his eyes.

Bucky finds Milo terminally boring. Like coma-inducing boring. Whenever Milo shows up, Bucky can't stop yawning. He says it's as if Milo absorbs the atmosphere, depriving his brain of oxygen, although I have yet to experience this phenomenon.

"Hey Frannie. Hey Bucky," Milo says. "How's it going?"

"Just waiting for orientation to start," I say.

Bucky stifles a yawn and nods in agreement, his eyelids at half-mast.

"You guys get your test results?" Milo asks.

"Duh," Bucky says. "Of course we got our results."

Before getting promoted from the fifth grade, we all took a test of two hundred questions that ranged from our personal interests to favorite enthusiasms to general knowledge, such as:

1) Who painted the Mona Lisa?
2) List three leisure activities you've engaged in during the past week.
3) What is your favorite color?
4) How many seconds are there in the month of August?
5) If given a choice, would you prefer ice cream, pizza, or Brussels sprouts?

I've decided the question about Brussels sprouts is a red herring. Any eleven-year-old kid who says they would prefer Brussels sprouts to ice cream or pizza is obviously attempting to skew the Bell curve.

The answers are then fed into a computer program, which spits out anywhere from one to ten potential careers for each student. The more potential job options you receive, the more tables you get to visit. Unless all of your career matches fall under one category.

"How many career matches did you get?" Milo asks.

"Five," Bucky says. He only received two potential careers on his test results but he won't tell me what they are.

"I got three matches," Milo says, sounding neither impressed with Bucky's number nor disappointed with his own. "Scientific researcher, accountant, and computer programmer."

While those jobs seem like a good fit for Milo, the thought of spending eight hours a day, five days a week stuck in front of a computer monitor or working with numbers and spreadsheets fills me with a sense of dread. I may as well spend the rest of my life in detention.

"Felicia got eight matches," Milo says.

"Eight?" I say, not concealing my surprise. Even Bucky's half-lidded eyes widen when he hears the number.

I received six potential careers on my results, which is twice the district-wide average. Eight is an anomaly. Nine is the most anyone ever received and that only happened one time, more than a decade ago.

"She says her results show that she might have a career as an actress." Milo looks back and forth between Bucky and me. "Pretty cool, huh?"

As far as I know, no one from Descartes has ever tested positive for a career in the performing arts. We tend to excel more in the areas of philosophy, science, or mathematics. But every now and then, you're bound to get an outlier. I just wish I'd been the outlier rather than Felicia. Although I wouldn't be interested in a career as an actress or a dancer or a stand-up comedienne.

What I'd really like to do is work with animals. Become a veterinarian or a dog trainer. Maybe get a job at a rescue shelter or a wildlife sanctuary. But my test answers didn't indicate a good fit for a career as a veterinary technician or a zoologist. It might have helped had I attended Goodall Grammar or Attenborough Elementary, instead.

My biggest problem with the entire process is how my future is about to be determined based on my answers to two hundred random questions. I mean, who came up with the questions? How do they know they actually work? What if I don't like my assigned career? What if I'd rather do something else? Do I have any other options?

I shared these concerns with my parents, who went through the same process when they were my age. My father was assigned a career in sanitation maintenance while my mother ended up as an administrative assistant. Fortunately, genetics and parental lineage don't factor into the career distribution process.

Still, I wasn't thrilled with my test results when I brought them home. Sullen and pouting is how my mother described me. My fourteen-year-old sister, Lulu, called me a Frannie Frowner, while my father told me to get over it. But if getting over it means having to grow up and have a career in environmental economics, I'd rather be morose.

"Don't worry about it, honey," my mother assured me. "You'll be fine."

I'm glad she feels that way, but how can my mother know I'll be fine? If she'd been assigned a career as a psychic, maybe even as a stockbroker or a meteorologist, then I'd be more willing to believe her. But last I heard, administrative assistants aren't known for their expertise in divination and prognostication.

Sometimes I feel like one of those flyers for lost animals that I see posted all over town, taped to light posts and stapled to telephone poles:

LOST
Eleven-year-old girl
Precocious and disillusioned
Awkward present but bright future
Last seen looking for answers
If found, please call or text...

Whenever I see a flyer for a lost dog or cat, I wonder what happened to them. How they got lost. If they chased after a bird or a mouse or some bright, shiny object and lost track of their surroundings. Or if they ran out the door from their assigned fate in search of a better life.

Not that I'm projecting or anything.

Milo doesn't ask me how many career options I received on my test results or what they are, and I don't offer any answers. Instead, he and Bucky and I just stand there in an awkward silence watching all of the other students until the bell rings, signaling the start of the job fair.

"Well, I guess it's time to get going," Milo says. "See what the future holds." He looks back and forth from Bucky to me with a bright, beaming smile before he makes his way through the crowd of students to stand in line at the Finance & Economics table.

As the other incoming sixth graders make their way to the tables, Bucky and I stand in the middle of the gymnasium and watch the flow of students circling around us. It's as if we're standing in the eye of the storm of growing up, Hurricane Puberty, and once we step out of the calm center we'll get caught up in the spiraling winds of adolescence before we're swept away to adulthood. And I'm not in any hurry to step out into that storm. I want to stay in the eye as long as possible.

As if reading my thoughts, Bucky lets out a big sigh. "Well, I guess we can't put this off any longer."

With that, he steps out into the swirling flow of students and is swept away in a flash flood of future property managers and prospective computer programmers. I lose sight of Bucky until he surfaces at the back of the line for Academics & Philosophy.

That little weasel. He probably got Professor of Philosophy or Dean of Students and didn't even tell me. I bet he's probably even excited about it and was just playing glum to make me feel better.

After a moment of unexpected envy mixed with pangs of jealousy, I turn away from Bucky and survey the other students and tables.

In addition to the tables for Academics & Philosophy, Finance & Economics, and Performing Arts, there's also Health Care & Medicine, Mathematics & Science, Professional Athletics, Real Estate & Property Management, and Computer Sciences, among others. I take out my test results and look them over, hoping they've magically changed and I'll have the chance to become a veterinarian or a zookeeper or maybe even a marine biologist. But my career choices are the same as before. So I fold up the piece of paper, stuff it back into my pocket, and let out my own sigh before I walk toward my first and only table: Mathematics & Science.

The Mathematics & Science table encompasses everything from natural to social to applied sciences, along with careers in statistics, stock market analysis, engineering, and teaching—which pretty much covers all six of my computer-generated career options: observational astronomer, environmental economist, market research analyst, mathematical logician, sports statistician, and high school calculus teacher.

I still don't understand how I ended up being matched with these careers from answering questions about my favorite television programs and how often each day I think about sports, but apparently the selection method is a proven process, even if each middle school uses its own method.

At John Venn Middle School, career matches are formulated using logical relationships between overlapping test answers and general interests, while Hermann Rorschach Middle School uses a process that involves analytical interpretation and complex algorithms. I don't know if one or the other process produces more accurate results, but I didn't have a choice as to which middle school I want to attend so the point is kind of moot.

Because it covers so many different careers, the line for the Mathematics & Science table is one of the longest, so it's going to take a while until I get to talk to someone about my future. On the bright side, at least I don't have to get back in another line.

None of the other kids in line attempt to engage in idle chitchat or even make eye contact with me or with anyone else. Instead, they're all business, staring straight ahead while occasionally leaning to one side or the other to see what's taking so long.

While Mathematics & Science has one of the longest lines, the shortest line belongs to the Celebrity & Glamour table at the head of the room. These are the jobs and careers most every kid dreams about: professional athlete, movie star, Broadway actor, best-selling author, supermodel, fashion designer, celebrity chef, talk show host, world-renowned artist, pop singer, and rock star, among others. The Golden Ticket table is what the kids call it.

I've never dreamed of becoming a movie star or a pop singer or a celebrity chef. Ever since I can remember, my dreams have involved helping animals and taking care of them. Just the thought of spending all day long with animals makes me happy, so a couple of weekends a month I volunteer at the SPCA to socialize stray dogs and cats who are waiting to find new homes. While I know someone will eventually adopt them, I still feel sorry for all of the animals that got lost or abandoned somewhere along the way.

All the way on the other side of the gym from the Golden Ticket table are three tables that fall on the opposite end of the career spectrum: Retail Sales & Food Service, Administrative & Office, and Customer Service & Janitorial.

No kid dreams about growing up to be a plumber or a janitor or an assembly line supervisor. And the idea of making a living as a shoe store salesperson or a coffeehouse barista never enters our minds. But the five most common jobs in the country are:

1) Retail salesperson
2) Cashier
3) Waiter / waitress
4) Office clerk / secretary
5) Customer service

While most of the students at the job fair don't start out standing in line for a career in retail sales, customer service, or office admin, that's where the majority of them will end up—even if they went to Descartes Elementary or Isaac Newton Academy. It's one of the truths of growing up that adults don't tell you: although many kids dream about becoming an all-star athlete or an award-winning actor, the odds are they'll end up working in the food service industry or answering phones for technical support.

My parents didn't tell me about any of this because that would be like telling your child there's no Santa Claus or Easter Bunny. But older sisters who have set sail for a career in customer service aren't bound by the same code of conduct as parents and are more than happy to dash their younger sibling's childhood innocence on the rocky shores of reality.

Sometimes I wish I were an only child.

So even though I'm resigned to a career as a logician or a statistician or a high school calculus teacher, at least I don't have to worry about waiting tables at Red Lobster or working behind the perfume counter at Macy's.

At the Celebrity & Glamour table, one of the students lets out a loud, enthusiastic *whoop*.

But as unglamorous as a career in food service or retail sales might sound, at least if you have a job title like waiter or sales clerk you pretty much know what to expect. But some of these other job titles and career options don't make any sense.

What's a procurement analyst? Or a human resources generalist? Or a global chief information officer? What does a senior account executive do? How does a business development representative spend her day?

A lot of us think these job titles are made up and that they don't really exist. And if they do exist, we don't understand why anyone would ever want to do them.

When I finally reach the front of the table, a woman with dark hair and dark-rimmed glasses greets me. "Hello young lady," she says with a bright, cheery smile as if she enjoys crushing the dreams of sixth graders. "And what are we here for today?"

Without saying anything, I hand her the sheet of paper with my test results.

"Observational astronomer. Environmental economist. Market research analyst. Mathematical logician. Sports statistician. High school calculus teacher," she says. "That's quite the variety of careers to choose from."

"I suppose," I say, the ennui flowing out of my pores.

I know I should probably try to sound more enthusiastic, but it's like trying to get excited about a bowl of store brand vanilla ice cream when what you really want is an Oreo cookie sundae made with gourmet hot fudge and organic whipped cream.

The woman types something on her keyboard, most likely my name but it might as well be a life sentence in observational astronomy. It's probably pointless for me to lobby for a different career, but at this point I figure I don't have anything to lose.

"What I'd really like to be is a veterinarian," I say. "Or a zoologist. I like the idea of helping animals."

"Yes," the woman says, typing. "Your test responses indicate you have a high level of empathy."

"They do?" I lean over to look at the laptop screen to see what she's reading but from my angle I can't see anything except glare.

The woman looks up from her computer and smiles. "I also see you're quite proficient at math."

I just nod and hold my breath. Not that I want to fan any flames of optimism, but the fact that she mentioned my empathy and math skills makes me wonder if there's a chance she might consider sending me over to another table, like Health Care & Medicine or Zoology & Animal Husbandry. I've never heard of a student being assigned a new career option at orientation before, but there's a first time for everything.

"Your responses indicate that you tend to be idealistic rather than pragmatic," the woman says.

"What?" I try to work my way around the side of the table to look at the laptop screen but there isn't enough room for me to maneuver. "Where does it say that?"

"And when it comes to athletics, you rated below average in general interest."

While I'm not a big fan of spectator sports, I don't understand how that's relevant. But whatever optimism I had begins to flicker.

"Your responses show that while you care about the environment, it doesn't rank in your top five concerns," the woman says. "And when it comes to astronomy, you're not a huge fan of star-gazing. Plus you don't care much for space operas."

"What does that have to do with anything?" I ask.

"And that leaves us with your best career match," she says.

"Wait!" I say, hoping for a last-second stay of execution. But it's too late. The woman types something and hits ENTER.

The printer spits out a strip of paper that the woman tears off and hands to me. And just like that, my childhood is over and my future is set in stone. Or at least in 12-point bold print.

HIGH SCHOOL CALCULUS TEACHER

"Congratulations!" The woman flashes her sadistic, dream-crushing smile. "With your empathetic nature and love of math, I'm sure you'll make a wonderful teacher. Best of luck with your career. Next!"

A boy half a foot shorter than me nearly shoves me out of the way in his excitement to get his assignment. I walk away from the table like a reanimated corpse, staring at the strip of paper in my hand as the optimism for my future dies out.

Not that there's anything wrong with being a high school calculus teacher. Teaching is a noble profession. And I'd rather be a high school calculus teacher than an environmental economist or a market research analyst, whatever that means. It's just that I wanted something different from what my test results indicated.

But apparently *different* isn't allowed.

I watch the other students who have received their assigned futures, most of them happy and smiling, high-fiving or fist bumping one another. Some of them have more than likely had their dreams realized, while the others at least have something to look forward to. Somewhere they can fit in and contribute to society, even if they don't realize that's why they're happy.

Bucky and I had planned to meet by the stage but I don't see him anywhere and the thought of sticking around inside the crowded gymnasium with all of these eager, happy students makes me want to puke. Sometimes I can't help my propensity for exaggeration. So I stuff my assigned career into my back pocket and go outside and sit down on a bench.

While I'm waiting for Bucky, more than a dozen students file out of the gym and walk past, all exuberant smiles and playful laughter. I watch them go, thinking about how they've found their proverbial pot of gold at the end of the rainbow. Or maybe they haven't found their pot of gold but something nearly as valuable: a purpose, even if that purpose was dispensed to them rather than discovered on their own.

I take out my assigned future again and study it, trying to manufacturer something akin to enthusiasm. But unlike the other purpose-laden students, I'm just as lost as before.

A few minutes later, Bucky shows up wearing a grin as big as Texas.

"Where did you go?" he asks.

"Out here, obviously."

"Why?"

"Because I needed some air."

"Oh," he says, nodding as if he understands. "So what did you get?"

"What did you get?"

"I asked you first."

"I asked you second," I say. "That means you have to go first."

"Since when?"

"Since always."

Bucky looks around as if in search of an arbitrator who can give a ruling on who goes first, then he shrugs, digs his four-inch strip of paper out of his back pocket, and holds up his official Job Fair Career Evaluation for me to see:

PROFESSOR OF PHILOSOPHY

It figures. Bucky gets the career he coveted and I'm stuck teaching derivatives and integrals to a bunch of apathetic teenagers.

"So what did you get?" Bucky asks.

I consider showing him my one-inch-by-four-inch strip of paper with my life sentence printed on it, then I change my mind and get up and walk away without saying anything.

Bucky catches up and falls in beside me, though he has to walk nearly twice as fast to keep pace since my legs are a good five inches longer. It's like a Dachshund trying to keep pace with a Labrador.

We walk in silence for several blocks before we come to a corner where the pedestrian crossing signal stops us with a solid red hand. Next to me at eye-level, taped to the traffic signal post, is a color picture of an orange and white cat above a hand-written note:

HELP ME GET HOME TO MY HUMANS
My name is Titan & I'm a 12-year-old male Bengal cat. I was accidentally let out the front door of my house & got lost & need to get back home. Because I'm friendly you may have found me and tried to help me. If you recognize me, please call my mom at this number...

I take a photo of the flyer with my cell phone and save the photo in the album Lost Animals, then I enter the phone number into my contacts list under the name Lost Cat – Titan and make the photo the profile picture for the phone number.

I have dozens of numbers for lost animals in my contacts. Lost cats with names like Titan and Snickers and Griffen. Lost dogs with names like Milton and Bangers and Tuck. There are a couple of lost rabbits and parrots in there, but the majority of them are dogs and cats. I've been saving the information of all of these lost animals for the past couple of years, just in case I run across one of them so I can help them to find their way back home. So far, I haven't found any of them, but it makes me feel like I'm doing something that matters.

I look at the flyer and study the photo, wondering if the people who put up the flyer are out looking for Titan or if they've given up. Sometimes I think about the people who post about their lost animals and I feel sorry for them. I feel their sadness. But most of the time I feel worse for the animals because they're out there in the world, lost and scared, trying to find their way back to their humans.

When the signal changes, Bucky and I cross the street and continue walking in silence. The entire time I scan the bushes and the front yards and the trees, just in case I might catch a glimpse of Titan. But he's nowhere to be found. A few blocks later, Bucky and I split up and go our separate ways.

"I'll see you later," Bucky says with a smile and a wave.

I respond with a half-hearted wave sans the smile and trudge down the street, occasionally glancing left and right looking for Titan, but mostly I stare at the ground three feet in front of me, bemoaning my fate. I finally look up when I reach the street corner and see another Lost Pet sign, this one stapled to a telephone pole:

REWARD!!!
Lost Dog – Mini Australian Shepherd
Name: Frannie
Age: Two Years Old
Friendly and Affectionate
Reward: $2,500.00

Rewards are pretty common on lost animal flyers, but $2,500 is a lot of money. Not that the money would be the driving force behind my efforts, but I wouldn't turn down the reward, that's for sure.

I take a picture of the flyer and enter Lost Dog – Frannie into my cell phone. This is the first time I've come across a lost animal with the same name as mine. Legally my name is Frances but no one calls me that except my parents and my sister, and she only does it to torment me.

I've never met any other Frannies or Franceses and don't know of any except for that movie actress my parents like and that television host who's always talking about other celebrities, but they don't count. I mean, it's not as if I know them personally. But now there's this lost two-year-old Australian Shepherd and I can't help but feel a connection with her. And it's not just because she shares my name.

We're both of us lost creatures, waiting to be found.

For several minutes, I stand on the corner and stare at the flyer for Frannie, imagining what she's feeling, wishing I could find her. I wouldn't even care about the money. I'd just care about helping her get back to her family.

I look away from the flyer and scroll through my list of phone numbers for lost animals. There are so many of them who should be home with their families, being loved and fed and appreciated. Instead, they're out on the streets or locked up in a cage or hiding somewhere, confused and frightened. I wonder what that must be like for them, searching for their humans or their homes and finding only strange faces and unfamiliar places. Someone should be out there searching for Frannie and Titan and all of the other missing dogs and cats and rabbits and birds.

As I'm standing there thinking this, a text message from my mother pops up on my phone:

What career were you assigned honey???

I take the strip of paper out of my back pocket and unfold it.

Not that I couldn't remember my assigned career, but I thought maybe while it was in my pocket it might have magically transformed into something like veterinarian or animal behaviorist or professional dog walker. But it's still the same as before:

HIGH SCHOOL CALCULUS TEACHER

I look from the piece of paper to the text message from my mother to the flyer on the telephone pole and stare at the photo of Frannie. When I look back at my pre-ordained career, I decide I don't care what the piece of paper says. I don't want to spend the rest of my life doing something that was assigned to me based on some theoretical interpretation of a bunch of answers I gave on some stupid test. I want to do something that matters to me. Something I care about. Something that gives me a sense of purpose and nourishes my soul.

After a few more moments, I put away my cell phone without answering my mother's text, crumple up the piece of paper, and throw my assigned future into a nearby garbage can. Then I start walking along the sidewalk, meandering back and forth through the streets, searching for Titan and Frannie, calling out their names, determined to find the lost creatures and bring them home.

Intervention for a Lycanthrope

We've all been there before.

You're at a party or a family gathering. Maybe a birthday, a holiday dinner, or a casual get-together with friends. Everyone enjoying the evening and the festivities, caught up in the camaraderie and good will, sharing drinks and laughter and memories, when a friend or partner or family member turns into a werewolf and runs amok, slashing up the sofa, urinating in the punch bowl, and disemboweling one of the guests, ruining everyone's night.

It can be difficult to approach a loved one who suffers from lycanthropy, especially during a full moon or when they're in heat. There's never a good or opportune moment to talk about the proverbial elephant in the room. And chances are when confronted, the werewolf will refute that they have a shape-shifting problem or claim that they have it under control, making it difficult to have any kind of open, honest dialogue, often leading to trust issues and territorial markings.

So more often than not, friends and family members find it easier to ignore the problem and wait until the transmogrification phase passes, pretending that everything's normal, hoping the problem will just go away. While it's awkward to know what to say to a werewolf, this avoidance approach doesn't benefit anyone. Instead, it just makes the situation worse and results in a never-ending cycle of broken promises, property damage, and dismembered carcasses.

Most of the time, people aren't aware that a friend or a loved one suffers from lycanthropy until it's too late. While the warning signs are common, it's easy to miss them if you don't know what to look for or if you're blinded by love. If you're not sure whether someone you care about is a werewolf, there are a number of obvious warning signs:

- Secretive behavior
- Angry or aggressive outbursts
- Increase in physical strength and howling
- Stocking excessive amounts of shaving cream and hair care products
- A growing fascination with lunar cycles
- Urinating in public and/or territorial spraying
- Increased appetite for rare or raw meat (including small farm animals)
- Aversion to sterling silver, especially knives and forks

People who struggle with lycanthropy often live in denial about their situation and are unwilling to seek help or treatment. They don't recognize the negative impact their shape-shifting behavior has, not only on themselves but also on their friends and family. Confronting them on an individual basis can often lead to hurt feelings and shredded torsos. Rather than going it alone, you may want to consider seeking professional help before things get out of hand or someone loses a limb.

During the Middle Ages, someone afflicted with lycanthropy was treated using surgery, medicine, or, in certain cases, exorcism. The use of silver bullets wasn't a viable option, as handguns and firearms in general weren't in widespread use until the latter part of the 14th century. Prior to that, if you wanted to use silver in order to "treat" a werewolf, you would have to melt the silver into a knife or the tip of a spear. But silver wasn't readily accessible or affordable to the masses. And no matter what century you're from, hand-to-hand combat with a werewolf is a bad idea.

Over the past 600 years, most of the surgical methods used during the Middle Ages have proven to be ineffective, not to mention barbaric. While a number of the medieval medicinal remedies can help to alleviate some of the symptoms associated with lycanthropy, they're not a silver bullet, so to speak, but just a temporary solution to a more deep-seated issue. And these days finding a certified exorcist can be tricky, as the deregulation of the exorcism industry has led to numerous unlicensed demonologists who don't know an evil spirit from a migraine. (While silver bullets are easier to come by than they were in the fifteenth century, they should be considered as a last resort for treatment, especially in today's animal rights friendly environment.)

One modern alternative to exorcism and pharmaceutical treatment is the Miller-and-Rollnick Model of intervention, also known as The Motivational Interview Style. This approach is based on the idea of pursuing behavioral change through the guidance of a trained therapist or counselor to help the subject focus on something positive rather than focusing on his or her destructive behavior.

Unfortunately, the number of therapists who are trained to treat werewolves has dwindled in recent years due to the removal of requisite classes from course curriculums, as well as due to an increase in the mortality rate of qualified therapists. So if you are able to find a lycanthropy therapist, be prepared to pay a premium for their services. You might also have to sign a contract that requires you to cover any medical expenses the therapist might incur during treatment and, in some cases, authorizes the therapist to put the werewolf down should the werewolf become hostile.

Once you've found a therapist who is trained in lycanthropy and skilled in Motivational Interviewing, the therapist will meet with the afflicted during weekly one-on-one sessions that focus on five key components:

1. **Express Empathy**

   Developing trust and a sense of unity between the therapist and the werewolf is essential to a successful treatment program. It's important that the therapist not try to establish any kind of dominance during initial sessions as this could trigger the shapeshifter's more aggressive personality traits and render communication difficult. Often the therapist will show that he or she is not a threat by getting down on all fours while maintaining a respectful distance. Once trust has been gained, some therapists will also incorporate social grooming into their treatment. Offering small rodents as rewards can also be beneficial in creating a mutual bond.

2. **Develop Discrepancy**

   The werewolf is invited to express and discuss his or her personal goals with the therapist. Most lycanthropes don't tend to think big picture when it comes to planning for the future. Career. Marriage. Retirement. These aren't important objectives. Instead, goals are visceral and short-term and typically involve growling, snarling, howling, and tearing the throats out of livestock. The therapist should recognize these goals without dismissing them or belittling them, while verbally pointing out how the werewolf can achieve or alter these goals without killing other living creatures.

3. **Avoid Arguments**

   The therapist should never initiate or engage in arguments with the lycanthrope, as this is counterproductive to a positive outcome and often leads to bloodshed. This can be the biggest challenge of the treatment process as werewolves are, by their nature, hot-blooded and argumentative creatures. When dealing with a quarrelsome lycanthrope, it's a good idea to provide him or her with positive responses rather than negative ones. Adopting a hunched, passive posture and avoiding direct eye contact can also help to defuse a hostile situation. Licking the muzzle of the werewolf or thrusting the tongue between their front teeth also shows submission. The therapist may also choose to lie on his or her back, hands drawn close to the body, with the belly and throat exposed. Whimpering is optional.

4. **Roll with Resistance**

   It's inevitable that resistance of some kind will manifest during the treatments. More often than not, this resistance involves various levels of growling and snarling, as well as the spraying of urine, which can be caused by anxiety or the innate desire of the werewolf to mark his or her territory. The werewolf may also casually threaten the therapist with dismemberment and disembowelment. Motivational Interviewing encourages the therapist and the lycanthrope to work through these resistances without escalating hostilities or resorting to violence. Most therapists, however, will keep a revolver with silver bullets handy, just in case.

5. **Support Self-Efficacy**

   In Motivational Interviewing, self-efficacy is the manner in which individuals view their own competence and perceive their own ability to change their lives. When it comes to dealing with lycanthropes, the therapist encourages the werewolf to realize that he or she is capable of many things, including possessing the strength to give up mutilating co-workers or devouring neighborhood pets. While howling at the moon is typically discouraged since it tends to lead to the terrorizing of communities, it can also provide the werewolf with the self-confidence he or she needs to move forward toward a more normal, less destructive lifestyle.

Sometimes the honest and open conversational style of Motivational Interviewing can get the ball rolling on the road to recovery. Or at least lead to a reduction in hospital bills. But in cases where the werewolf refuses to see or acknowledge that there's anything wrong, or if he or she ends up killing or dismembering the therapist, a group intervention can provide an alternative approach for a structured environment to encourage behavioral changes.

A group intervention is an organized coordination of family, friends, and co-workers who care about someone who is struggling with an addictive or destructive behavior. The result is a pre-arranged gathering at an agreed upon location in order to confront the werewolf about his or her lycanthropy and encourage them to accept treatment. The group intervention is often conducted in consultation with a doctor, a licensed counselor, or an intervention specialist, and involves friends, family, co-workers, and anyone who cares about the well-being of the werewolf.

This approach to treating lycanthropy is based on The Johnson Model of intervention, often called The Ambush Style. As the name implies, this is a surprise attack, which is not something you should enter into lightly when dealing with werewolves who, historically, do not respond well to surprises or attacks. An intervention is a highly charged situation with the potential to cause anger, resentment, and a sense of betrayal, so you should take all necessary precautions before confronting your werewolf. This can include providing participants with pepper spray, stun guns, and body armor. Just in case.

A successful intervention with a lycanthrope must be planned carefully in order to get the intended results. A poorly planned intervention can make the situation worse, resulting in injuries, hospitalization, and significant property damage. The last thing you want is to have to deal with medical bills, lawsuits, or the loss of a security deposit. In order to avoid unnecessary and costly expenses, you'll want to take the following steps prior to holding your intervention:

1. **Make a plan**

   A family member or a friend of the lycanthrope proposes the intervention. Once enough support is received from members of the werewolf's social circle, a planning group of loved ones is formed. Ideally, each member of the planning group will take on a specific responsibility, decreasing the individual burden and stress on each participant. If you're not sure how to go about planning the intervention or need some professional guidance, it's a good idea to consult with a qualified counselor, psychologist, intervention specialist, werewolf behaviorist, or an old gypsy woman.

2. **Gather information**

   Members of the planning group investigate the extent of the lycanthrope's problem by interviewing as many friends, colleagues, and family members as possible. During this stage, the group may also choose to research available inpatient and outpatient werewolf treatment programs, including rehab centers, holistic healing programs, and Werewolves Anonymous.

3. **Form the intervention team**

   The planning group forms the intervention team. Team members set a date and location for the intervention and work together to present a consistent, rehearsed message and a structured plan. Non-family members of the team help keep the discussion focused on facts and shared solutions rather than on emotions, which can run high when discussing treatment that includes options such as shock collars and euthanasia. It helps to have everyone on the same page; otherwise, you can find yourself embroiled in endless and unproductive discussions about the philosophical differences between curses, afflictions, and addictions.

4. Decide on specific consequences

If the werewolf doesn't accept the terms of the suggested treatment, each person on the team needs to decide what action he or she is willing to take, such as moving out, filing a restraining order, taking away visitation rights of children, or hiring a werewolf hunter. This, however, can get rather costly, as the price for werewolf hunters has spiked in recent years due to increased demand and specialization. Not to mention the rising cost of health insurance. Some less severe and expensive options for dealing with a recalcitrant werewolf include hanging mistletoe around all of your doors and windows, planting a Mountain Ash tree in your front or backyard, and using wolfsbane. Also known as monkshood or aconitum, wolfsbane is a powerful repellant that can be planted around the home, distilled in oil and burned as incense, or added to water as a repellant. In general, werewolves hate getting wet. Filling squirt guns and super soakers with a mixture of distilled or brewed wolfsbane and water is an effective and inexpensive method for chasing off incorrigible lycanthropes. Mixing in some holy water can help to add an additional supernatural repellant.

5. Make notes on what to say

Each member of the intervention team should write down specific incidents in detail, describing instances when the werewolf's behavior and actions caused hardship or problems, such as emotional distress, shredded clothing or home furnishings, and the expense and embarrassment of having to reimburse neighbors for medical bills or mutilated pets. Discuss the emotional and financial toll of the werewolf's behavior while still expressing compassion and concern, along with the belief and expectation that the werewolf can change. Your werewolf can't argue with facts or with your emotional response. For example, you can begin by saying something like:

"Every time you shapeshift in your sleep I'm afraid you're going to slash open one of my arteries" or "I was upset and hurt when you killed and ate the family dog."

6. Hold the intervention meeting

Without revealing the reason for meeting, the lycanthrope is asked to come to the site of the intervention. It's important to remember that werewolves don't react well to surprises and attacks, so be prepared for the possibility of violent outbursts and resentful spraying. It's always a good idea to keep some Nature's Miracle handy to help combat the smell, just in case. Once your loved one has settled down or been subdued with wolfsbane or tranquilizers, you'll need to take the following steps:

- Forcefully present reality to the lycanthrope. Don't *accuse* him or her of being a werewolf, but provide hard evidence that this is the reality. Photos of property damage, eviscerated animals, and dismembered friends, family members, or co-workers should be shown during this portion of the intervention.

- Members of the core team should take turns expressing their love, while at the same time sharing their concerns and feelings and discussing their emotional and physical wounds, detailing the damage the lycanthrope has caused. Specific and concise examples are best, as werewolves don't do well with abstract concepts or generalities. "You bit off two of my fingers" is much better than "You crippled my hand and made it impossible for me to tie my shoes."

- Team members guarantee their support of the werewolf, offering a treatment plan with clear steps, goals, and guidelines. Again, specifics are better than generalities as they offer less room for interpretation. Werewolves are notorious obfuscators. Having a health care professional in attendance can help to clarify treatment and facilitate this portion of the intervention. However, finding a health care professional who is willing to attend can be problematic, as most insurance companies don't cover werewolf interventions.

- The lycanthrope is asked by an appointed team member to acknowledge that he or she has a problem and to voluntarily check into an agreed upon treatment program. Each team member will reiterate what specific actions or changes he or she will make if the werewolf doesn't accept responsibility and agree to treatment. (Refer to Step 4: Decide on Specific Consequences.) Don't make any threats unless you're committed to follow through on them. Werewolves can sense weakness and will attack instinctually so stick to your guns. If you've brought firearms to the meeting, this applies both literally and figuratively.

- At this point, team members and any remaining friends and family who are still alive—or not seriously injured and bleeding out—should help with the immediate transfer of the werewolf to a lycanthrope treatment facility.

7. **Follow up**

A spouse, family member, or any close friend who is not hospitalized or suffering from post-traumatic stress disorder should remain involved after the intervention. This is a crucial step in helping the werewolf to remain in treatment and avoid relapsing into shapeshifting fits of destruction and rage. This involvement can include attending counseling sessions with the werewolf, seeking your own therapist and recovery support group, or learning how to perform an exorcism. Once the treatment program has been completed, changing patterns of everyday living can help to keep the werewolf calm and make it easier for him or her to avoid falling into old habits and destructive behaviors. Some suggestions for managing behavioral patterns include attending yoga classes, performing daily meditations, and giving them a daily wolfsbane and Xanax smoothie.

If you find that neither the one-on-one therapy nor the group intervention provides any lasting solutions, other options for behavioral modification include behavioral shock collars, lobotomy, and transmogrification reversal therapy. Whatever your decision, be aware of the efficacy of each option, as well as the financial and emotional costs associated with them. Should you have to resort to using silver bullets to put down your werewolf, it's prudent to seek legal advice to verify the relevant lycanthropy rights laws in your state.

Living with a lycanthrope can be a highly stressful and difficult situation, fraught with numerous challenges both emotional and physical. But it doesn't have to mean the end of your relationship or your life. Finding the right therapy or process that works for you is the key to finding success and, ultimately, to finding happiness.

Acknowledgments

Several of the stories in this collection were published in previous anthologies and likely wouldn't have been written or imagined into existence had it not been for the invitations to contribute to the anthologies. So I would like to thank Cameron Pierce and Rose O'Keefe with Eraserhead Press; Jennifer Brozek and Katie Cord with Evil Girlfriend Media; and Eugene Johnson and Charles Day with Evil Jester Press. Thank you for providing me with the motivation and inspiration to write those stories and for giving them their first home.

All of the stories in this collection received invaluable feedback from numerous readers and I'm indebted to their contributions. A big thank you goes out to Rachel Moore, Keith White, Judith Wrubel, Jeffrey Whitehead, Loren Rhoads, Eunice Magill, Jim Saltzman, James Goudreault, and Bill Breedlove. The next drink is on me.

Special thanks to Lynne Hansen, who not only created the incredible cover art for this collection, but who provided support and guidance for some of the formatting challenges I encountered. The world needs more people like you.

Finally, I'd like to thank my family and friends for all of your support and encouragement over the years. You're the best support group a writer could ask for. And, of course, thank you to my fans. Without you, I'm just screaming into the void.

About the Author

S.G. Browne is the author of the novels *Breathers, Fated, Lucky Bastard, Big Egos,* and *Less Than Hero*, as well as the short story collection *Shooting Monkeys in a Barrel* and the heartwarming holiday novella *I Saw Zombies Eating Santa Claus*. You can learn more about his writing at www.sgbrowne.com.